C000077583

Reverberation

....

Saint Lakes Book Nine

April Kelley

Hard Rose Publishing

Copyright © 2021 by April Kelley

All rights reserved.

No portion of this book may be reproduced in any form without written permission from the publisher or author, except as permitted by U.S. copyright law.

Cover by Miblart

Edited by No Stone Unturned

Cover content is for illustrative only, and any person depicted on the cover is a model

Published by Hard Rose Publishing

This is a work of fiction. Names, characters, places, and incidents are either the product of the author's imagination or are used fictitiously, and any resemblance to actual persons, living or dead, business establishments, events, or locales is entirely coincidental.

Contents

Chapter One

Vaughan Somerset was pretty sure his nipples had melted somewhere between dropping off the council member at Blackwing Coven and saying goodbye to his brother Owen. And also, his last flight to the desert had taught him how much he loved vegetation—green trees clumped together really did it for him. The vast forests that made up most of Saint Lakes made him giddy. Or it would if he wasn't so damn tired. So maybe he just felt weird. All worked up and shaky with the thought of being home. He missed Saint Lakes. And he missed one person in particular, not that he would ever say it aloud.

Saint Lakes' airport only held his small cargo plane and one other little puddle-jumper thing that belonged to Amos, the airport's caretaker.

Vaughan grabbed his tattered backpack and stepped off the plane. He threw the worn blue bag over one shoulder as he left the hangar, waving to Amos. He intended to drive himself home, but Amos stood on his front porch with his hands on the rail and questions on his old, wrinkled face.

Amos was a wolf shifter who had been around the world and back again about a million times before he'd settled in Saint Lakes. He had bought the land and built the airport well before Vaughan was born, and probably before Saint Lakes had even become a shifter town. He had taught Vaughan how to fly and helped him to buy his plane. They'd even built Vaughan's hangar together.

Vaughan owed him a lot, including the conversation Amos wanted. As tired as Vaughan felt, he sighed and turned back, crossing the tarmac again.

"Cloudless day. Heard it's supposed to rain, but the weatherperson lied the past three times I've listened." Amos starting the conversation with the weather meant he had something on his mind. Vaughan had been around the man long enough to know that.

"Before this morning, you listened six years ago and sixty before that, right?" Vaughan stepped onto the front porch with a grin.

Amos shook his head with narrowed eyes. The smile sneaking onto his face gave away how he really felt. "Get in the house, smartass. I have a sandwich and some tea with your name on it."

"'Smartass' isn't my name. That sandwich and tea must be for one of my other brothers. They're the only smartasses I know." Despite Vaughan's teasing, he went into the house, dropping his bag just inside the door. He took off his shoes because Blackwing Coven was a sandy hell that didn't give up on trying to make a sinner out of him even with a thousand miles and distance. Tracking it into Amos's house would piss the man off something fierce.

Vaughan went to the table and sat in front of the bacon sandwich. By the gods, Amos's bacon sandwiches were the best thing on Earth. Well, almost the best thing. Vaughan knew of something, or rather someone who was the best thing on Earth. And man, did he miss his dragon shifter.

He admired the goodness before taking a big bite.

Amos chuckled when Vaughan moaned. "Is one sandwich gonna be enough, boy?"

Vaughan shook his head, not wanting to talk with food in his mouth. His mother had taught him better than that, and he followed that rule whenever it crossed his mind.

"When was the last time you ate?" Amos stood at the kitchen counter, building another sandwich. He had his back turned.

Amos had passed the age where the body slowed down in aging. Gray hairs mingled with the black, and his blue eyes held a world of experience. Most of Amos's life was a mystery to Vaughan. Amos preferred it that way.

Amos's shoulders were square, and he held them back. He had the posture of a much younger person. Tattoos peeked past his T-shirt sleeve and flowed down his arms.

"Don't remember the last time. Probably yesterday." The last thing he remembered putting into his mouth was some jerky one of the paranormal council bear enforcers had thrust at him before take-off.

Amos turned from the counter, grabbing Vaughan's empty plate. He loaded another sandwich on it and set it in front of him again. Vaughan still had the first one firmly in his grip. The thing was almost but not quite halfway eaten, and Vaughan didn't plan on stopping until he'd consumed the entire thing.

"What's going on that the Alpha's working you so hard?" Amos sat across from him with what Vaughan thought of as Amos's dad stare.

Vaughan chewed and swallowed before answering. "You know Owen's mate, Damian, right?"

"Not personally, but word is he's the shoot-first-and-ask-questions-later type."

"Yeah, well, he got that way because he had a shitty father. Ever heard of Blackwing? It's a vampire coven out west."

Amos's dark brows drew together. "Can't say I have."

"Militia-type compound. Rough bunch who think the humans will wage war and want to get ready, even if it means abusing each other." Vaughan took another bite. Eating gave him time to think.

"That's probably on the mark."

Vaughan nodded. "Maybe. We need to stand united. Not go off half-cocked, killing everyone with different DNA and a viewpoint."

Amos smiled, reaching across the table to pat Vaughan's forearm. Holding the sandwich made the gesture awkward but did nothing to diminish the sentiment. "I'm proud of you, boy."

Vaughan smiled. "Thanks."

Amos took his hand away. "So what about Blackwing has Saint Lakes so tied in knots?"

"It doesn't. Not really. But Blackwing's leader tried to hurt Damian's brothers. Turned into a battle, so I had to transport everyone. The council got involved because of the abuse. Apparently Blackwing didn't know torture was illegal." They were damn idiots but then, Vaughan didn't know crap about running a clan or coven. Still, he didn't have to know any of that to know how to be a decent human being.

"Our Alpha has Blackwing set straight, I hope?"

"Well Damian and his brothers did most of it but yeah...between Damian's brother and Vesh Arnauld, the council member I just dropped off there, everything is under control."

Amos gave Vaughan a knowing look. "Until paranormal existence is all over the news."

Vaughan nodded. "But we'll have Blackwing on our side, and that's a good thing. We might have killed their old leader, but we wouldn't have beat the coven in a fair fight." Vaughan took a bite out of his sandwich. He made a noncommittal sound. The more food that filled his empty stomach, the more fatigue took over his body.

"Finish eating. And then I'll drive you home. You're too tired to drive yourself."

Vaughan shook his head. "I can call home and have someone pick me up."

"It's late."

It *was* late. Well after dark. But a certain someone waited for him under the guise of working. "Someone's always up at Mom's house."

Amos leaned in, tilting his head as if studying a wild animal. "I've known you your whole life. Hell, I helped raise you, boy. You have never turned down a ride if you're tired."

Vaughan chuckled even as he shook his head. "You're a nosy old man."

Amos sat back in his seat and crossed his arms over his chest. "It's one of those biker dragons, isn't it?"

Vaughan didn't blush very often. Not much got to him, but heat climbed from his chest to his neck. He had the kind of skin where red blotches would form, which only added to his embarrassment.

"Sully's a wolf." Vaughan took the last bite of his sandwich, focusing on it instead of Amos.

"He isn't the one, though. Is he?"

Vaughan shook his head. "Can we not talk about it?"

Amos chuckled. "You're acting like that time you liked the Sinclair boy. You were what, fifteen years' old?"

"Sixteen." Vaughan wanted to roll his eyes but that would prove Amos' point about him acting like a lovesick teenager.

"You never keep shit from me." Amos's narrow-eyed gaze drilled into Vaughan's soul.

"It didn't start out as anything more than fucking." And that was the very reason Vaughan insisted on keeping it a secret. He didn't need a lecture from anyone, including Amos.

"But you fell in love." Amos nodded and pursed his lips just enough that Vaughan knew he rolled the information around in his head, deciding it was true.

"Yes. And now I don't know where I stand with him." Vaughan didn't have to ask Amos to keep the information to himself. Amos always had Vaughan's back.

The corners of Amos' lips turned up and his eyes sparkled with some memory or other. "I've never met my mate, but I've loved before."

Vaughan darted his gaze to Amos. "What happened?"

"Nothing I want to talk about. And I don't have any sage advice, so you're shit out of luck there too."

Vaughan grinned around another bite. "No old man wisdom about how I should wait for my fated mate? Why fuck it up, blah, blah."

Amos lifted an eyebrow. "So that's what has you so secretive. You think Estelle won't approve, or maybe it's Garridan who scares you. He's a pretty traditional shifter. The most traditional in the clan."

"It's not the only reason. Garridan isn't the Alpha. Ladon is, and he won't care. Ladon will kick ass if someone has something negative to say. And it isn't anyone's business who I fuck."

Vaughan couldn't deny just thinking about having the conversation sent his nerves into overdrive. If he knew how Bandos felt about him, it would make coming clean a hell of a lot easier.

"It's still no one's business, even though it's more than that."

"We haven't talked about it. Bandos and I, I mean. I'm not sure if he feels the same way."

Vaughan yawned and sagged into the kitchen chair.

"Better call him before you fall over from exhaustion."

Vaughan must've looked like shit for Amos to drop the conversation. He would've kept Vaughan talking for hours any other time.

Vaughan nodded and pulled out his cellphone. He had Bandos' cell number programmed with the title *eggplant*. His phone wasn't capable of using emojis for contacts. The word implied basic feelings that Vaughan had surpassed weeks ago. The word made Vaughan feel guilty even though they hadn't ever called each other anything other than fuck-buddies. It made Vaughan feel like shit for taking things to the next level. As if he needed Bandos's permission to feel anything more.

He texted, *You still awake?*

Bandos replied right away. *Yep.*

Can you pick me up at the airport?

Be there in five.

Bandos would never say he waited up, but then he didn't have to. The truth lay in the quick reply and in the five-minute arrival time. That niggling, doubtful voice said maybe Bandos had stayed up working and just had his phone close.

Whatever, he'd get to see Bandos regardless of his motivation.

Vaughan put the phone back into his pocket and picked up his sandwich again.

Amos's expression suggested he understood the turmoil flowing through Vaughan's veins. Hell, he probably did. They'd been best friends, despite their age difference and a few other things that shouldn't have made them compatible but never really fucking mattered.

"Thanks for the sandwich."

Amos nodded.

Vaughan waited on the porch with Amos. He leaned against the rail. The wooden posts held him up as much as they held up the roof.

Amos sat in a chair with his elbows on his knees and his hands steepled under his chin. He appeared ready to pop up if Vaughan showed any signs of teetering too far in either direction.

When Bandos pulled his motorcycle in front of the house, Vaughan grabbed his backpack and stepped off the porch. He waved to Amos.

Amos stood, gripping the railing.

Bandos took his helmet off and raised a hand in greeting.

Amos didn't return the gesture but appeared as if he wanted to see into his soul and find out his intensions toward Vaughan.

"Thanks again, old man." Vaughan grinned, not wanting to give too much away.

Bandos handed Vaughan the helmet. "Put that on."

Vaughan took it but eyed the thing with suspicion. "What will you wear?"

"Only have one."

"And my head is more fragile than yours?"

Bandos had a sexy way of smiling with his eyes, as if he found Vaughan funny but didn't want to encourage him at the same time. "Just do what I say."

"So you're hard-headed enough to not need protection. Got it." Vaughan put it on and took a step closer to Bandos. "Do up the buckle thing, will you?"

Bandos kept the bike between his legs as he leaned closer to Vaughan. "What's that guy's problem?" he whispered as he fiddled with the buckle.

"He knows about us." Vaughan kept his eyes on the way Bandos concentrated.

"What about us?" Bandos met his gaze as if daring Vaughan to say something, although the gods knew what he needed to hear. The way he posed the question sounded a little like an accusation.

"He's my best fucking friend, okay. I tell him stuff."

Bandos's eyebrows went up. "Like?"

"Like how I needed a ride home because I'm so fucking tired I can't see straight. So will you please stop fishing for whatever the fuck you want me to say?" Vaughan didn't have bad moods very often, but when he did, he didn't mince his words.

His grouchy ass needed a bed.

Bandos had dimples when he smiled and sometimes when he appeared concerned, only they didn't pop as much as when he was happy. He finished securing the helmet and ran his hand down Vaughan's arm. "Where do you want me to take you?"

"Is that an offer?" Vaughan smiled.

"Yep. Get on."

Vaughan climbed behind Bandos, wrapping himself around him.

"Don't fall asleep." Bandos didn't wait for a response. He revved the engine and took off. Vaughan waved at Amos without taking his helmet-covered head from Bandos's wide back.

The lake air rode along beside them as they roared toward the cabin Bandos shared with Rocky and Sully.

Sully was out rescuing someone, so they wouldn't have to sneak around because of him. Rocky was the problem, and Vaughan couldn't see how they'd fool someone who searched for the truth for a living, and was a paranormal who would smell Vaughan as soon as he entered the house.

Vaughan could smell the differences in the lakes. There were three that made up Saint Lakes. Every one of his siblings had a cabin on the waterfront, including himself. He hadn't been to his house in a while, though. Not since before the battle. He'd been too busy. Between the problems starting with the humans and his cargo business, he hadn't had time.

Bandos slowed down and turned. The bike engine quieted to a purr and then he pulled to a stop, shutting it off.

Vaughan continued to lean against him, not wanting to let him go. The leather of his jacket felt cool beneath Vaughan's hands, and the thing smelled like Bandos—like cinnamon and a hint of something spicier, although Vaughan hadn't been able to figure the scent out.

"You gonna let go?" Bandos had a deep voice that contrasted with his youthful face. It washed over Vaughan like honey, coating every molecule in his body.

"I'm still debating that. I could fall asleep just like this." Vaughan closed his eyes, proving his point if only to himself.

"Or...we could get off the bike and go inside."

Vaughan hated to ask, but he had to know the answer. "What about Rocky?"

"He already knows."

He lifted his head and stared at Bandos's back. "How?" Although he already knew, he still wanted to hear Bandos's answer.

"I don't keep secrets from Rocky or Sully. I couldn't anyway because you're loud when you come. It's a small cabin." The way Bandos said it sounded as if he spoke about sunny, mild weather.

Vaughan climbed off the bike, taking a step away. "Why'd you give me shit about Amos knowing if you told Rocky and Sully?"

Bandos sighed. "I wasn't giving you shit. I was asking what you told him."

Vaughan had half a mind to turn and walk his ass to his cabin, which was closer than his mom's house. Instead, he lifted his eyebrows and grinned. "What do you tell Rocky and Sully?"

"The truth."

"Which is? That I'm always that loud when we fuck?"

Bandos chuckled and shook his head. "Something like that. And I told them we've been seeing each other."

"And they gave you shit about waiting for your mate, right?"

"No. They both know better than that. They asked me if it was serious."

"And you said..."

"That we haven't talked about it much."

Vaughan opened his mouth to speak and then closed it again. He had to think about the next thing he said because he would end up spilling his guts, and it wasn't the time for the discussion. Instead, he pointed to the helmet's strap. "Take this off me."

Bandos stepped up to him. His big body gave off enough heat to warm Vaughan to his core. Vaughan was always cold when exhaustion set in. It was one of those weird things his body did. That, and he had a headache that had started about the same time he had landed his plane.

Bandos fiddled with the buckle. His fingers brushed gently against Vaughan's skin. "It's the truth. We haven't talked about anything."

"I know. And now isn't the time to have our first official argument." That could cause a breakup and probably would, because Bandos just might have a few commitment issues. "Can I get a raincheck? Please."

Bandos smiled even as he concentrated on the buckle. "A first official argument sounds serious."

Vaughan put his hand over Bandos's mouth. With his other hand, he gripped Bandos' nape and pulled him closer. Vaughan leaned in, kissing Bandos on the forehead. "Shut it for now."

Bandos chuckled and wrapped an arm around Vaughan's waist, pulling him into his side. "Let's go inside. I'll tuck you in."

"Must be serious if I get to spend the night." Vaughan grinned as he let Bandos lead him inside.

"I thought you didn't want to talk about it."

"Not right now."

"Then you probably shouldn't talk about how you never let me spend the night either."

Vaughan sighed. "I know. Sorry I'm so tired during our first official sleepover."

"We're having a lot of 'first officials' tonight." Bandos opened the door and led Vaughan inside.

All Vaughan saw was the bed. It was enough to bring tears to his eyes. He dropped his bag where he stood and fell onto the mattress. The pillow smelled like Bandos, which allowed his mind to settle.

He had enough wherewithal to not let his dirty shoes touch the mattress. He felt Bandos take them off, as well as his socks.

"Turn over," Bandos whispered.

"Don't wanna." Vaughan pulled the pillow closer.

The bed dipped, and then he felt Bandos cover his back. Bandos pressed his stubbled cheek against Vaughan's. "Come on, baby. Turn over so I can make you more comfortable."

Baby. That was another first.

Chapter Two

S ince the battle with Stavros had come and gone, they could go back to their own homes. He loved his family, but all those grown-ass people under one roof did not make for a Zen situation. Between the arguments and the overall lack of space at his mother's house, Vaughan was happy he was back home in his empty cabin by the lake. The only problem was he wished Bandos had visited.

Not that Vaughan had invited him.

Vaughan had his sliding glass door open even though there was a bite in the air. The screen blocked the bugs from getting in and the house was warm enough all by itself. He stared at the lake.

The moon shone off the water's surface, sparkling like diamonds in the ripples. Something was swimming about. He could see it gliding close to the shore. Maybe it was an animal. Turtles liked that particular spot in Saint Lakes. It was probably a clan member. If Vaughan had to venture a guess, he would say it was Henri, who lived across the lake. Henri was Rocky's mate, although the two hadn't connected the way fated mates should. That was Henri's doing, although Vaughan didn't know why he held back.

He hadn't nosed around Rocky and Henri's business because he had been flying cargo and people around a lot lately and didn't have time to find out what was going on between them. He also had problems of his own, not that he would've called Bandos a problem. That Vaughan was in love with him, but they weren't true mates, was the actual issue. Damned if he could do anything about it.

Vaughan had on pajama pants and nothing else. The air was cool, blowing across his bare chest. It was the first night he'd spent time in his cabin for longer than he could remember. He usually stayed with his mom, but he needed the down time.

Vaughan rubbed at his chest. Yep. It was love.

Damn it.

Vaughan sighed and turned, walking over to the coffee table and his phone, pulling up Bandos's phone number and pressing the green call button.

When Bandos answered, Vaughan could tell he hadn't been sleeping, although he sounded exhausted. "Hey. Do you need me to pick you up from the airstrip again?"

"I'm home. Got in about forty-five minutes ago." Long enough to shower and change his clothing for the first time in over thirty-six hours. Fatigue set in, but he wanted to see Bandos more. "I miss you."

Yeah, maybe that little confession took things to the next level. Bandos would either deal with it or he would call whatever they had off. Either way, Vaughan didn't want to fake it anymore. He had feelings, and by the gods he wanted to let himself experience them.

"Me too, baby." Oh, that smile. It came through in every syllable.

Vaughan had an image of Bandos in his mind. He had memorized Bandos's smile for when they couldn't be together. He hadn't done it on purpose. It had just sort of happened when he hadn't been paying attention and before he knew it, he had a clear picture in his mind whenever he needed to see it. He called it his fix because Bandos's dimples could cure just about any illness.

"Can I come over?" Vaughan probably hadn't needed to ask, but sometimes Bandos worked late. All his computer shit was at Mom's house, so he might have been there until the early hours. But Vaughan had it on good authority that Bandos was home, which meant he was just a few cabins away. Vaughan could walk over with little effort.

"How do you know I'm home?"

"I have eyes everywhere."

"Hm...either Lucas knows about us or Jules said something."

Vaughan chuckled. "I called home when I landed. Jules was waiting for Hacen to get out of a meeting. I might have gotten him to mention who was in the house."

Vaughan put on his shoes and left, shutting the glass door. He wasn't worried about thieves. No one in Saint Lakes would steal anything from anyone, but especially not a wolf shifter who could follow their scent. He followed the lake but stayed on the phone.

The moon gave enough light for him to see even without shifting to his wolf's vision.

"I think Ladon knows." If the information worried Bandos, it didn't come through in his voice.

"Hm." Vaughan suspected the same thing. If Ladon knew, then it was likely Jules knew as well. Ladon and Jules were as close as best friends and pretty much always had been since Jules's gotcha day.

When had they decided that keeping their relationship a secret was a good idea? Vaughan sighed. Oh yeah. It was when they had been fuck-buddies. Fucking wasn't all they had anymore.

He was leaning toward telling the clan and seeing if anyone had a problem with it. Maybe he didn't care about their reaction. Maybe.

"Are you going to say anything else about that besides grunting at me?" Bandos wanted to talk about every damn thing.

Vaughan didn't see the point. At least not yet. "No."

"The alpha of your clan knows about us and you have nothing to say?"

"Ladon might be the alpha, but he's my little brother. I know him well enough to know he won't have a problem." It would be the rest of the clan. And Mom would have a conversation with him.

"Then why are we sneaking around, Vaughan?"

"A better question is why you're trying to start an argument."

"I'm not."

He knocked on Bandos's bedroom window as gently as he could so as not to wake Rocky, who probably knew he was there anyway because his bedroom window was the one right next to Bandos'.

Vaughan would keep up the pretense because that was what they had agreed on when they'd started fucking. So what if the sneaking had been his idea in the first place and Bandos had gone along with it because he was getting his dick wet, so what the fuck did he care?

Feelings happened, and that changed things.

Bandos lifted the window, so Vaughan ended the phone call. He handed it to Bandos, who took it and stepped back, giving Vaughan room to climb through.

Bandos set the phone on the nightstand and turned, pulling Vaughan into his arms, holding him close. "Not trying to argue. I just don't know where I stand with you."

Vaughan ran his hand across Bandos's wide shoulders and sighed. "I could say the same thing, Bandos."

Vaughan grinned, wanting to change the subject. He wiggled his eyebrows. "Did you get more lube?"

Bandos chuckled. "Yeah."

"Then why are you still talking?" Vaughan didn't wait for Bandos to answer, but kissed him before sucking on Bandos's bottom lip. The quickest way to make Bandos forget was to kiss him as if they wouldn't get another chance to lock lips. "You love kissing more than fucking."

Bandos bit at Vaughan's lips playfully, letting him know what he thought about his assessment. "I love kissing *you*."

Vaughan smiled. "Prove it."

Bandos was big like all dragon shifters. Tall with muscles all over. Vaughan was only a couple of inches shorter, but he was a lot leaner. When Bandos lifted him off his feet and carried him to the bed as if he weighed nothing, it didn't surprise Vaughan. He was no lightweight, but Bandos didn't seem phased at all.

Vaughan's shoes were slip-ons and fell off easily along the way.

Bandos laid him on the bed, settling over him all while continuing the kiss.

Vaughan wrapped his legs around Bandos's waist.

Bandos had an advantage over Vaughan, having just his boxer briefs and nothing else on. Vaughan's pajama pants created more of a barrier between them.

Bandos didn't seem bothered by the obstacle. He cupped Vaughan's cheek and assaulted his senses with his lips. It was so fucking good.

Vaughan moaned, humping into Bandos, wanting some sort of friction on his hard cock. It seemed to do the trick in getting Bandos to focus on something other than Vaughan's mouth.

Vaughan let his legs fall apart when Bandos moved away.

Bandos stood, taking his underwear off.

Vaughan got naked as well, reaching for the nightstand drawer and pulling it open. Bandos grabbed the lube and then settled over Vaughan again. Neither of them cared enough to close the drawer.

Instead, Bandos fisted Vaughan's dark hair, tilting his head back and licking a path from his neck to his ear. "You're fucking sexy." Bandos whispered the words as if it was a dirty secret.

By the gods, Bandos could reduce him to the things he felt. He stole everything else.

Bandos kissed the place where Vaughan's neck and shoulder met. "Maybe I should bite you."

Vaughan sucked in a breath and then moaned when Bandos nipped playfully on that spot. He didn't draw blood or create a mating bite, but damned if Vaughan didn't want him to.

It was in Vaughan's nature to say something witty, but nothing came to mind other than his willingness to let it happen. "Yeah."

Bandos licked the spot again before pulling back, meeting Vaughan's gaze. The resignation was unmistakable, and it didn't go away when he put lube on his fingers.

Vaughan cupped Bandos's cheek when he looked away. Bandos rubbed around his pucker and he nearly forgot he had something to say. "I want you to, Bandos."

"It's not the time." Bandos buried his finger inside Vaughan up to his second knuckle. When he met Vaughan's gaze again, he seemed closed off. And then he said, "I'm going to fuck you until you scream."

He rubbed Vaughan's prostate. It stole Vaughan's brain cells, and he forgot what they were talking about. "By the gods."

Vaughan lifted his hips, demanding more, and Bandos gave it to him, pulling out part way before pushing in again. It took three thrusts in and out before Bandos added a second finger.

After that, he didn't waste time with teasing. They both wanted each other too much. Bandos removed his finger and lined up his cock, pressing in until just the head penetrated him.

Nothing else mattered but the moment.

Vaughan's eyes shifted with no effort. The only reason the difference registered was because his world lost a little color and his sense of smell kicked into overdrive. It hadn't happened during sex before.

Bandos sucked in a breath, his own eyes turned reptilian, and he pushed into Vaughan as if punishing him for giving him feelings.

Yeah, they both knew what it meant. The difference was the formation didn't piss one of them off. Beyond the clan wigging out, Vaughan welcomed the love. He wanted it more than his next breath.

In the plane, when he had time to think because there wasn't anything else to focus on but his own thoughts, he had figured out that Bandos was all that mattered. Maybe he didn't know what to do with that information, but he welcomed the knowledge.

Based on Bandos's sudden change in behavior, he wasn't as welcoming about the feelings they shared, although he had been before, which confused Vaughan more than anything.

Vaughan pulled his legs back, lifting his hips. His eyes closed when Bandos's cock rubbed over his prostate, sending white-hot bursts of lightning through his body.

Bandos reached between them, taking Vaughan's cock in his hand. He pumped it a couple of times before Vaughan came. Bandos wasn't very far behind. His movements became erratic, and he pressed in as far as he could get, holding it for long seconds before he slowly relaxed.

Vaughan wrapped his arms around Bandos, keeping him close. He smiled when Bandos settled on top of Vaughan as if he intended to sleep like that.

Vaughan opened his mouth to speak, but Bandos cut him off. "I don't want to talk about it."

Bando brought his clean hand up to Vaughan's hair, lacing his finger through the strands, and he turned into Vaughan, burying his nose in his neck, kissing him before settling again.

"What did you think I was going to say?"

"I don't know. I just know whatever it is, I don't want to talk about it."

Vaughan chuckled. "Okay. But what if it was just to tell you that was very satisfying?"

Vaughan felt Bandos's lips turn up into a smile against his skin.

"You weren't going to say that."

"Maybe I was. You'll never know now."

Bandos met Vaughan's gaze. Humor lit his eyes. "Was it? Satisfying, I mean."

"Yep. You?"

"Always." Bandos kissed him but kept it to just a peck. When he pulled back again, his expression was serious. "I know we need to talk, but can it keep until the morning? We're both tired and I don't want to argue."

Vaughan yawned, which made Bandos smirk.

When Bandos got up, probably to grab something to clean them, Vaughan closed his eyes. He was asleep in seconds.

Chapter Three

B andos set his phone's ringtone to make the traditional phone sounds, so when he woke that was how he figured out it was his phone going off and not Vaughan's. Vaughan had a different ring tone for everyone. It was ridiculously cute and a couple of them were annoying, although Bandos would never tell Vaughan for fear of the relentless teasing.

Vaughan had half the blankets off his body and seemed to press into Bandos for warmth. They spooned.

Bandos straightened the blanket, so they covered more of Vaughan before reaching for his phone on the nightstand. As soon as Bandos had it, he saw the screen read *Somerset*, and then the time.

It was after three o'clock in the morning, so it had to be Shawn. No one else would call him that late.

He pressed the green call button and whispered, "Yeah."

"I found something." Yep. Shawn.

Vaughan mumbled in his sleep and turned, pressing his cheek against Bandos's neck.

"Wait. Are you in bed?"

"It's in the middle of the night."

"Right. And I just heard someone else's voice. Who are you fucking?"

"What do you want, Shawn?"

Shawn chuckled. "Fine. I found a message about the fae."

"The missing dude?" There weren't very many fae left in the world. The one they were searching for might even have been the only one left. Bandos had done a little research and found out the fae had unique abilities. When matched with a male witch, they could enhance the other's magic. It could cause either growth or destruction, depending on the end goal.

One of the Somerset siblings had overheard Stavros talking about a fae when they were investigating, and that bought everyone a clue as to the real danger. It was a shame the real bad guys were a few powerful humans who would probably start a world war, and not the leader of a small coven of vampires. It was up to the paranormal council to fix it, and Bandos wanted to help. Finding the other missing piece of the trouble train would go a long way to working things in their favor.

"Yeah, but someone deleted part of the message. Not sure how to find it or if it's even possible."

"Oh, it's possible." Bandos sighed. "I'll be there in a few minutes."

"Tell whoever it is you're fucking I said hello."

Bandos shook his head. There was no one who gave him more shit than Shawn. Not even Rocky or Sully, who had been his best friends for more years than Shawn had been alive. Their personalities meshed, and they had become fast friends. "Bye, pest."

Shawn chuckled. "Bye."

Bandos ended the call with a smile and put the phone back on the nightstand before wrapping his arms around Vaughan again.

By the gods, he didn't want to get out of bed. Vaughan's body was warm, and he was an aggressive cuddler.

Bandos rubbed the side of his cheek against the top of Vaughan's head. "Vaughan." Even though he whispered, the words still sounded too loud.

He hated waking him. Lately, Vaughan went on one run after another and hadn't been sleeping as much as he needed.

Bandos kissed the part of Vaughan he could reach.

He would leave a note right before he left, telling him where he went. He might text as well. That should cover all the bases.

And then he pictured Vaughan trying to maneuver around Rocky, who was a silent observer on the best of days. Sometimes he assessed everything and everyone around him with a smile on his face, and other times the grim reaper had nothing on him. Bandos didn't want Vaughan to have to deal with Rocky if he decided stoic-asshole was his mode of communication.

Knowing Rocky, he wouldn't say a word because he knew Bandos and Vaughan had kept their relationship a secret.

He never thought he would love someone again. After Shephard, he didn't know he had it in him to even want to try. Vaughan had worked his way under Bandos's skin and then deeper until he held Bandos's heart in his hand.

Bandos had never been the type to wear his emotions for all to see. That was half their problem. Vaughan didn't know where he stood, and Bandos wouldn't continue as a dirty little secret. Fuck-buddies was something different. He could do that without telling anyone because they hadn't involved emotions. But they both knew they weren't that anymore.

For someone like Vaughan, who hid little and when he did, it was with humor and teasing, Bandos's closed-off attitude probably left him feeling as if he were alone in what they had.

They needed to talk.

When Bandos moved, he did so as slowly as possible. Scooching away an inch at a time so Vaughan wouldn't get aggressive and pin him to the bed. He would never leave if that happened, and there was a fae who needed rescuing.

The tactic worked. He cleared the bed and Vaughan rolled onto his stomach.

Bandos had adjusted the water to the shower and stood under the spray when someone knocked on the door. The knock wasn't heavy-handed but mindful of the hour and another person sleeping in the house, which told him it was Vaughan.

Rocky would have rapped his knuckles against the door once and then entered, not caring about anyone or Bandos's bathroom usage. Bandos could take a shit and Rocky wouldn't give a damn.

"Come in, baby."

The door opened and closed right before Vaughan pulled the curtain back and entered the shower.

Bandos smiled and pulled Vaughan into his arms.

Vaughan's curls were all askew, more than normal, and his expression was a little disgruntled, but he welcomed the embrace.

"Do you know what time it is?"

"Shawn called. He needs my help."

"It can't wait until late morning? And when I say late, I mean *late*. Eleven-thirty at the earliest."

Bandos chuckled and turned them so Vaughan was under the spray, giving him an opportunity to warm his skin. "It has to do with the fae.

I have evidence that suggests he needs rescuing, but we don't know where he is yet. Shawn might have found the missing piece."

"Missing piece?"

"Investigating is sort of like putting a puzzle together, only I have to find all the pieces first."

"Makes sense." Vaughan tilted his head back and let the water run through his hair. He sighed and smiled. "I'm a little more awake now."

"You should go back to bed, baby."

"Nah, I'm good. I want to talk to you, anyway."

"We can do that after I come back."

"Which could be this time tomorrow."

He got laser-focused on whatever he was doing and lost track of time. "I'll take a break if I go that late."

"I'm fine, Bandos. Really. It's just Mom's house. I can crash when we get there."

Bandos let it go and grabbed the bottle of shampoo. He squeezed some onto his hand, applying it to Vaughan's hair. "I know we need to talk."

Vaughan kept his eyes closed as Bandos worked the lather into his curls. He opened his mouth to speak, but Bandos cut him off.

"I think I need to start the conversation, baby." Bandos focused on his task. Something about the moment made him nervous. Old memories made him gun-shy. "I had a mate."

Vaughan stiffened but didn't speak.

"It was a long time ago. Back when a lot of shifter clans didn't mix species or mate outside of one man and one woman. I was a kid. Barely twenty-two and a little pissed off because my father tried to marry me off to some older dragon shifter who wanted kids but didn't have a mate. And she was female. I knew I liked boys almost from day one, so the thought of a female mate wasn't appealing. Shephard belonged to the clan a town over and they were wolf shifters."

"Double whammy. Different shifters and gay. That sucks."

Bandos helped him rinse his hair.

"Yeah. And he was the alpha's son, which meant he had fewer choices than I did."

"So what happened?"

"We did what we were told but agreed to see each other in secret."

"Oh." Vaughan winced. "I wish I would have known that. I wouldn't have suggested keeping our...thing on the down-low."

"I know. It's fine." Bandos hoped that was true by the end of their conversation.

"I have a feeling the story doesn't end well." Vaughan opened his eyes and met Bandos's gaze.

Bandos reached for the hair conditioner and put some on his palm. He bet that if Vaughan didn't have conditioner, there was no getting through those curls with a comb. "No, it doesn't. It's why I waited so long to tell you how I feel."

"And how is that?"

"I'm in love with you."

Vaughan released a breath as if he had been holding it for months. The smile turned into a grin. "Gods, so am I. I have for a while now."

Bandos smiled.

Vaughan turned them in the shower as Bandos worked the conditioner through his hair. "It's your turn. Dip your head back."

"Do you want to know what happened or not?" Bandos did what he was told, though, letting Vaughan take care of him.

"You can talk and let me wash your hair at the same time."

"Well, his father caught us together. He went to my father, and they decided we would marry women of their choosing the next week. I decided to leave and asked Shephard to come with me. He refused.

"On the day I intended to head out, his father came to my house with a bunch of his clan members and beat the shit out of me. My father stood and watched them do it and then kicked me out of his house. I found out later that Shephard had told his father what I had planned. He didn't stop that little going-away present."

Vaughan cursed as he put shampoo into his palm and worked it into Bandos's hair. "The fucker. Tell me which clan he belongs to so I can kill him."

Bandos smiled at Vaughan's protective instinct. "He died a long time ago. More years than you've been alive. The woman he married raised their children a little more liberally. They turned out better without him."

Bandos let Vaughan rinse the soap from his hair.

"Do you talk to them?"

"She reached out when he died. Said she thought I should know. We've been friends since."

"How did he die?"

"A human saw him in wolf form in the forest and shot him."

Vaughan finished rinsing his hair and then worked conditioner into it before getting under the spray again, tilting his head back. "I'm sorry that happened to you, but I'm glad too. I know that probably makes me a shitty person because I benefited from it."

Bandos smiled. "It was difficult for the first few years, but Rocky and Sully got me through it."

"Wait." Vaughan met his gaze. "You knew them way back then?"

"Yep. Rocky was in my clan. Sully was in Shephard's. In fact, Sully was Shephard's best friend. They came to my defense when Shephard's father beat me and left when I did. We've been together ever since."

In true Rocky fashion, he knocked on the bathroom door with one quick rap and then the door opened. "I have to pee."

"Hi, Rocky." Vaughan grinned.

"Vaughan."

"How's your turtle shifter?"

Rocky made a noncommittal noise.

"I'll take your silence for not well. Want some advice?"

"No."

Vaughan spoke as if Rocky had answered differently. "Buy two copies of the same book. Make it something nonfiction and steeped in history. Read one copy. Then give the other copy to Henri."

"Which part of history?"

Vaughan chuckled. "Doesn't matter. He loves it all."

"Fine." Rocky turned on the water for the sink.

"You're welcome."

The tap shut off and then Rocky left the room without a word.

"He really needs to work on his manners. Mom would have a field day with his attitude."

Bandos chuckled when he heard Rocky yell, "Fuck you, Vaughan."

Chapter Four

Time had slipped away, and Echo Daydale had lost the ability to tell what day it was. He knew the time, though. The tower room had a window that was so high on the wall it was set just beneath the ceiling. The sun's rays streamed through the panes of glass, touching Echo's skin when he sat in the right spot. Every day Echo would take in as much light as he could.

When his mother had been alive, she had always told him to go outside. "Get your nose out of that book, Echo, and go play. The sun doesn't shine for everyone."

Even as a child, he loved his books and learning. He likened himself to a sponge, absorbing everything he could. His mother had been right about needing the sunlight, although he hadn't realized what she had meant by saying everyone didn't have access to the sun until he could feel the vitamin deficiency taking hold.

He had read a medical book once that said some humans were allergic to the sun. It seemed unimaginable until the day they had kidnapped him and put him in the tower room of a castle as if he were a princess in one of those cartoon movies.

His mother hadn't let him watch them because she said they promoted women's dependence on men. He hadn't told her he had maybe wanted to wear one of those pretty dresses and hang off the arm of a prince, especially if said prince was his mate. But overall, he agreed with her.

His mother might have been fae, so they lived by a separate set of standards, but she had mingled with humans for most of her life. They lived in a human village, mixing in as best as they could with enchantments to round their ears and adapted some of their culture.

His mother's feminist attitude was one of those things he'd latched onto. His father had rolled his eyes whenever she'd gotten on one of her soapboxes, and said little. He'd spoken through his actions, supporting her when her boss had tried to cut her pay and hours, saying she didn't work as hard as the men. They both had understood the necessity because she worked the construction site alongside his father.

And Echo had learned his body parts did not make him special or superior. And they didn't mean he couldn't wear a dress if he chose. His parents would have supported his choices. Perhaps Father would have taken longer to come around, but Mother would have taken a flamethrower and cleared away all the bigots.

Echo sighed at the disappearing rays.

The stone floor was dirty. Still, he sat where the rays touched, dirt or no.

His clothing had taken a beating. He tried to clean them as best as he could in the bathroom sink, but the only soap was what he used on his body. It wasn't adequate enough to do as thorough a job as he would have liked.

The level of loneliness he had felt before getting kidnapped was nothing compared to what his life had become. They confined him to the room. He had prided himself on his introversion, but his nature wasn't enough to save him from insanity.

Little pieces of himself floated to the window and through the tiny crack where the glass had broken long before he had gotten there.

The castle was hundreds of years old, but someone had restored it at some point. Whoever owned it probably had a lot of money. Echo imagined old castles weren't cheap.

The last of the rays disappeared, leaving Echo feeling a little desperate.

It had been months. At least a few. Had it been more than a year? He had lost count of the days a while ago. A part of him regretted losing focus, and a part of him was grateful. Knowing might have reduced his level of hope. He hadn't had a lot of that, anyway.

No one would look for him. His parents had died long before his kidnapping. Maybe his boss would have a few things to say about him missing so many days of work. Mr. Farrell wasn't emotionally intelligent enough to connect Echo's past behavior of never even being late one day the entire three years he had worked for him to not showing up as any cause for alarm.

Sandy, his co-worker, may very well have found it alarming. And perhaps she had gone to the police and filed a missing person's report. She and his best friend, Helena, were his only chance of gaining his freedom.

His hope had thinned out until he hung by it as if it were a bunch of balloons. All but one had popped. It wasn't enough to keep him in the clouds. The closer he came to the ground, the more he realized he would crash and break off a vital part of his sanity. He was helpless to stop it.

Echo sighed and focused on the page number in his book. He'd have to ask the night guard for another book soon. The vampire who came at night liked him. Or he supposed he did, since he was the only one who ever showed kindness.

He shut his book and stood, stretching out the cramps in his muscles from sitting on the hard ground for so long. He brushed off his trousers as best as he could. Dust particles clouded the air around him as he worked the dirt off.

Perhaps the night guard would lend him cleaning supplies. He had asked before and nothing had come of it. It was worth trying again. What harm would a bucket and cleaning solution cause?

Echo made his way into the bathroom to relieve himself and wash his hands since he could feel the grit clinging to his fingers and palms. Modern plumbing inside a castle seemed odd, and he still didn't take it for granted.

Any castle he had ever seen had been from afar. He had never been close enough to understand how one functioned in a modern world. They all looked so medieval and untouchable.

He appreciated how he could turn a knob and water would flow.

It was as he grabbed the soap that the vision hit him.

The last one had come before the kidnapping. He'd seen a male witch almost die at the hands of a vampire coven. It had happened somewhere in the States. He wasn't sure how he knew the location. Sometimes little bits of knowledge popped into his mind without him knowing the reason or cause. Every vision meant something significant would happen. He'd had a vision of the accident on his parents' construction site days before it happened, which had changed his life forever. Even that had meant more than just the knowledge that it would affect him. The construction company employed half the town, and after the accident, the company had gone under. Those who hadn't lost their lives, lost their jobs. Their small town hadn't been the same since.

The witch was special. He was important, although Echo wasn't privy to that information. He had counted himself lucky to have seen the outcome of the witch's ordeal because it had ended with the witch alive.

Echo concentrated on the scene playing out in his mind. He saw himself in a photograph through someone else's eyes. It was as if he were another person. Echo didn't know who or what their importance was. The person met the gaze of a male. A large, strong-looking shifter who had lovely green eyes that reminded Echo of the green hills near his hometown.

Something upset the males in his vision. Echo couldn't tell why. All he knew was they were important to him somehow.

He added two more balloons to his bouquet of hope, and it was just enough to keep him from crashing.

For the first time in days, he smiled.

Chapter Five

Vaughan sipped on his third cup of coffee and contemplated making Bandos take a break as he leaned against the counter in front of the coffee pot. He'd been there for a couple of hours, staying in the kitchen because he didn't want to hover, and he would if he made his way closer to Bandos.

He had an ache in the pit of his stomach and he didn't know why. The feeling made him uneasy in his own skin until everything around him felt shaky, including his budding relationship.

Maybe it had something to do with his plan to come clean about them. It wasn't as though he expected a bad response from his family. Some of the more traditional clan members might have an issue, but overall, they wouldn't get much resistance. The family would accept and love without conditions, like they always had. He expected an uncomfortable conversation with Ladon, mostly because Vaughan knew his little brother would tease him. Vaughan would do the same if the circumstances were reversed.

Hell, the only reason Vaughan had kept it secret for as long as he had was because he didn't know where he stood with Bandos. Bandos didn't exactly give anything away. Or hadn't until the shower earlier.

That conversation changed a lot, including him gaining a protective instinct because of Bandos's past.

Maybe that contributed to the unease.

Maybe he shouldn't have come with Bandos. He could've still been in bed with Bandos's scent on the blankets.

The door to the kitchen swung open, and Magnus stopped in his tracks when he saw Vaughan. Magnus had on pajama pants and a T-shirt that was probably Ladon's, given how big it was on him. Magnus wasn't a little guy, but Ladon made him appear about the size of a teenage boy.

Magnus blinked twice and then recovered as he made his way across the room. "You're here because..."

Before Vaughan could answer, Ladon entered the kitchen, scratching his bare belly. He kissed Magnus on his way to the coffeepot. "I'll get us some coffee, baby. You can sit down."

Magnus smiled and sat at the table.

Vaughan took the pot from Ladon. "Your coffee tastes like shit. Let me do it."

"Thought you would be sleeping." Ladon grabbed two mugs from the cupboard and put them on the counter.

Vaughan made a noncommittal grunt because he knew where the conversation was going and he wanted to draw it out some, give himself time to think through his answers. He filled the pot with water and poured it into the machine.

"Didn't you get in late?" Ladon leaned against the counter.

"Yep." Vaughan emptied the reusable filter into the trash before rinsing it out.

"Why are you here?"

And there it was, the perfect opportunity to come clean with his alpha. He would have liked to tell his mother first because she would kiss him on the cheek, tell him she already knew, and call him dear at least once. It would fill Vaughan with all the gooey good things his mother's warmth often did.

He could probably handle telling Ladon.

Probably.

"Shawn found something regarding the fae. Called Bandos. Since Bandos getting out of bed woke me, I thought I might as well come with." Vaughan grabbed the ground coffee and the measuring spoon and put the correct amount into the filter thing.

Magnus chuckled. "You owe me twenty bucks, babe."

Ladon grinned and poured coffee into each mug. "You want some advice?"

Vaughan smiled. "Sure."

"Never bet with an investigator. Bandos will figure shit out way sooner than you. My investigator mate knows all, so Bandos probably does too."

Vaughan chuckled. "I'll remember that."

"So Bandos, huh." Ladon regarded him with raised eyebrows.

"Yep."

"He's not your fated mate." When had he and Ladon become friends? Vaughan had somehow blinked and missed Ladon maturing into someone he could have a serious conversation with.

"And yet I love him anyway."

Ladon nodded. "Okay."

"That's it? Just 'okay'."

Ladon shrugged. "I won't tell you who to love. No one will, Vaughan. You have my word on that."

"So you think the clan will have issues."

"I didn't say that. They didn't when Tim's ex-wife left him, and it was a big fat fucking clue that Tim and his ex weren't fated mates. Why would they act any different with you and Bandos?"

Vaughan didn't think they would. "At first it was just a fuck-buddy situation, so why say anything, ya know?"

"Yeah. It's nobody's business."

"Exactly." Vaughan sighed. "Now, if I don't say something, he becomes a dirty secret, and I don't want him to feel that way."

Ladon raised his eyebrows. "It's like, *serious*, serious, then?"

"Yeah."

"Oh." Ladon shook his head. "Man, you have not thought it all the way through, have you?"

"Not at all." Vaughan knew what Ladon was getting at. Finding his fated mate would create issues, but it might never happen, so why borrow trouble.

"Well, I like Bandos and for what it's worth, I think you guys are good together."

"Thanks, Ladon."

"Thomas might help you." Ladon had a good suggestion.

Thomas, one of Jules's mates, was a warlock. His magic came from the ancestors.

Vaughan would talk to Bandos about it and see what he thought. They had nothing to lose but their approval of the ancestors, and they were all dead.

"Thomas connected himself, Hacen, and Jules, and it was an effortless process, even under the stress of their situation." Magnus brought his mug to his lips and sipped.

Vaughan nodded. "Yeah, I bet he pissed Stavros off with his little stunt."

"It gave Nicolono ammunition to use Jules as his punching bag. That's about it. Thankfully, you all rescued Jules or he would be dead by now. Nicolono had lacked a conscience so it wouldn't have taken him long to get sick of Jules, even if the ancestors hadn't taken away the mating pull." Sometimes it was easy to forget that Magnus had worked for Nicolono before coming to Saint Lakes. In fact, the only reason Magnus had come to the area was because Nicolono had hired him to kidnap Lucas. Instead, Magnus and Ladon had found each other. They seemed happy since mating.

Maybe mating had matured Ladon. Becoming the acting alpha had done wonders too. No doubt that was a demanding job that would've made even the most immature child grow up, and Ladon had always been a little ahead of his age, anyway.

Shawn came through the door with a couple of papers in his hand, heading straight for Ladon. He handed them over without a word.

Bandos followed at a less excited pace. He darted his gaze to Vaughan, which meant whatever information they had found would take Vaughan away again. Bandos didn't like it, although his expression wasn't easy to read.

Yet another reason asking Thomas for help would be a good idea. Given Bandos' past, Vaughan would have to plan what he intended to say. He'd never been good at smooth talking and he doubted he could talk Bandos into anything, including feeling the mating pull again.

He had said he loved Vaughan, but the question remained, how much? Enough to put his feelings to the test? Vaughan had his doubts.

Vaughan crooked a finger at Bandos when he hesitated to come over. Once he was close enough, Vaughan leaned against him until Bandos took the hint and wrapped an arm around Vaughan's shoulders and pulled him closer. Bandos kissed him on his temple.

Ladon studied the papers, going through them one at a time until he made it through the last one. Once he did, he focused on Bandos. "Can you get information about the building?"

"Oh yeah. I have some information on my laptop." Bandos rubbed Vaughan's shoulder. He probably didn't know he was doing it.

Ladon pulled out his phone and focused on it. Knowing him, he called a meeting. "Give me the basic gist of what we're talking about here."

"Well, it's exactly what the message calls it. An old castle with an interesting history. It's changed owners a lot. Mostly because it takes a small fortune just on the upkeep, not to mention the actual restoration of a building like that. Beyond an excellent security system, that's all digital and easy to hack. I didn't find any other security measures."

Ladon nodded. "Meeting in an hour in the office."

Bandos nodded and leaned into Vaughan. "Prepare to leave. Again."

"I figured. I'm ready to go." Vaughan always had a bag packed with everything he needed. He kept it in a compartment on his plane and replaced everything when needed.

"You're working too much and not taking care of yourself."

Vaughan smiled. "Are you volunteering for a job?"

Bandos's eyes sparkled with humor. "What's it pay?"

Vaughan wiggled his eyebrows but didn't comment because his little brother was in the room.

Chapter Six

B andos sat on the couch with his laptop on the coffee table in front of him. He needed to bring up the document he'd created containing the information about the castle. Given its historical value, there was a lot, and none of it was significant to the fae in question. The only value was the drawing someone had done of the inside. It made planning a rescue easier. Or potentially, if the restoration stayed true to the original plan.

"A castle. Seriously." Ramsey put the printed conversation on the desk. He was the last one to read it. "That seems...a little over the top."

Vaughan sat next to Bandos, watching the laptop screen as Bandos moved around the Internet. "Yeah, well, the person who owns it is probably a vampire."

Bandos nodded. "That would be the coven nearest to it, but a woman vampire is listed on the deed. She's not important other than she has connections to Delano Archer. It seems Delano intervened in Stavros' plan to ship the fae to the United States. According to the logs I found, Stavros intended to mail the poor guy here in a damn crate.

Delano's the reason the fae isn't dead from dehydration or at the very least malnourished. He had the fae taken to the castle, and I'm pretty sure they haven't moved him since."

Ladon asked, "What do we know about the castle?"

"It has a fairly rich history. A battle had destroyed most of it about four hundred years ago, but someone had it rebuilt, and the current structure is around three hundred years old. It suffered some decay, but the current owner has restored it." Bandos turned his computer around. "So this is a drawing of the original structure."

"Original. Not the current one?" This question came from Garridan, who had always been smarter than most had given him credit for. Bandos could relate on some level. First impressions told most that Bandos was the big, young jock type. It didn't matter that he wore a lot of leather and rode a motorcycle. He'd never played a sport in his life, and his years expanded more than a human lifetime. Still, he didn't look like a computer nerd older than most in the room.

Bandos smiled. "And there's the problem. There's no way to tell if they restored it to its original form. Not even the one from three hundred years ago. And the historian who drew the sketch took an educated guess."

Garridan sighed. "And security?"

"High tech, but nothing I can't get through. I don't know about inside."

"Any thoughts on where the kidnappers might keep him?" Ladon directed the question toward Fane and then met Rocky's gaze.

Fane stood from Ramsey's lap and walked the few steps to get to Bandos's laptop. He sat on the floor in front of it and scrolled when he needed the drawings for another floor.

Rocky sat next to Vaughan, so the computer was close even if the screen wasn't facing him. Fane turned it so Rocky could see and then stood, sitting on Ramsey's lap again.

"The rooms are large and fairly open," Rocky commented.

"Except for the upper-levels. Those need to be checked first. If he's not there, then go down to the dungeon," Fane said.

Vaughan chuckled. "Dungeons and castles. It sounds ridiculous."

"I watch television with Ramsey sometimes. Castles always have dungeons," Fane said.

When Bandos turned to meet Vaughan's gaze, Vaughan winked. To the rest of the room, he said, "Can't argue with that."

Rocky nodded. "I agree with Fane. They probably don't have a lot of prisoners so the upper-levels would be where I would check."

"What do we know about the nearby coven?" Ladon asked.

"Nothing, really. They seemed to stay out of trouble, despite their connection to Delano. They're also small. Less than two hundred members. What they lack in numbers they make up for in money, though. Still, I have a feeling the only reason they're helping Delano is because his coven is one of the largest in the world."

Ladon sat back in his chair and tapped a finger on the arm before turning to Magnus. "You know Delano, right?"

"Yeah. I know him. He follows the money and not much else."

"How likely is it that Delano will join forces?"

"Before Jules killed Stavros? I would say not at all. After? It's likely. Especially given how some human politicians know about us. Senator Fowler has a lot of clout. He'll be a problem at some point. I would say Delano's probably underestimating him because he's human. Sorta has a prejudice where they are concerned. It's not likely he'll come around until the senator makes a big move."

"Until it's all over the television, you mean?" That came from Garridan, whose eyes shifted to his dragon's and his fangs dropped.

"Pretty much, yeah. That's what I think he'll do." Magnus put a hand on Ladon's shoulder. "Why did you ask?"

Bandos hadn't seen a lot of insecurity in Ladon. He seemed conscious of his experience or lack of, which wasn't a bad thing unless he displayed that sort of uncertainty in front of his clan. It said something about Ladon that he let his guard down around his inner circle. It meant Ladon leaned on them when he needed to the most. It was the mark of a good leader.

"I'm just thinking ahead. Like if we go in and take the fae, would that piss Delano off enough to side with the humans later on?" Ladon turned his gaze to Garridan. "What do you think?"

The pride in Garridan's expression was unmistakable. His role as the Somersets' father suited him well.

Bandos had known Garridan for more years than some people had been alive, Vaughan included. Going feral had changed him in a lot of ways that made Bandos feel a little guilty for leaving his friend with a monster like Stavros. Not that Bandos had known. It was nothing for decades to go by without communication for shifters, especially those born before the age of telephones. Shifters lived a long time and Bandos, Rocky and Sully had led a nomadic lifestyle until recently. They hadn't even known Garridan was in distress. The excuses didn't change one fundamental fact. They hadn't been there for their friend when he needed them the most.

The old Garridan, the one Bandos had known before, shone through when he looked at Ladon. The paternal instinct was loud and clear.

"Your thinking is sound. We'll want to extract him with as few casualties as possible," Garridan answered.

"Send in two or three at most and tell them to be as silent as they can," Fane interjected.

With any other alpha, Fane inserting himself into the conversation might have ended with a punishment, but Ladon didn't seem to hold on to formality. Plus, it was stupid not to take Fane's advice as he was better at fighting and strategizing than anyone Bandos had ever met.

"Bandos, can you get around the security from here?" Ladon asked.

Bandos wanted to lie because it meant he would get assigned to the trip. "Probably, yeah. It's a good system, but not that good. I'd like to go, though."

Ladon raised his eyebrows and smirked. "And why is that?"

Bandos cleared his throat. "Vaughan will have to transport, right?"

Ladon nodded.

Bandos raised his eyebrows. No words were necessary. Everyone in the room knew about their relationship just based on his statement and facial expression.

He half-expected there to be silence. Instead, Ramsey cursed, and Fane gave him a smug smile. "Told you," Fane said.

Garridan gave Bandos a narrow-eyed stare. Bandos expected the dad-talk at some point.

Vaughan put a hand on his knee. "I'll be okay."

Vaughan, rejecting Bandos's help, pissed him off. "You're overworked. If I don't come, you won't take care of yourself. And you'll be even worse when you get home."

"I promise to eat all my veggies. Now stop worrying about me."

"I'm serious."

"I can see that." Vaughan met Ladon's gaze. "I'm fit to fly either way."

Vaughan could take or leave him.

Bandos put an arm around Vaughan's shoulders and held him close. "I can get through their security better if I'm there. And Rocky can vouch for me."

Rocky made a noncommittal sound and shrugged. "He does all right."

Vaughan whispered in his ear, "You're overreacting but it's sexy."

Bandos rolled his eyes and ignored Vaughan's teasing. He focused on Ladon instead. "I'm also big enough to carry the fae out if needed."

Bandos hoped for the fae's sake that his time in captivity wasn't so detrimental to his health, but it was something they should plan for.

Ladon raised his hand, silencing Bandos's argument. "I think it's good that you go. We need someone else."

"Um." Vaughan raised his head. "I'm going to be there anyway, so why not?"

"Because you're about as silent as a train." Ladon rolled his eyes.

"Hey, my ninja skills aren't as on point as Fane's, but I can follow Bandos's direction. I do just fine when he's fucking me. Tell him, baby." Some of the words that came out of Vaughan's mouth were unbelievable.

Bandos sighed but otherwise didn't contribute to the conversation. Vaughan had taken it to a place he would rather not go, at least not with anyone besides Vaughan.

Ramsey snorted out a laugh, and even Fane chuckled.

Rocky smiled, which was as good as an outright laugh.

Garridan was the one who stopped Vaughan before he really got started. "This is not the time, Vaughan."

"Sorry," Vaughan said, but Bandos could tell he wasn't. He would keep going if it were anyone else reprimanding him.

Bandos thanked the gods for Garridan's parenting skills because he didn't want to have a discussion with the alpha about his and Vaughan's sex life.

"I can't send back-up easily," Ladon warned.

"It should be an easy extraction. The coven doesn't seem prepared for trouble. It tells me they don't make a habit of seeking it out." As much as Bandos didn't want Vaughan to put himself in danger, facts were facts. As someone who was good at gaining concrete information, he wouldn't put any more emotion into the discussion than he already had. Plus, Bandos could protect Vaughan if needed.

"Okay, so what do you know about the fae?"

"In terms of what? His history? A fae's abilities? His physical stats?" Bandos asked.

Ladon sat forward. "I just want to know that you know who to grab. And before you start in on me on how you're not stupid, Vaughan. It may not be obvious if the person is unconscious. Do we even know the person's gender?"

"I wasn't going to say you were stupid," Vaughan protested but grinned, which meant he had witty, teasing thoughts.

Bandos turned his computer around and pulled it closer before typing. He found the picture he wanted. Before he could turn it again, Vaughan snatched the computer from the coffee table and held it to his face as if he had a problem with his sight.

Bandos scowled and went to take the computer back, but then Vaughan's eyes shifted to his wolf's and his fangs dropped. Vaughan cursed and stood before handing the computer back to Bandos.

Bandos took it and watched Vaughan as he left the room. He sent the picture to the copy machine and waited for it to print before turning the computer around to show everyone. He set it back on the table before standing and grabbing the computer printout.

Bandos half-expected to find Vaughan pacing in the kitchen, but he wasn't. Jules and Thomas were there instead. Jules stood at the sink, filling the coffee carafe with water. Thomas stood next to him with his head on Jules's shoulder. Both wore T-shirts and matching plaid pajama pants.

"Can one of you point me in whatever direction Vaughan went in?"

Thomas pointed to the sliding glass door without moving or saying a word.

Bandos didn't waste time. He headed outside, chasing Vaughan all while his heart rose into his throat because he knew what kind of bug had crawled up Vaughan's ass and it didn't bode well for their budding relationship.

He followed Vaughan's scent to the front of the house and saw him leaning against the siding.

Vaughan didn't look his way, although he stiffened. "Are you ready?"

Bandos didn't stop until he pressed against Vaughan, boxing him in with his arms. He tried to get Vaughan to meet his gaze, but Vaughan kept his eyes averted to the ground. "No. I have to go back in and talk to the alpha about your mate."

Vaughan shut his eyes. "I don't know that for sure."

"Not until you meet him." And when that happened, Vaughan would know the fae was his. Bandos didn't have a doubt in his mind.

He could feel Vaughan's firm body against his own. Nothing in Bandos's life had felt so right. Vaughan had entered his life just in time to exit it and leave Bando less than whole.

Vaughan opened his eyes and snapped his gaze to Bandos. He had never seen Vaughan even close to angry, and maybe he wasn't all the way to that emotion yet, but he was close. "We don't know, so don't make a big deal out of it until we do."

Bandos showed Vaughan the photo printout. "You partially shifted looking at this. I think we both know what that means."

"Nothing." Vaughan raised his voice and threw fire at Bandos with his eyes. "It means nothing."

"Why are getting upset?" Bandos would think Vaughan should feel some level of happiness.

"Because you're getting ready to dump me over it."

"I never said that." But he couldn't deny his thoughts leaned in that direction.

"I can see it on your face."

"Maybe we should know for sure."

Vaughan sighed. "That's what I fucking said two seconds ago."

Bandos leaned forward, pressing his cheek against Vaughan's. "My feelings for you won't change."

Vaughan wrapped his arms around Bandos's waist and held on as if his life depended on it. "Isn't that supposed to be my line?"

"It is, yeah."

"Then ditto. And I mean it. We can figure this out without it changing things between us."

Bandos moved away. "Your mate changes everything."

Chapter Seven

E verything to do with planes came automatically. The sequence of what Vaughan had to do to get the plane ready was like meditation. Instead of focusing on his problems, he did his job. Thinking was never a good thing. Whatever it took to not have to think about what bothered him. But it was just the two of them and Bandos was in a mood.

Bandos hadn't said more than two sentences since they'd arrived at Saint Lakes airport. He sat in the co-pilot's seat and focused on his laptop.

Vaughan knew whatever Bandos read had to do with the fae, and as curious as he was about that, he wouldn't poke the dragon by asking. The last thing Vaughan needed was for Bandos to think he wanted to mate with the fae. Maybe he did, maybe he didn't. Reacting to one picture didn't mean he wanted to declare his undying love for someone he had never even met. But Bandos thought he would, which was ridiculous.

"Did we pack a bag for the fae? Just in case he needs clothes." They didn't know what condition the poor guy was in. Hell, just the thought of the fae injured and unkempt made Vaughan's eyes shift to his wolf's.

"In the back."

The radio crackled to life, giving him instruction to prepare for take-off. Vaughan spoke back and continued readying the plane.

"Did you get toiletries for him?"

"Yes. I got everything your mate would need. I promise." And so it began. They were about to talk about the elephant on the plane. Maybe that was a good thing.

"Stop it."

Bandos made a noncommittal noise at the back of his throat.

"You're starting an argument."

"It's a fact, Vaughan. You denying it is making it worse."

Vaughan rolled his eyes and started the engine. Bandos put his computer away and put on the headphones.

"You know as well as I do, your wolf is going to go nuts when you get one whiff of his scent." Bandos grabbed the edge of his seat when Vaughan put the plane in reverse and backed up. It wasn't until he pulled onto the runway that he relaxed.

"Are you a nervous flyer? Because if you can't handle it, you need to move to the back."

"Don't change the subject."

"I'm not. I'm trying to fly a plane, which you need to let me do." Yep, they definitely had their first fight. No doubt about it.

"Sorry."

Vaughan taxied down the runway and then took to the air. It wasn't until he had the proper elevation that he spoke to Bandos again. "I love you."

"Vaughan."

"It's true. A mate won't change my feelings. And it won't change yours either. So I suggest we either talk about something else or come up with potential solutions to this problem that doesn't include you roaring out of Saint Lakes on your bike."

"You think I'll leave the clan?"

"I think you'll do what you *think* you have to, but you forget I have a brother who has two mates."

"Two *fated* mates. That's different."

"I don't see why it has to be a big deal."

"You'll have instincts toward him you don't with me."

"I would have instincts toward anyone who looked like him. And yeah, maybe some of it is because he's my mate, but not all of it. He looks as young as you do."

"I'm three times your age, Vaughan." Bandos sighed and shifted in his seat. "And his."

"Great, but that's not my point. I'm just saying he looks innocent. And he looks small. Like Jules."

"He's shorter than Jules." Bandos supplied that little tidbit of information without looking Vaughan's way. "Five-foot-five-inches and around a buck-forty."

"Thank you for sharing that, but that just proves my point."

"I know." Bandos shook his head. "He looks...fragile. I doubt he is, though. He's a fae. Fae know the future and can amplify other's abilities. That's why Stavros wanted him and Lucas. With Lucas killing and healing so easily, the fae would make it possible for him to do that to an entire species at one time."

Damn. "That's a massive extermination." What did it mean that he was a little proud to know his fae was a badass? As bad ass as his dragon.

"Yeah. That's why we need to keep the fae safe. No one deserves what they're doing to him." Was that a protective instinct, or was Vaughan projecting?

"We'll protect him, baby."

"He'll need all of Saint Lakes. So will Lucas." Bandos cleared his throat. "His name is Echo."

Vaughan swallowed the lump forming in his throat. He didn't want it to matter, but it did. Putting a name to the face made him more real. He wasn't just a picture anymore.

Echo.

By the gods.

"Watching you bond with him is going to be fucking torture, but I don't plan on leaving Saint Lakes."

"Maybe he already has a mate. Same as me. Did you ever think of that?"

"I'm not your mate, Vaughan."

"You are, and I'll fucking bite you to prove it. Just wait until we land."

"It's not that simple."

Fuck. "Yes. It is. Nothing has to change."

"This changes everything."

"Okay, fine. But we don't know how yet. We won't know until after we meet him, so stop with the negativity."

"I'm being realistic."

Vaughan sighed. "Look, I get your caution. You had a mate who not only left you but also allowed a beat-down. You can compare me to him, or you can keep an open mind and see if you can trust me."

Bandos cursed. "I'm starting to like your teasing side better. What does that say about me?"

Vaughan chuckled. "That you're a glutton for punishment and also, you know I'm right."

After a few minutes, Bandos said, "This isn't as simple of a situation as lack of trust."

"I know." That was more apparent than anything. "The flight is going to be a few hours. Maybe you should get some sleep."

Bandos shook his head. "I'm good."

"Fine. But I'm done arguing. I mean it."

Bandos made that noncommittal noise again. "He has two jobs. He works as a barista in a café and a cook in a restaurant. The same person owns both places."

"Okay."

"He doesn't have family, but a few of his friends filed missing persons reports and put fliers around his hometown, so he has people who care about him."

"No one should be alone."

"I'm pretty sure he wanted a cat because he kept tried to adopt one right before Stavros had his people kidnap him."

"A cat."

Bandos nodded and rubbed circles with his thumb on Vaughan's thigh.

"What else?"

Chapter Eight

As forests went, it wasn't the densest one Vaughan had ever been in. The ones surrounding Saint Lakes had way more trees. Comparatively, Saint Lakes looked like a northern jungle, not that such things existed but it had a similar density sometimes. Everything was evergreen because there were more pine trees. But the forest they were in had moss growing everywhere, including up the sides of trees. The bright green made it seem like the land of the fae.

Vaughan would never have said it aloud, but he didn't know what he was doing. He shouldn't have pushed so hard to go in the field. He was good at transporting, not rescuing pretty fae men.

He had wanted a chance to prove himself to Bandos, not that he had anything to prove. He probably should have adopted that attitude a lot sooner than when they were about to rescue a fae from a castle.

Bandos seemed so sure of himself with the investigation and rescue. Flying a plane paled in comparison, especially since all he would have done had he not spoken up was wait for the rescue team to finish and worrying about Bandos getting hurt. And maybe he would have worried about the fae as well, not that he wanted to admit it. At least not to Bandos, who already didn't trust Vaughan.

So yeah, maybe he listened to his ego. Since he was following Bandos through a forest that made him feel like a hobbit. His height and lean build made him more elf-like, plus he liked to think he was sexy enough to be one. He needed pointy ears, and he would be all set.

"Do you think I'm pretty enough to be elf? Like the ones in Tolkien's books," Vaughan whispered while staring at Bandos' ass.

Bandos carried his laptop under his left arm. When he turned to meet Vaughan's gaze, he handed it over. Bandos shook his head and rolled his eyes as he turned back around.

Vaughan held the computer in front of him as Bandos took his phone out of his pocket and stopped walking again even as he kept his eyes on the screen. "So? Am I?"

"I've never met an elf, so I don't know."

"But you saw the *Lord of the Rings* movies. Do I look like the elves on there?"

"No. Your ears aren't pointy enough. And I think you'd need longer hair." That Bandos indulged Vaughan spoke of his affection.

"But I'm tall enough and lean, right?"

Bandos made a noncommittal noise in the back of his throat and turned toward the left. "We need to go toward the east."

"Right?" Vaughan dragged out the word.

"You're so pretty you could model underwear. Now will you concentrate?"

Vaughan grinned. "You're not just telling me what I want to hear, are you?"

Bandos sighed. "We're getting close, so I'm going to need you to be serious."

"I'm being serious."

"No, you're not. You're in teasing mode. Flip the switch."

Maybe he should come clean. "This whole thing makes me nervous." His adrenaline made his heart pound, which made his breathing heavy. Traipsing through the forest in his human form didn't help.

Bandos didn't even turn around. "It'll be okay."

"I have a bad feeling." It sat in the pit of his stomach. "And I have zero skills to lend toward this mission."

"Just follow my direction."

Vaughan sighed. "I will. I trust you."

"Good." Bandos turned to meet his gaze again. "Because I trust you too."

He wasn't just talking about Vaughan's ability to follow directions, but with the mating situation as well.

Vaughan closed the distance between them and kissed Bandos. He kept it brief. "No pressure, right?"

Bandos smiled. "No pressure, baby. I promise. Let's rescue him first, yeah?"

Vaughan kissed him again and then let go.

Bandos continued walking, and Vaughan followed as he prepared to take orders from his dragon.

Vaughan kept his mouth shut, which wasn't easy for him. He had a lot on his mind and wasn't one to hold back. Shelving all of it to focus on his task wasn't exactly his strength unless it came to flying.

It wasn't even ten minutes before they saw an enormous stone building emerging just beyond the trees. Bandos stopped and crouched next to a tree almost large enough to hide his wide shoulders. Vaughan squatted next to him, handing the computer over when he reached for it.

Bandos opened it and set his phone on the moss. The computer didn't take long to boot up and before Vaughan knew it, Bandos was typing away.

He cursed under his breath but didn't stop what he was doing.

"What's wrong?" Vaughan whispered, leaning into Bandos.

"Their security system has a wall I need to get around. I didn't expect it."

"'A wall'?"

"I can tell you the technical term if you really want to know."

"Firewall, right?"

Bandos smirked. "Pretty much."

"So you're trying to hack into it by putting malware on it." Vaughan could fly a plane and fix a motor, but he wasn't a computer genius like Bandos. Still, he knew more than the basics.

Bandos met his gaze with raised eyebrows. "You should help me like Shawn does."

Vaughan started to reply but stopped himself when he heard voices in the distance. He stiffened and his eyes shifted. He mentally prepared himself to shift.

Bandos closed the computer lid so the artificial light wouldn't draw attention. They both seemed to hold their breath as the voices drew closer.

Bandos shifted his hands. His green eyes turned reptilian, and he growled low in his throat. Vaughan found Bandos's response sexy, but the timing for such thoughts wasn't right so he tried to shelve them.

Vaughan smelled the threat before he saw them. The scent of lavender covered the area, but it grew stronger the closer the voices came.

Vampires.

It meant they were in the right place.

When the vampires came within sight, they both had guns strapped to their hips but nothing else separated them from looking like normal people. They spoke in an accent so heavy it was difficult to make out the fact that they spoke English. Vaughan understood about forty percent of the conversation. It seemed mundane anyway. As best as Vaughan could tell, they talked about the difficulty of getting pregnant and how one of them had a mate who needed an heir. The woman seemed genuinely upset.

Vaughan assumed they were doing a perimeter check since they were scanning the area. Bandos and Vaughan hid themselves and stayed downwind so they wouldn't have sensed them no matter how good they were.

They passed without incident and Vaughan relaxed. Bandos didn't, though. He might have shifted his hands to his human form again, but his eyes stayed reptilian. His growl was a deep rumble that got deeper when Vaughan moved his weight from one leg to the other.

"Stay close." Bandos never stopped the subtle aggression.

"Oh-kay." Vaughan hopped over, trying not to stand and show himself to the vampires who weren't that far away. He couldn't help grinning.

"Shush." Bandos opened the computer again and did his thing.

Vaughan's grin widened, but he kept his mouth shut. The last thing he wanted was to make Bandos's job harder. He was already protective, and that would likely get worse when they entered the castle.

He'd seen Bennett get protective of Lucas, and Ladon got that way with Magnus too. He knew dragons were protective toward their mates. He never thought Bandos would go all dragon mate on him, but he liked it.

"Got it." Bandos closed the computer and tucked it between two moss-covered tree roots. He leaned into Vaughan. "They should come back around in the next five minutes. We'll head to the west side of the building. If the construction stayed true to the original building, there should be a window."

"What if there isn't a window? What's Plan B?" Vaughan pressed his cheek against Bandos, wanting the contact.

"There's a door that leads into the kitchen. It's exposed inside and out and not a great idea, but it's the only other way inside that won't get us caught." Bandos breathed in Vaughan's scent.

"Will you fit through the window?" It was a legitimate question.

"I don't know, but you will. In the eventuality that I don't, I want you to stay put until I get to you."

"Understood." Vaughan heard voices again.

Bandos pulled Vaughan close, nearly making him fall on his ass. Vaughan almost cursed but stopped himself before he could let it spill. He narrowed his eyes, but his annoyance was lost on Bandos who watched the vampires as they scanned the area.

They were still discussing fertility. It sounded as though the woman had decided on calling a local vampire specialist. She didn't call them a doctor, but that was what Vaughan thought they were. Since neither lady seemed evil, Vaughan hoped things worked out for her.

The ladies weren't their enemy. Hell, the vampire coven wasn't evil either. Not anymore than Saint Lakes. They were just on the opposite side. The question was for how long, because the fact was, they had a common enemy in the humans and that meant they would fight side by side at some point. The enemy of their enemy was their friend and all that.

Once they were out of sight, Bandos stood, helping Vaughan up. He sighed and pulled Vaughan into him, kissing his temple. "Follow me."

Vaughan could obey when he wanted to and following Bandos wasn't a hardship. "Has anyone ever told you how nice your ass is?"

"Be serious."

Yeah, that would not happen because Vaughan needed something so he wouldn't focus on his heart trying to beat its way out of his chest and his stomach churning with nerves. "I am being serious."

So not every castle had a moat filled with gigantic scary creatures with large teeth. And there wasn't a drawbridge. There probably had been a wall for protection at one point but it had either decayed, or someone had taken it out long ago. The castle stood alone like a king without a court, which made it easy for them.

The danger lay in leaving the cover of the trees and entering the grassy yard.

Bandos, in particular, made a big, noticeable target. At least from anyone coming in front of them. He blocked someone's view of Vaughan.

They ran across the yard. "Watch the windows," Bandos whispered.

Vaughan scanned each window as they moved, not seeing anyone, but the sun reflected off the glass of a few of them so he couldn't see inside. If someone wanted to take them out with a bullet, they wouldn't have been able to stop them, so looking for trouble was almost a moot point.

Vaughan breathed easier when they made it to the castle. He raised his eyebrows upon seeing the size of the window. Even he wouldn't fit unless he turned sideways. "Yeah, you aren't getting through that. I might not either."

"The drawing I found was crude. They weren't blueprints." Bandos peered inside before lifting the window. When the thing raised, he took Vaughan by the arm, pulling him over. "Do not and I mean under no circumstances, unless your life is in danger, leave the room."

Vaughan rolled his eyes. "I got it."

Bandos stood behind Vaughan with his hands on Vaughan's waist. "I'll lift you."

"You know, for someone who was about to break up with me, you sure are protective." Vaughan gripped the windowsill and used his arms to lift himself. He would have to go headfirst and turn his body sideways to get through.

Bandos moved from Vaughan's waist to his ass. "I never said I would break up with you."

Vaughan concentrated on squeezing through the window. At one point he thought he would get stuck. Not even going sideways seemed to work at first. But, minus a few scrapes, and with Bandos pushing him inside, he gave birth to himself, but in reverse.

Vaughan landed in what appeared to be a sitting room with a modern couch facing a fireplace. Above the mantle was a large television. As castle rooms went, it wasn't what Vaughan had expected.

Vaughan poked his head out of the window in time to see Bandos make his way along the side, so he shut the window and settled in, preparing to wait.

Vaughan had never been good at being bored. A few years ago, Mom tried to get him to meditate, and it had been a disaster for them both. Vaughan hadn't been able to stay serious, which frustrated Mom to the point she'd kicked him out of the living room.

Bandos wasn't the type of guy to take a break from working either. He got laser-focused on something and was like a cat hunting down a rat. He didn't let go until he found what he needed to solve the puzzle. It made him good at investigating, but they weren't settling into a relationship. Between Vaughan's boredom and Bandos's laser-focus they hadn't tried very hard. Or they hadn't before going on a rescue mission.

The fae changed things.

Vaughan sighed and leaned against the wall, close to the only door in the room. He stayed out of target range, not wanting to get hit by it if someone entered. His position allowed him to hide as well. It would give him an advantage for a few seconds, which was enough time to run or fight.

Waiting gave him time to think.

Vaughan was trying to curb his attitude. A photograph had pissed him off, and he didn't want that to extend to the pretty guy in the picture. The fae's smile had etched itself into his brain and he couldn't let go, which did little to curb the anger.

It felt like an assault on his feelings for Bandos.

It left him uneasy because he had told Bandos to trust him to make things right, but he didn't trust himself. The whole thing unsettled him, making him feel the same way he had when his mother had tried to teach him meditation techniques.

Footsteps sounded outside the room, and then the door handle squeaked when someone turned it.

Vaughan stiffened and his eyes shifted. He prepared to shift but held back, hoping it was Bandos.

When a redheaded vampire poked his head inside the room, making a mediocre attempt at a scan, Vaughan held his breath. Even half an attempt wouldn't do much to keep Vaughan out of the guy's line of sight.

Before the vampire could turn his head in Vaughan's direction, he seemed to crumple to the floor.

Vaughan blinked once, staring as he tried to make sense of what he'd seen. And then Bandos entered. He dragged the vampire inside.

Vaughan let out a breath he didn't realize he held. He took a step in Bandos's direction. "Did you kill him?"

"No. He passed out." Bandos let go of the vampire's arms and then grabbed Vaughan's hand. "We don't have a lot of time before he wakes up and alerts everyone. After that we're screwed."

Vaughan nodded and let Bandos pull him along.

Chapter Nine

The visions had stopped surprising Echo long ago. Each glimpse into the future was like a nugget of gold. The importance was subjective. The value only made a difference if he quantified it, so he had learned not to. He had learned not to think about his visions in terms of his life changing, and he never tried to stop what he saw, even when he knew the moment would cause him pain.

He tried to think of each vision as his imagination until he came to the period of time in which it would occur. Some fae focused on their visions so much they suffered through their present state. Echo suffered with the memory.

His latest vision stole his breath, causing him to stop reading in the middle of a sentence. He could feel the book slip from his fingers, and then the vision sucked him in as if his future and present meshed. He couldn't tell the difference.

He forced himself to focus on each breath he took into his lungs, calming himself so he could think about what he saw with some level of objectivity. He reserved his feelings.

Echo saw a big male. The one with green eyes who he had seen in an earlier vision. Perhaps some type of shifter. The wisdom in his eyes spoke of his true age, even if his physical appearance did not. He held himself with confidence. Each stride spoke of it as he carried Echo's battered body. A wolf walked behind them, growling as if protecting them from a threat.

In the vision, Echo wrapped his arms around the big shifter, taking in the scent on his shirt. Despite the blood and dirt, he smelled like cinnamon, and something about that calmed Echo. Despite the aggression, the wolf also made whatever the situation bearable.

Vampires lurked nearby, ready to strike. Echo wasn't ready when it happened. The vampires tore into the wolf, biting and tearing his flesh with his claws. The big shifter tried to keep Echo safe, but he couldn't fight with so many and ended up dropping Echo as he shifted.

A dragon. Echo had never met that kind of shifter. There weren't many left in his land anymore. They had migrated west to the new world long before the Spaniards had begun exploring.

The dragon's color was a deep blue, so dark he appeared black when he fell into the shadows.

Echo had always been a passenger within the vision, keeping emotions out of it as much as possible. He couldn't with the one he was experiencing. The wolf and the dragon meant something to him. They tethered themselves to each other and to him as well, although he wasn't sure how.

"No!" He knew he yelled because the sound vibrated off the tower walls. The him in the vision sat on the ground, unable to move, crying as if that was his only choice. "Help them!"

The dragon took to the sky. Echo tried grabbing for him, but he couldn't get close enough. He just kept floating away. He lost control of the vision. His mind popped out of the future and brought him back to his present circumstances.

The door to his room opened, and the guard entered, scanning the room as if he looked for a threat. He scowled and his eyes glowed red as if expecting an attack. When he turned to Echo, his lips curled in disgust.

"What the fuck is your problem?"

Echo couldn't stop the emotions. He couldn't help the tears or the fact that he still felt unbalanced by what he'd seen.

He grabbed the book and held it to his chest, needing something to ground him. He turned his face to the sun. Connecting to the earth would bring him a small measure of peace. The rays streaming through the window were all he had. And perhaps the stone he sat on. Humans had used the stone to make something, but they were still part of the natural earth.

"Freak." The door closed and the lock mechanism fell into place as the guard left.

Echo liked the other guard better. He didn't call Echo names and treated him as if he were a person. Echo suspected the one guarding the door didn't know very many people beyond his own kind, which made him ignorant.

Echo opened his book and focused on the words, escaping into the pages for a little while. It would free him from the vision.

He didn't even get through one paragraph when something banged against the heavy wooden door. Echo slowly put his book on the stone floor and backed away until he felt the wall at his back.

He opened his senses. Banging and scraping were his only indicators of trouble.

And then someone growled. It sounded familiar, and that was when Echo knew.

The tears came. For the first time in his life, he felt the need to change the future. He wouldn't be a passive observer, suffering the memory any longer, and he wouldn't live in the moment. The future would wreck him if he didn't concentrate on changing it.

Echo shook his head as soon as the door opened and stood, ready to run.

The dragon shifter dragged the vampire guard by his bare foot. He laid on his stomach with his hands tied behind his back with what looked like one of the man's socks. The vampire's had sharp claws. He hissed as he wiggled around, trying to get away.

Blue, as Echo named the dragon in his mind, had reptilian eyes but otherwise appeared as human as Echo. He left the vampire in the center of the room. Blue kneeled and got in the vampire's face. "We're not here to hurt anyone. The fae is his and we're taking him home."

The vampire showed his fangs.

"Keep your mouth shut until we leave, and you'll live. Yell for help and I'll kill you. It's as simple as that." Blue sounded as if he were having a conversation about the weather, but the threat must have taken hold because the vampire's eyes widened, and he stopped hissing.

When Blue turned his gaze on Echo, his eyes softened. Even though they were reptilian, the tenderness was unmistakable.

When the wolf entered and Echo saw his human face for the first time, he held his breath. He had never seen a more handsome person, but that wasn't what stunned him the most. It was the way he grinned.

"I believe you meant to say *the fae is ours*." Wolf took a deep breath in through his nose and his fangs dropped as he stalked toward Echo.

Echo shook his head and held out his hands. His chest ached and he couldn't get it to stop. "Leave me here."

His body rebelled the closer Wolf came, and he dropped his hands, stepping closer.

"We have to go." Wolf stood over him. "Shit."

"Please." Echo shook when he remembered how the vampires over-powered Wolf. "Leave. Before they hurt you."

Wolf wiped away Echo's tears with his thumb. "It's okay now. We're here."

"Yes. That's the problem." Echo wanted to fall into Wolf's protection, but doing so would come at a cost.

Wolf turned, meeting Blue's gaze. "We're having an issue."

The dragon stood and crossed the room. He put his arm around Wolf's waist and stood next to them, boxing Echo in as if they created a different kind of prison. Blue was bigger than Wolf, but both were tall and a lot bigger than Echo. Echo only came up to Wolf's shoulder, so next to Blue, he had never felt smaller.

He should have felt claustrophobic with them caging him and being so close, but they provided a wall of protection. He could breathe without fear for the first time in so long it was overwhelming.

He let out a hysterical chuckle as he braced himself with a hand on Blue's wide chest when his knees threatened to buckle. The tears clogged his throat, cutting off his bout of insanity. He fisted Blue's shirt, and that seemed to spur both men on.

Wolf said, "Bandos." The alarm in his voice was unmistakable.

Blue lifted Echo into his arms. The feeling of his hard muscles felt familiar. Wolf growled.

The vampire hissed at him as if he thought he was the target, but Wolf focused on Blue as if he were a threat.

Blue shook his head and sighed. "Lead us out."

"Sorry." Wolf turned and grabbed the vampire guard's keys off his belt. The growling stopped. "I don't know why I did that."

"Just keep your eyes open."

When they all left the room, Wolf locked the door behind him, leaving the keys dangling from the lock.

Echo touched Blue's neck, getting his attention. When their gazes met, he said, "I saw this. The vampires will overtake you."

"When?" It surprised Echo that Blue didn't come at him with disbelief.

"Outside. In the forest as we're making an escape. They injure you both."

"You're sure that's when?"

Echo nodded and laid his head on Blue's shoulder. "If you just leave me here and run, you'll make it."

"Since that's not happening, do you have a Plan B?" Wolf was the one who asked.

Echo sighed. "No."

Blue smiled, trying to reassure Echo. "Find a hiding spot inside the castle. We'll take off at night."

"They'll smell us. Especially you. The cinnamon scent is rolling off you."

Echo breathed in Blue's scent. He smelled good. As good as Wolf.

His mother had once had a conversation about fated mates, and she had mentioned scent. Fae had the same senses as a human. There wasn't much removing them from humans other than where they originated and the magic they held. But his mother had said he would know his mate because he would smell good. So what did it mean that he liked both of their scents?

Blue rubbed Echo's arm. "We'll head down to the lowest spot."

"Hot air rises, baby."

"Shut up, Vaughan." Despite his words, he chuckled.

Echo opened his eyes and met Blue's gaze. "He's a smart ass, yeah?"

"Better than a dumb ass." Wolf stopped and turned, putting a finger to his lips. He pointed around the corner.

Blue nodded and whisper in Echo's ear. "I'm gonna put you down. You stay between us."

Echo nodded but didn't speak. His heart beat hard, and he didn't know how to calm down. So he focused on Blue.

Blue put Echo on his feet, gently pushing him behind Wolf.

Wolf reached back, using his arm to box Echo in.

Echo held his breath.

When Wolf shook his head and then backed up.

Blue wrapped his arm around Echo's waist and lifted him off his feet again. Blue turned and took him into the first room he came to, with Wolf following.

Echo covered his mouth to keep from voicing his fear. He still squeaked, but he hoped only Blue and maybe Wolf heard him.

Blue pressed him against the wall just inside the door. "Shh. We'll keep you safe."

When Wolf slid in beside them, he had a scowl on his face. "They're going to check on him," he whispered. His lips nearly touched Blue's ear.

Blue nodded. "Plan C?"

Wolf shook his head. "We get the hell out of here."

Blue sighed. "Shift."

"You want me to shift and...what? Take out a coven?"

Blue growled. "Do what I say. Now."

Wolf backed away, pulling his shirt over his head. "I'm just saying. Of the two of us, you're the one who should shift."

"Vaughan."

Voices sounded outside the corridor, so everyone remained quiet.

Wolf stopped and growled, gripping the nape of Echo's neck and probably would have drawn him closer if not for the hold Blue had on him.

When Wolf growled at Blue, he raised his hands and backed away. A light left Blue's eyes and Echo scowled at Wolf. He found himself smashed against Wolf's chest like a coveted doll.

The voices disappeared. Blue looked at the stone wall to the left of Echo and Wolf. Wolf had let up on his hold so Echo could at least breathe again.

"You'll be apologizing to Blue for mistreating him."

Wolf met Blue's gaze and mouthed the nickname.

Blue shook his head. "We'll talk about it later. Get him out of here. I'll lead this time."

Wolf nodded and wrapped an arm around Echo's waist, pulling him closer. When Blue stood in front of them, Wolf touched his shoulder with his free hand. "I don't know why I keep growling at you. My wolf is confused."

What had Echo just stepped into?

Chapter Ten

Vaughan had expected the protective instinct. He'd felt it when he'd seen Echo's photograph, so he figured it would punch him in the gut. He didn't expect his reaction to extend to Bandos as well. He promised Bandos he would fix the fated mate thing. But maybe that was a promise he couldn't keep.

Vaughan took in Echo's scent as he leaned down, whispering in his ear. He smelled like an orchid Mom had in the south-facing window in the living room. It only bloomed twice a year, but when it did, it smelled like chocolate and roses. "Why do you call Bandos Blue?"

"His dragon is beautiful. Almost as beautiful as his human form. Has he never shifted for you?" Echo braced himself with a hand on the stone wall as he walked between Bandos and Vaughan. He seemed calmer, which was good. He wasn't resisting the rescue the way he had when they first found him.

His clothing had seen cleaner days and smelled as if he hadn't taken them off in months, possibly longer. Echo's skin appeared about as clean as he could get it stuck in a castle with questionable plumbing, and none of that took away from his prettiness.

"I've seen him shift a few times. How the hell do you know the color of his dragon, though?"

"He shifted in my vision. He tried to protect us from the vampires." Echo seemed to shutter as if he had a chill.

They would have to pay attention to his health. Vaughan knew little about fae. For all he knew, Echo was one of a kind. He seemed as fragile as a human. Living in a drafty castle for however long they held him captive, he might catch a cold like a human would.

"So that's a real thing for you. You're psychic?" Did it make him an asshole that he wanted to ask Echo to tell his future or whatever?

"Are you trying to be funny?"

Bandos chuckled but grabbed Echo's hand, quickening his pace.

"No. But do you think I am?" Because that went a long way toward getting to know him better.

"No. You should try again when we're all safe."

Bandos snorted and then tried to stop himself when he came to a corner.

Vaughan grinned and put his hand over Bandos and Echo's.

Bandos tried to pull away, but Vaughan tightened his hold.

Echo scowled, unhappy about being stuck in the middle, but Vaughan didn't care. He had something to prove.

And look at Vaughan, not growling.

"It's clear." Bandos pulled them both along.

They were all so close their bodies were touching. Vaughan felt Echo's back against his chest. "You think Bandos is beautiful?"

"Shush," Bandos whispered.

"Yes. Don't you?" Echo answered as if Bandos hadn't just spoken, which Vaughan found hilarious.

"Yeah. He's gorgeous." And he could've waxed poetically on just how pretty Bandos was, especially when he was naked. And his cock did magical things.

"Will you both stop talking?" Bandos whispered.

"Probably not." Vaughan grinned.

Echo covered his mouth. "I'm sorry if the conversation makes you uncomfortable. Wolf and I will stop if you are."

"'Wolf'?" That was the nickname he got?

"You are a wolf."

"So I was in this vision of yours too?"

"Seriously, you need to shut up. Someone is coming." Bandos opened the first door on the left and dragged them both inside.

Vaughan let go of Bandos's hand so he could close the door behind them.

The room they were in was a bedroom with an enormous bed against the left wall and a stone fireplace with a dark wood mantel. The room was sparse and the bed just a bare mattress. Clearly, no one lived in the castle, which made hiding easier.

The castle wasn't as elaborate as Vaughan had imagined. Even if the furnishings were as elaborate as a king's, it still wouldn't have matched the vision in his mind because everything was gray and brown. The floors and walls were stone with wood in the right places, holding the building together.

Their one big win was the fact that the castle was massive, which made the hide-and-seek game they were playing easy. The problem was they were on the tower floor, so they would lose the game soon.

Vaughan met Bandos's gaze and he could see he thought the same thing.

Echo leaned into Bandos's side with his head resting on his arm. Vaughan knew Bandos well enough to know he wanted to pull Echo into his side, but wouldn't because Vaughan's wolf had had a reaction earlier.

Vaughan moved in on Bandos, gripping his nape as he met his gaze.

He could feel Echo pull away so he could watch them, and something about that made the moment less about survival and more about connection. For once, Vaughan kept his mouth shut. Instead, he held Bandos's gaze.

He half-expected Bandos to shut himself off, but Vaughan could see how he was trying to trust. Some of his hope had died, though. The resignation was there, and he didn't hide it.

"Now isn't the time for this, Vaughan," Bandos whispered.

"What better time is there? We're hiding." And maybe Vaughan needed a distraction. If he thought about the danger they were in, he would go insane.

Vaughan kissed Bandos. He kept up the press of lips past what was usual but didn't deepen it. When he pulled back, he whispered, "You're my mate too."

"We're not fated."

"Aren't we, though? Garridan was held captive for almost as long as I've been alive, but we rescue him just in time. He calls Rocky and you guys come to Saint Lakes. I would say that's fate." Vaughan smiled.

Echo cleared his throat. "Would you like privacy? I'll give you as much as I can."

Bandos was the one who answered, but he didn't take his eyes off Vaughan. "No."

"You're part of this." Vaughan didn't either. It was about him reassuring Bandos.

"And if I don't want to be?" Echo asked.

Vaughan met Echo's gaze. "We're mates."

Echo set his pretty lips into a hard line and gave Vaughan a pointed stare. "I'll have a say." He wiggled his finger between Vaughan and Bandos. "And how do you know I don't already have a love somewhere tucked away?"

Vaughan turned his gaze to Bandos, gauging his reaction. Bandos raised an eyebrow and even though he wasn't smiling, Vaughan could see the amusement in his eyes. Bandos thought Echo was cute. Maybe he even thought he was sexy.

Vaughan let himself fully imagine what it would look like if Bandos and Echo kissed, and while he felt a spark of possession toward them both, he didn't growl. His wolf didn't react at all.

"Do you?" Bandos's question brought Vaughan out of his own head. It took him a few seconds to realize Bandos was asking if Echo was in a relationship with someone.

"That is not the point. The point I'm making is you two seem intent on deciding for me." Echo's voice raised enough for Vaughan to shush him. He acknowledged him with a nod.

"That's a good point. And we're not trying to take your choices from you. We only just acknowledged our feelings for each other. And then Vaughan saw a picture of you and knew you were his mate. We're just trying to see where our love fits in to all that." Bandos had never been more candid.

Echo scowled and averted his gaze. "You've been looking for me."

Bandos nodded.

Echo met Vaughan's gaze. "You rescued me because I'm your mate?"

Vaughan sighed and pulled Echo into their circle, wanting to protect him. "It's complicated. My brother mated with a witch. A male witch. He's wanted by—"

Echo held up his hand. "A male witch and I could give life or take it away to millions all at once. Being kidnapped makes sense now."

"Yeah. Once we figured out you were in danger, Bandos and Shawn, another one of my brothers-in-law, started looking for you through the Internet. It took a long time to find you, but they finally did."

"I'm on the Internet?"

"Everyone is," Bandos whispered.

"Bandos is a computer genius." Vaughan couldn't help it. He was proud of Bandos's ability.

"I wouldn't go that far. It's mostly just experience." Bandos smiled.

Echo smiled back, and it completely transformed his face. Bandos and Echo liked each other. That much was clear, so Vaughan had to stay out of the way of that.

When Echo turned his smile onto Vaughan, it felt like a gift. Instinct kicked in and Vaughan kissed him. A part of Vaughan expected Echo to back off, but he let the kiss happen. He even wrapped an arm around Vaughan and leaned into it.

Vaughan turned into him, taking Bandos with him almost without thinking. Bandos was an anchor. He was steady no matter the situation. Maybe that was experience, like Bandos claimed, or maybe it was something else. Whatever the reason for his nature, he balanced Vaughan.

Echo wedged between them, leaning mostly against Bandos.

Bandos cursed, which put Vaughan on alert. So he ended the kiss.

Echo pressed his forehead against Vaughan's arm and sighed.

Vaughan met Bandos's gaze, wanting to know if something was wrong.

Bandos shook his head. "It's fine."

"No. What's wrong?" Vaughan would find out what Bando's problem was so they could talk about it. He wanted the three of them to work and for that to happen Vaughan had to facilitate the communication. If he waited for Bandos, it would never happen.

"Nothing's wrong." But Bandos's cheeks were a pretty pink, so something was going on.

"Are you jealous or..."

Bandos sighed. "Echo got hard, which made me hard."

Echo groaned and pressed into Vaughan even more. "By the gods."

"Oh." Vaughan grinned, which made Bandos smile.

"You're not reacting," Bandos whispered.

"Oh, I'm having a reaction." Vaughan's dick was at half-mast and if he pictured Echo rubbing against Bandos, he would get all the way there.

Bandos chuckled. "I meant you're not growling at me."

"I don't feel jealous. I feel protective." Vaughan wanted to keep things light, but it was the moment for the discussion they really needed to have. He patted Echo, getting his attention. When their gazes met, Vaughan said, "I apologize in advance for talking about you like you're not here."

Echo nodded but didn't comment.

Vaughan met Bandos's gaze. "You're twice as big as him. My wolf doesn't trust you not to break him. Hell, my wolf doesn't trust me not to break him."

Echo squeaked and his mouth hung open. "Should I take offense?"

Bandos was the one who answered him. "No. It means you have a wolf shifter bodyguard. That's a good thing."

Vaughan didn't avert his gaze from Bandos when he spoke, even though he spoke to Echo. "You have a dragon shifter, too."

Bandos nodded. "The difference between you and me is the mating pull."

Before Vaughan could respond, he smelled a vampire close enough to hear them talking. He put a finger to his lips. His heart beat harder and his adrenaline kicked into overdrive. The time for pretending they weren't in a deadly situation was over.

Bandos's eyes shifted and his fangs dropped. He wrapped his arm around Vaughan's waist and lifted him out of his way.

Vaughan pulled Echo into him, trapping him against the wall, protecting him with his body.

Echo fisted Vaughan's shirt. "Are they coming in?"

Vaughan nodded and whispered, "Right outside the door."

"Please don't get hurt." Echo met his gaze and refused to look away, so Vaughan didn't either.

It wasn't until the door burst open and a group of pissed-off vampires stormed into the room that Vaughan averted his gaze. He closed in on Echo, making sure he stayed safe while keeping an eye on Bandos. If Bandos couldn't fight them by himself, Vaughan would step in. In the meantime, he would protect their fae.

Chapter Eleven

Echo held his breath when Wolf moved enough to give him a view of Blue. He fought two vampires and seemed on the winning side of things. Three more entered the room. One had a gun strapped to her hip, but she didn't pull it on them. Still, Echo couldn't take his eyes off it. It meant instant death if she took it out of the sheath.

When they closed in on Blue, Echo cried out. "No! Don't hurt him. I'll go with you." His instinct kicked in and he tried to go to Blue, but Wolf held him back. "I'll go with you. Stop! Please."

Wolf cursed under his breath, and that had Echo shifting his focus. "They're hurting him."

Wolf nodded and pulled his shirt over his head, tossing it to the floor. "Stay here. Don't move. Okay?"

Echo nodded and wiped his eyes. "Hurry."

Fists hitting flesh was all he heard, and each blow made Echo wince. He felt each one as if they punched him.

Wolf kicked his shoes and socks off. His pants came next, along with his underwear. Echo grabbed his clothing and held it to his chest.

Wolf shifted. Echo had never seen an actual wolf before. He hadn't even seen one in a zoo. He had dark gray fur that looked soft and thick.

When Wolf lunged at a vampire, his huge jaws clamped around the woman's neck and the blood flowed down her body as if Wolf had turned on a faucet with his teeth, Echo froze. He pulled Wolf's clothing to his nose and drew in his scent.

The vampire with the gun seemed to realize they were no match against two shifters, especially two who fought so well.

She turned to Echo, closing the distance.

Echo stopped breathing when fear lodged in his throat. He backed away, scooting along the wall until the fear gripped his chest, making his lungs ache. He turned to run but he was no match for a vampire's speed, and when she caught him, it felt as though a stone had hit him from behind. He screamed when her claws pierced his sides.

He tried to crawl away from her, but with every inch, she dug her claws in farther.

And then she gave him an opportunity to get away. As soon as he got to his feet, she buried her claws into his skin. He cried out from the pain and arched his back to dislodge her.

She treated him like a rag doll, using him as a hostage. His adrenaline took over, and he stopped thinking about anything but survival. She turned him just right for her holstered gun to come into view so he flipped the leather strap and pulled the gun free.

He had never fired one, but he's seen enough on television to have developed somewhat of an instinct. At least he knew where the trigger was, and he knew how to aim.

As soon as he pointed it at her, the gun went off as if on its own. The power of the gun and the way it knocked him off his feet, scared him more than the vampire's claws did.

The top left side of the vampire's head blew off and she staggered before falling to the floor. A part of her body laid across Echo's legs.

His ears rang. He didn't even hear the gun clatter to the floor when it left his shaking hands. He backed up, trying to get away from the vampire and her blood that would touch him in the next few seconds.

And then the smell of cinnamon washed over him right before Blue lifted him off the floor. Echo shook as he wrapped his arms around Blue's neck, holding on as tightly as possible.

His life depended on Blue and Wolf. He hadn't thought he had anyone looking for him capable enough of orchestrating a rescue. He had worked out ways to escape but had executed none of them. Getting rescued by shifters hadn't entered his mind.

"Are you hurt?" Blue asked, nearly yelling so Echo could hear him.

Echo nodded. "Vampire clawed me. What about you and Wolf?"

"We're both good. No worries, little fae."

Blue met Wolf's gaze. "Lead us out, baby. Take out anyone who gets in our way."

Wolf was still in his animal form, but he seemed cognizant. He forged a path past the dead vampires, growling at each of them as if they were still a threat.

Blue winced as they followed Wolf out of the room. "Vaughan, we need to get to the plane fast. He's bleeding. I can feel the wetness of it on my arm. And I can smell it."

Echo shut his eyes and tried to forget the pain in his side and back. Having it spoken about made him feel it even more.

They headed down a staircase. Echo remembered it from when they'd brought him to the tower room when he had first come to the castle. Something about it made the rescue feel more real than it had before.

The stone walls had electric sconces lighting each side. They made the whole place look scary. Nothing about it said modern except for the way the light was powered. That a dragon shifter carried him to safety said as much. Even with his bandana and leather vest with a patch on the back, the whole thing left Echo feeling as if he had traveled in time.

And then two vampires came around the corner of the spiral staircase. Wolf lunged at them, taking one down. They both tumbled for a few steps. Wolf yipped in pain, but recovered quickly enough for him to snarl again.

Echo's heart lodged in his throat and all he wanted to do was help Wolf. He tried to get Blue to put him on his feet, but he held onto Echo.

Blue ran after Wolf and the two vampires. Echo saw the vampire who had gone ass of head down the steps with Wolf lying in a heap at the bottom of the staircase with glassy eyes and a twisted body. The other vampire laid on the stairs, bleeding from his neck. His body shook and he could barely take a breath.

Echo's stomach turned, and he buried his face in Blue's chest, shutting his eyes.

"Are you okay, little fae?" They must have passed the dead bodies at some point and, although Echo chose not to look, he couldn't keep the scene out of his mind.

He shook his head. "My stomach. Is Wolf injured?"

"He's good still. Are you gonna puke?" Blue pulled him closer, which surprised Echo. Given the question, he thought Blue would put him on his feet, but it seemed as though he cared more about comforting Echo than getting stomach bile on his shirt.

"Maybe."

"Do you want me to put you down?"

Echo shook his head. "Unless you want to."

"I don't. I like carrying you."

Echo met his gaze. The surprise made his stomach calm some. "Are you sure?"

Blue's cheeks turned pink, but he smiled. Wasn't he cute when he tried to flirt. Even if the moment was inappropriate.

"I like it too." Plus, he wasn't entirely sure he could walk without it hurting a lot. "Thank you for taking my mind off...the gore."

They were almost at the bottom of the staircase when a vampire stepped into view. He stalked toward them with a knife in his hand. The way he held it suggested he knew how to use it. He kept his arms away from his body, leaving his chest open as if he were getting ready to attack a human. Maybe that had encompassed the vampire's experience up to that point.

Wolf lunged toward the vampire's vulnerabilities. His weight sent the vampire to the floor. Wolf had the advantage of being fast and he fought well.

Echo's father had taught him a few tricks on how to protect himself. It had annoyed him at the time because he had been barely a teenager and hadn't wanted to learn it. But his father had been a strong fae who had fought for paranormals in wars he never talked about. Echo's mother had mentioned the war a few times, which clued Echo into the fact his father had suffered from the trauma. But he was a great warrior and had wanted Echo to know how to use his abilities to his advantage.

Echo regretted acting like an annoyed teenager. Had he known their time was limited and that he would come to a moment in life where defensive maneuvers were necessary, he would have paid closer attention.

The knife clattered to the stone floor when the vampire fell. He scrambled to get away, but Wolf was too heavy. He growled, showing his teeth, but didn't use them on the vampire.

Echo didn't know why he gave the guy a warning instead of killing him on sight like he had all the others. Maybe it was because he realized that without the knife, the vampire wasn't a threat.

When Wolf moved away, the vampire laid there with wide eyes. Wolf walked over to the knife and picked it up with his teeth, carrying it as they headed down another set of stairs.

Getting out of the tower did the trick, it seemed, because they didn't encounter anyone else. The castle was big enough, and the coven was on the smaller side. It left them a lot of opportunity to hide even while descending to the lower floors, because more than one staircase led to the same places and the vampires couldn't cover every inch. Trying would spread them too thin. The castle's size worked against them, but Echo could see it being an effective protection for someone with an army.

At some point Echo heard metal clatter on stone and realized Wolf had dropped the knife, but he didn't know why until he turned and saw four vampires standing in the great hall.

Blue put Echo on his feet, leaving him next to a door. When Blue started taking off his clothing the way Wolf had, Echo figured he would shift. Blue dropped his shirt and pants on the ground as he stripped. He revealed his muscles with each thing he took off. Echo's body would have reacted if it weren't for the moment. Hearing the fighting forced him into the reality of his present situation.

The great hall was massive, but would it allow something the size of a dragon to fit inside? Not that Echo knew how big a dragon was. He assumed a lot. Echo was about to find out, though.

Wolf already fought off the vampires, snarling and biting. He moved like a predator. The vampires closest to him sensed the danger and hesitated.

When Blue shifted, his big scaly body took up a lot of room. He blocked Echo and seemed to be cognizant of his tail because he didn't hit Echo with it, and it was close enough for that to happen.

Echo couldn't see the fighting because Blue blocked his view, but he heard flesh giving way and bones breaking. It turned his stomach. He put his hands over his ears and shut his eyes, and tried not to think about his shifters getting injured.

He wasn't sure how long the ordeal lasted. It wasn't until someone touched his shoulder that he thought to open his senses. He backed up before taking his hands away from his ears. And then he smelled pine and cinnamon. He opened his eyes and saw Blue first. Wolf stood next to Blue, licking him on his bare thigh. And then Wolf turned his gaze onto Echo and growled.

Echo wasn't sure why until he realized where Wolf stared. When he looked down at his shirt, he saw the blood. The wetness caused the material to cling to his skin. The pain, which he had gotten used to, washed over him with a vengeance. Not even his adrenaline kept it at bay.

Blue didn't acknowledge Wolf's lick, but dressed faster than anyone Echo had ever seen. He closed the distance between them and didn't hesitate to lift Echo into his arms.

And then Blue turned the knob on the door and head out. Doing so was awkward because he held Echo, but he seemed to manage. As soon as they were outside, and Blue ran toward the forest, he knew he hadn't done enough to keep his vision from happening. Maybe there wasn't a way to stop it. He had to live through it. Somehow, he had to figure out a way to do that.

He didn't have to look to know Wolf followed behind them or that he growled the entire time.

The hurried way they traveled through the forest made their path obvious, so Echo concentrated on covering their trail, even though he knew the vampires would catch up at some point.

The moss sprung back to life behind them, and the trees bent to conceal them. He didn't need to see that either to know it was happening. He took a deep breath of clean air and let his connection to the earth grow deeper. He shut his eyes and focused all of his attention on the natural world surrounding them.

It was something he could do to create distance, which they needed, and prolong the inevitable outcome. It would buy them time. Maybe they could come up with a plan to thwart the attack.

The smells hit him—earthy, natural smells that he hadn't experienced in longer than was healthy for a fae. His mother used to tell him fae belonged to the forest. He hadn't even known how being locked in that room affected him until he wasn't anymore, and vowed to walk on his own two feet amongst the trees if they reached safety.

The sun had sunk into the earth, sending it into dusk, but it didn't take away from the air caressing his skin or the slight dampness. He heard a small animal skitter amongst the trees and sensed something larger watching them. With Wolf growling and Blue's dragon so unmistakable, even when he was in human form, whatever it was didn't pose a danger.

It probably wasn't a threat regardless, because Echo was pretty sure it was a red fox. While they were sometimes curious creatures, they weren't dangerous.

The fox eased something inside Echo, and he relaxed even more.

Birds sang and flittered around the tops of the trees, not worried by their presence. Even though they made a lot of noise.

Blue didn't speak. He seemed to focus on getting them all to safety, wherever that was.

Echo couldn't go home. The kidnappers knew where he lived. It wasn't safe there anymore.

The air changed and fear crept in as if a ghost possessed his soul. Echo took a deep breath, but he couldn't seem to get it past the lump in his throat. Perhaps it was the shadows creeping in that set the scene, but somehow Echo doubted it. "The vision."

"Vision?" Blue asked without losing his focus.

"They will overrun us. They attack Wolf first." No sooner did the words leave his mouth than vampires emerged through the trees, fighting their way through sagging branches. But breaking through created enough of a distraction that Wolf was prepared.

It wasn't the same as in his vision. The vampires hadn't caught them off-guard.

Blue put Echo on his feet when the vampires became too many for Wolf to fight alone. Still, Wolf had an advantage.

Blue stripped and shifted, taking to the air almost as soon as his body changed. The shifting happened almost as fast as the snap of his fingers. The density of the forest wasn't a hindrance to get the air underneath his wings. He seemed to scan the area, choosing a vampire a good distance away from where Wolf fought. As soon as he got close enough, the vampires swarmed him.

Echo couldn't stop the emotion, so he let the tears flow. He wedged between two roots and then used his magic to cover himself with branches. No one would get to him.

When Wolf yelp and then backed up, Echo panicked. He already had his magic at the front of his mind, so using it was second nature.

The moss grew around all the vampires' legs, rooting them in place. Echo turned his gaze on the ones attacking Blue and did the same thing.

Blue got away, hovering above the scene as if confused by the sudden change in events. When the branches of the trees pierced the vampires' chests, Blue flew even higher as if wanting a better view. His gaze landed on Echo and stayed there.

Echo focused on the vampires around Wolf, who had backed away and cocked his head. He sat and watched as the vampires struggled against their bindings.

Echo left one vampire alive, but branches killed the others. The one who had been left alive, crumpled, passing out. When he awoke, he would tell the rest of his coven what had happened and maybe that would scare them away from Echo.

Wolf yipped and backed away, stumbling before he turned and headed straight to Blue. Blue saw him coming and shifted as soon as his feet hit the ground. Wolf shifted and launched himself at Blue. He didn't stay there long, though. "Shit. Where's Echo?"

Blue nodded in his direction. He kept a hand around Wolf's waist as he led him over to him. Blue pulled on his underwear and pants before squatting in front of Echo. Their gazes met. "That's some trick, little fae."

Wolf kneeled next to him. "You did that?"

The tree branches slowly fell back into place as he nodded. "I'm chlorokinetic. All fae are."

"So much for not killing a lot of coven members. Hopefully Ladon won't be pissed," Wolf commented.

Blue shrugged. "Couldn't be helped."

Echo kept his eyes on them both, not wanting to see a dead body.

"Did you see that in your vision?" Blue asked.

Echo shook his head. "It ended right before. Telling you about the vision and you believing me might have changed the sequence of events."

He took a deep breath and let his nerves settle. "You both came through all right." The knowledge hit him, which brought tears to his eyes.

"Are you hurt?" Wolf asked.

"No."

"I doubt they even saw him." Blue grabbed his shirt, shaking it off before putting it on. He put on his socks and shoes next. And then held out his hand for Echo to take. "No one could see you, but you could see everything, couldn't you?"

Was that respect Echo saw in Blue's expression?

Echo put his hand in Blue's and let him pull him to his feet. He stepped over a tree root, but his legs were shaky. His puncture wounds ached. Between the pain and the adrenaline crash, it left him weak.

Wolf moved in behind him, putting a hand on his shoulder before lifting his shirt, searching his wounds. "We need to get to the plane and get him treated."

Blue nodded. "I can shift and fly him there."

"Yeah, do that." Wolf kissed the top of Echo's head. "I'll be there a few minutes after you, but I'll try to keep up as best as I can. The medical kit is in the compartment behind the cockpit."

Blue furrowed his brow. "If you're not there in thirty minutes, I'm coming after you, which leaves Echo alone and vulnerable, so run your ass off, do you hear me?"

"I hear you, baby." Wolf kissed Blue quickly before shifting and taking off toward the west.

"So I'm gonna shift and you climb on my back. Hold on to my neck, okay?"

Echo swallowed the fear and nodded. He wasn't a fan of heights, but if it meant he got away from the vampires, then he would do just about anything. Plus, he would stay with his shifters a little longer and that was a bonus.

Blue backed away and shifted before lying on the ground, waiting for Echo to climb on.

Echo's legs felt wobbly as he walked. Climbing on top of him proved a lesson in pain management, but he worked through it. As soon as he grabbed onto Blue's scaly hide, they were in the air, his big wings flapping. If anyone was on the ground and saw a dragon flying, Blue didn't alert anyone to that fact. So either no one saw or Blue didn't care.

Chapter Twelve

Bandos scanned the area around the plane from above before descending. He hadn't seen anyone from the air but he smelled humans as soon as he landed. The smell was strong enough that he knew someone had been close by in the last hour. It put him on alert. His thoughts went to Echo and getting him inside the plane as quickly as possible so he was less exposed.

Bandos could feel Echo shaking, which was another reason he wanted to get him inside. It wasn't that cold on the ground, but the higher they flew, the colder the air grew. Bandos's dragon form could handle it because his body regulated itself. Echo didn't have that luxury. His body worked like a human's, so the colder air made him hypothermic.

Echo pressed himself to Bandos's back, clinging like a monkey. Bandos had to reach behind him and pull Echo to his front, all while turning, which wasn't easy because Echo was too busy shivering to help. His only saving grace was Echo's size.

Echo wrapped his legs around Bandos's waist and his arms around his neck, burying his face against Bandos's skin. Bandos tried to use his body heat for warmth.

He smelled humans as he drew closer to the plane door. His eyes shifted and his fangs dropped. He went on high alert, sniffing for any signs of humans nearby. His senses told him they were long gone but someone had been inside at some point. Still, the scent was at least an hour old.

His chest ached thinking about Vaughan running into danger and hoped his instincts about the danger being gone was correct. Either way, he couldn't do anything about it. All he could do was focus on Echo and hope Vaughan stayed safe.

He would have to search the area but first he needed to get Echo warm.

He knew Vaughan had blankets in there somewhere, so Bandos made it his mission to find them. He found a stack in the back, along with three duffle bags. Everything they'd brought for Echo belonged to Shawn or Fane, except for a pair of shoes that belonged to Jules. None of it would fit. It seemed as if he had lost weight during his captivity, at least compared to the photographs Bandos's research had uncovered.

Based on how he'd taken out around twenty vampires all at once, he didn't need brawn to protect himself. He was also the prettiest person Bandos had ever seen, not that thinking it was appropriate or necessary.

If someone had been inside before, they were long gone. The plane wasn't that big and there weren't many places to hide. Perhaps it was another pilot interested in Vaughan's plane. Some of the tension leaked out of his body and he breathed a little easier.

Bandos grabbed a blanket and wrapped it around Echo as he headed into a warmer part of the plane. He sat on the bench seat and rubbed Echo's back, getting some of the heat into his skin.

The longer they sat there, the more Echo relaxed.

Bandos was still naked, and the closeness affected him. He wasn't sure Echo could feel his hard length until he pulled back and their gazes met.

"Sorry."

Echo's response was to move his hips into Bandos, letting him know his body had responded too.

Echo leaned forward as if he intended to kiss him, but Bandos put a finger on his lips, stopping him.

"You belong to Vaughan, little fae."

Echo scowled. "I believe we discussed it."

"But we didn't decide anything." And if they kissed, Bandos would want more.

Echo sighed and wrapped his arms around Bandos's neck again, cuddling close. "I suppose we need more talking."

He sounded put out, which made Bandos chuckle. "Are you warm enough?"

Echo nodded. "Your body is like a furnace."

"We need to treat your wounds." And Bandos needed to put on pants.

Echo climbed off Bandos's lap and sat in the seat next to him. All of his attention went to Bandos's hard cock.

All Bandos wanted to do was pull him back onto his lap and take both of their cocks in hand. He wouldn't do that to Vaughan, though. If it meant stepping away, then Bandos loved Vaughan enough to do it, even if it would kill his soul.

Bandos stood and went to the back of the plane, grabbing his bag. He unzipped it and dug around for a pair of jeans. He put them on, as well as a T-shirt. Socks and shoes came next. When he dressed, he grabbed the bag they'd packed for Echo and set it beside him.

After he got Echo settled and Bandos treated his wounds, he would look around the airstrip for threats.

"Some of that might fit better than other stuff, but it's all for you. I know you probably want to wash up, but I'd like to treat you first." The airport wasn't much bigger than the one in Saint Lakes, but it had a place Echo could take a shower if he wanted. Bandos had seen the building with a washroom when they had first arrived. It was smarter to get out of the area as quickly as possible because Bandos didn't want to risk Echo's safety if the humans nosing around Vaughan's plane turned out to be a threat. Still, as long as everything checked out and if Echo didn't take forever, they could work it in.

Echo pulled his shirt off, wincing when his arms were above his head, but he seemed fine once he put them down. He pulled on the wound.

Bandos went to the cabinet that Vaughan had told him held the first aid kit and rummaged round, looking for something that resembled a medical kit. It didn't help that Vaughan lacked organizational skills.

"Did you try the one on the other side?" Echo stayed on the bench seat, lying on his stomach. He kept his hands down at his sides and had his eyes closed.

Bandos switched his focus and found a bag marked with a big red cross on it. He grabbed a bottle of water from the pack on the floor and a cloth he had seen from the other cabinet.

When he made it back to Echo, he kneeled on the floor. He put everything next to him except the cloth and water bottle, wetting the fabric, and then attempted to wash the wounds.

Echo jumped and hissed. He moved his arms out of the way, though. He kept his eyes closed and let Bandos do what he had to do.

When Bandos went to his other side, Echo turned so the back of the bench was less of a hindrance. Bandos tried to be gentle, barely touching him, but he still caused Echo pain.

The wounds on his sides weren't as bad as the ones on his back. Those might need stitches. Bandos didn't know how fast a fae healed so he wasn't sure.

"What's your healing ability, little fae?" He wet the cloth again and wiped the last of his wounds.

The pain was clear in his voice when he spoke. "Humanlike."

"Do you scar?"

"No. I'll heal as if nothing happened."

That was a relief. It meant Bandos didn't have to stitch it up.

"I'm sorry for causing you pain." Bandos had never disliked something more and there was worse to come because he had to use some type of antiseptic, which would probably burn.

"You've nothing to apologize for. You're doctoring me."

Bandos rummaged around in the bag looking for something better to clean the wound with and found rubbing alcohol, which would sting but would do the trick. He scored some cotton pads next and poured some alcohol onto a couple of them. "This is going to hurt."

Just as Bandos dabbed at the cuts on Echo's side, Vaughan came aboard. He was in his human form, but still growled. His eyes were canine and Bandos could tell Vaughan wanted to shift completely. "I smell humans all over."

Vaughan is safe. Thank the gods.

The tightness in Bandos's chest eased and he could breathe again. "Me too. But they aren't here anymore."

"You're sure?"

Bandos nodded.

Vaughan went to the back without another word.

"Humans? On the plane?" Pain laced every word he spoke.

"Nothing to worry about." Bandos leaned forward and blew on the wound he had just doctored, trying to ease some of the sting.

Echo sighed. "I'll ask Wolf about it then. Since you want to placate me."

Bandos smiled and shook his head.

When Vaughan came in from the back, he had clothes on. He bent down and kissed Bandos on his cheek before moving around him and kissed Echo next. "Did you say humans were on the plane?"

Vaughan's eyes shifted again and he growled. "Yes."

"Is everything all right?"

"I hope so. We'll know when I start the engine." Vaughan met Bandos's gaze. "Are you searching the area?"

Bandos nodded. "Wanted to fix Echo's wounds first. The area is secure. I got an ariel view before landing. Echo's safe, baby."

Vaughan nodded and went to the cockpit.

"How did that situation end up about me? I thought we were talking about humans." Echo sighed.

Bandos smiled because Echo sounded put out and that was cute. "It's always about you where safety is concerned."

"Damn straight," Vaughan yelled from the cockpit.

"If you're a pilot, don't you think you need to concentrate on that and not on making conversation." Echo smiled and when he spoke again, he whispered, "I feel very safe here."

"I heard that. Wolf shifters hear everything." Vaughan didn't let anything go. He'd banter until Echo gave up. It was his biggest talent.

"Shut up and concentrate, Wolf."

The bickering struck Bandos as funny but he felt it was his duty to warn Echo. "He's going to irritate you on purpose now. You realize that, right?"

Echo opened his eyes. "He better not."

"He will. Vaughan has two modes and one of them is teasing."

"Is the other one fighting, because he does that very well?"

"He definitely fights better than anyone has given him credit for." And Bandos would bring it to Ladon's attention when they got home. "But no. The other mode is this emotionally intelligent person who can ask therapeutic questions regardless if you want to answer them."

"You don't like it when he tries to psychoanalyze you. Is that what you're saying?"

"He doesn't with me usually. Just everyone else."

"And why is that?"

Vaughan yelled from the cockpit again. "Because Bandos won't do anything until he's ready, so it doesn't matter what I say." He poked his head out. "Isn't that right, baby?"

Bandos stopped cleaning Echo's wounds long enough to flip Vaughan off.

Vaughan pointed to Bandos but met Echo's gaze. "My point exactly."

"Shut up, Vaughan."

Vaughan smirked and went back into the cockpit.

Bandos shook his head and put down the cotton pad. He found some antibacterial ointment and spread that on each puncture wound. The bandage pads had adhesive on them, which made putting them over the wounds a lot easier.

"Did you want to shower, little fae?"

Echo yawned.

Bandos chuckled and patted Echo's shoulder. He pulled the blanket over Echo and headed to the back to get another one. That one he put near Echo's head in case he wanted to use it as a pillow.

Bandos bent and gave Echo a kiss on his cheek on instinct, brushing his hair off his forehead.

Echo smiled but didn't open his eyes.

Bandos went to the cockpit, sitting in the co-pilot's seat. Vaughan did his thing. Bandos understood some of the more technical aspects of flying, so he could take a good guess at what Vaughan was doing.

"Aren't you going to scan the area?"

"Yeah. I think it's still necessary even though Echo's too tired to shower. I think whoever nosed around is long gone." Between being locked in that room for the gods knew how long and then their ordeal getting out of the castle and in the forest, Bandos guessed it had taken a toll on Echo.

Vaughan nodded. "The scent is at least an hour old. Maybe a little longer.

"Does the plane seem okay? You don't think anyone fucked with it?"

Vaughan shook his head. "It seems find so far. I'm taking extra time, testing and stuff."

Bandos nodded. While his instinct said they weren't in any immediate danger, he still felt uneasy. Something seemed off, but he couldn't pinpoint what.

"You like him." It wasn't a question, and Vaughan didn't lose focus on his task. Changing the subject was something Vaughan was good at. Something about bouncing around from one topic to the next helped him concentrated on one thing, which was weird but Vaughan wasn't exactly the most normal person alive. Bandos was the laser-focused type. He didn't like talking when he was trying to concentrate, so it was often a lesson in patience where those particular personality traits were concerned.

"Yes." It didn't matter what *like* meant. That was a broad term that could have meant anything, but all the ways he could have liked Echo, he did. He didn't bother denying it.

"Me too. And not just because he's my mate."

Bandos ignored the ache in his chest. "He's perfect for you."

Vaughan met his gaze but focused on the plane again. "I won't let you back off. That's a fact, Bandos. Wrap your head around it."

Echo stood between the seats with the blanket around his shoulders. He met Bandos's gaze. "Are you leaving to do a search or can I sit with you?"

Bandos opened his arms and waited for Echo to settle on his lap. He could hold Echo for a few minutes. He was safer in Bandos's arms anyway. If he'd felt the humans were close, he might have had a different answer.

Echo sat sideways, resting his head on Bandos's chest. His eyes closed almost immediately.

Vaughan smiled as if Echo just made his point for him. And maybe he had.

If it was two against one, Bandos was on the losing end of that scenario, but Bandos wouldn't come between mates. He hadn't liked it when it had happened to him, so he wouldn't do it to Vaughan. It didn't matter how much his heart ached or how much he loved Vaughan.

"We would have talked about this eventuality," Bandos whispered and wrapped his arms around Echo, trying to keep him warm. Bandos hadn't ever felt so comfortable cuddling with someone before. Echo fit against him as if it were magic.

"We didn't exactly have the time. And we're talking about it now. We've been talking about it since I saw the picture. It's time we come to some decisions. Don't you think?"

Bandos grunted. "I won't come between you."

"So in a few hours we're gonna arrive in Saint Lakes and you're gonna what, forget that you carry him around or like cuddling with him?" Or forget that he loved Vaughan. He knew that was where Vaughan would go next.

"I'm not gonna forget."

"But you're gonna get on your bike without a single word and never look back. Is that the plan?" Vaughan met his gaze. "If you do, then fuck you."

"Fuck you if you think this is easy for me." Bandos wouldn't let Vaughan talk to him like that.

Echo sighed and sat up straight. "I guess I'll have that shower since you two insist on arguing."

"Sorry, honey." Bandos kissed Echo on his temple and then pulled him back down.

Echo didn't protest and settled against Bandos again.

Vaughan smiled again. "Yeah, we'll shut up so you can sleep."

"I don't mind the talking. It's the arguing."

"Okay. No arguing then." Bandos met Vaughan's gaze and smiled. "I'll need to do a check soon."

"I'll be ready to go in a few minutes."

Bandos put his hand on Vaughan's shoulder, squeezing gently. "I promise to stick around long enough for all of us to talk. Let's just get home first."

Vaughan sighed. "I guess that's all I can ask for at this point."

Bandos stood and sat Echo in the cockpit seat. "I'll be right back."

"Let's hope you don't find anyone lurking around," Echo said.

"Amen to that."

It took him about twenty minutes. Not finding anything made him breathe a little easier. But the search was the first lesson in what it would take to keep Echo safe. He would always need to be vigilant because everyone wanted a piece of Echo. He would always be prey. And something about that made Bandos's stomach ache.

Chapter Thirteen

A better pilot didn't exist. The hum of the engines and the smooth glide through the air lulled Bandos to sleep right along with Echo. Of course, it didn't help that Echo straddled his lap. The blanket covered them both, and Bandos put the folded one behind his head.

His sleep was light enough he noticed Echo's heavy breathing. Bandos would categorize it as a light snore, but he would never call it that for fear Echo would turn his displeasure on him.

As far as Bandos was concerned, Vaughan could get that side of Echo. Bandos would take the cuddling. He felt better when Echo was close, so it was a win for him.

He felt just as protective of Echo as he did of Vaughan. The only difference was Vaughan was a lot more capable of a fighter than Bandos had realized. That eased the worry a bit. With Echo, there was nothing that would ease the worry except if he glued himself to Bandos.

Something banged as if a god had pounded their heavy fist on the side of the plane. The plane dipped. Bandos stiffened. He held onto Echo a little tighter.

It wasn't until he noticed the quiet and then Vaughan cursing from the cockpit that he went on alert. And then Vaughan used the word, "mayday" and said, "Shit, no communications?" He sounded confused but it was the fear laced through the words that had Bandos's heart pounding hard.

He rubbed Echo's back, trying to wake him. "Wake up, little fae."

Echo mumbled something, but then stiffened when Bandos took the blanket off him. "What?"

Bandos stood with Echo in his lap and then put him on the bench seat. He strapped Echo in with the chest belt and then fastened the one around his waist as well, making sure he stayed as safe as possible. "Don't take off your seatbelt unless Vaughan tells you to."

Echo's pretty eyes were wide with worry when he nodded. "What's happening?"

"I don't know, but I don't hear the engines." Bandos cupped Echo's cheek and then did the thing he shouldn't have. He initiated a kiss between them, keeping it brief. It still stepped on Vaughan's toes but if Bandos was right about what was happening, he wanted to die knowing he let Echo know how he really felt. "Stay here, honey."

Echo nodded and held onto the straps as if doing so secured him to the seat even more.

The plane lurched, sending Bandos into the wall next to Echo. He cursed and righted himself enough to head to the cockpit.

Bandos had never seen Vaughan panic. Not even when the battle had started between Stavros's coven and Saint Lakes. But Vaughan's expression said it all.

"By the gods, get strapped in, Bandos." Vaughan didn't take his focus away from flying. He kept his hands on the yoke and his eyes on the sky. "Does Echo have his seatbelt on?"

"Yes." Bandos sat. He was glad Vaughan's plane had chest straps. Bandos didn't know for sure, but he didn't think all planes had those types of belts.

"You should strap up in the back. It's safer." Vaughan did his best to keep them from nosediving.

Bandos wouldn't leave Vaughan to handle whatever was happening on his own. "What's going on?"

"The engine cut out and I have no communications. I think I know what the humans were up to."

Bandos sucked in a breath. The bang he had heard made sense. "They cut out the engine."

"More like blew it up with a fucking bomb. I think."

His heart pounded so loudly he heard it in his head. He knew what the lack of engine sounds meant, but he hadn't let the thought sink in the way it probably should have. "Fuck."

"Yeah."

"So what do we do?"

"Crash as gracefully as possible."

Bandos grabbed Vaughan's shoulder. "Fucking hell."

"That about covers it, yeah."

Bandos tried to get his brain past the crashing thing, and onto something that would help. "Where are we?"

"We're in the U.S. Northeast."

Bandos nodded. "Good. It's good we're not landing in the ocean."

"Oh look, an upside." The plane shook and Vaughan sucked in a breath. "Shit."

Bandos kept his hand on Vaughan's shoulder. "I love you. You know, just in case we die."

"I'll land it without killing us. And hopefully I won't break my plane." Determination crossed Vaughan's face as if the thought of not dying was a new concept he had to make happen. It didn't exactly instill confidence, but Bandos had faith in Vaughan's piloting abilities. "But I love you too."

Bandos turned to see how Echo was doing. Their gazes met and Echo gave him a thumbs up, but the fear in his eyes told the truth. Bandos nodded and turned back around.

The view outside the window showed treetops and not much else. Hopefully, there were houses amongst the trees, but he couldn't see any.

"We're going down in the trees," Bandos murmured.

"That's how it looks, yeah."

"No. I mean. We're going down in the forest." Bandos turned again, getting Echo's attention. "Think you can soften the blow from way up here?"

Echo concentrated. He had a green glowing aura around him when he shut his eyes. Bandos hadn't noticed it before, but he bet he had it when he saved their lives earlier. "I can lessen it, but that's all."

"That'll do, little fae."

When Vaughan stiffened, Bandos felt the air change. He knew they were close to the crashing part of their predicament.

Bandos faced Vaughan, not wanting to see outside the window.

Vaughan's jaw clenched. His arm flexed as he tried to maneuver the plane to their advantage.

The tops of the trees scrapped the bottom.

"The trees are rising to meet us. We're slowing down." Was that relief on Vaughan's face?

They sank and the plane shuddered. Bandos couldn't avoid watching their fall even if he wanted to because the trees scraped the windows. They moved so fast the greens and browns were indistinguishable. The branches acted like arms, trying to wrap around the plane, and while that slowed them, it didn't do enough to not feel the impact when it happened. The belly scraped the ground.

Bandos's head hit the back of his seat and the air left his lungs as if a vacuum had sucked them out. He had a sudden need to get to Echo. His eyes shifted and his teeth elongated. His hands grew claws as his dragon took over, but he turned them back so he could take off his seatbelt.

"Bandos! Fuck." Vaughan had too much on his plate to say anything more.

"Echo. I need to get to him." Bandos didn't waste time explaining. He stood and tried to make his way to the back. The distance felt like miles as he stumbled around. The plane shook and lurched. Tree branches broke as they raced along the ground, throwing him off his feet a couple of times. He stood, digging his claws into the metal of the fuselage to stabilize himself. If he weren't a shifter, he wouldn't have been able to move around at all, but he could pull himself along the wall.

Echo yelled, scowling but Bandos couldn't hear past the scraping and creaking of the plane crashing.

When he made it to Echo, he tried to sit beside him, but the plane hit something solid, sending Bandos ass over teakettle into hard metal. His head took the brunt of the impact.

Pain exploding through his brain was the last thing he remembered.

Chapter Fourteen

The first thing Vaughan realized when he came to was that nothing moved. He heard birds chirping nearby, but that was all. A part of Vaughan thought maybe he had died and was in some type of limbo, waiting to go to the next place, wherever that was. He recognized he was on his plane, but it didn't make a sound. Not a wheeze or a pop. Silence.

Vaughan's senses woke before the rest of him. The smell of blood came first, and it made him shift his eyes and teeth. He unclipped his seatbelt and tried to fight the nausea rising in his throat. He stood. His stomach turned. He grabbed the cabinet door and the bucket he kept at the bottom for cleaning. He got to it just in time to retch. There wasn't much in his stomach. He hadn't eaten since being in Saint Lakes, which seemed like years but was less than twenty-four hours ago.

When he finished, he put the bucket down, braced himself on the cabinet and pulled off his shirt. Kicking off his shoes took longer than normal because his stability sucked, but he got them off. His pants came next, and he shifted. As soon as he did, he realized the reason for his instability because the sharp pain in his head subsided a bit.

He hadn't had the time to contemplate his injuries until then. He must have hit his head. The smell of blood made sense. It was his own.

Vaughan's second thought was for Bandos and Echo. The need to protect made him tense. He sniffed the air but didn't smell humans like he had before takeoff, and that eased his worry a bit.

He shifted back and the rest of his headache faded. He might have a concussion, but he had bigger things to worry about, so he focused on taking in the scene.

As soon as he saw Bandos's prone, lifeless body, he ran to him. Bandos lay face down on the floor of the plane.

Vaughan's hands shook as he felt for a pulse. He held his breath until he felt the steady bump. The relief was so sudden, he couldn't keep the tears from his eyes. He pressed his lips to Bandos's cheek and kept it there for a few seconds, trying to gather his emotions enough to find out how Echo was.

When Vaughan straightened and scanned the area, there wasn't any sign of Echo. It was as if he'd disappeared. The panic was almost immediate. He held his breath for a second as he tried to scramble for reasons Echo wasn't in sight. Nothing eased the ache in his chest.

Was his sense of smell off? Had the humans taken Echo?

Vaughan stood and yelled, "Echo!"

The plane door stood open. He wasn't sure how he'd missed it. Between his head wound and finding Bandos lying unconscious, he couldn't rationalize his environment. He just knew he had to get Echo and Bandos in the same place. Once he'd done that, he would figure out what to do next.

"Echo!" He headed out of the door and shifted once his feet hit the ground. With his nose to the dirt, he followed Echo's scent. Over a ridge and on the other side, Vaughan found him picking what seemed like a weed. He had a bunch in one hand.

Vaughan shifted to his human form and closed the distance between them. He didn't breathe until he had his arms around him.

He still scanned the area, searching for any sign of danger, but he found nothing.

Echo stiffened and yelped. He recovered enough to straighten and turn to face Vaughan and then buried his face in Vaughan's chest. He had tears streaming down his face and sniffled. "Wolf."

"Are you hurt?" Vaughan rubbed Echo's back.

"Blue told me to stay in my seat." Echo's tears wet Vaughan's bare skin.

"What are you doing out here?"

"Gathering medicinal plants. It will help with your injuries." Echo pulled away, holding up the weed he had picked.

He gripped the nape of Vaughan's neck with his free so he could study the wound on Vaughan's head. When he took a big bite of the weeds and chewed, Vaughan thought he had lost his mind. Insanity wasn't a problem Vaughan could handle given their current situation.

"We need to get back to Bandos. He might wake up. If he finds us both gone, he's going to freak out." A dragon shifter in protective mode wasn't a good thing. Bandos had imprinted on Vaughan and, given how he put himself in danger as they were crashing, he probably had on Echo as well.

"The medication in the plant will help heal your wound. If you weren't a paranormal, I'm positive you wouldn't have woken up. I worried about you the most because I wasn't sure how bad the internal injury was." Echo spit a wad of green glop onto his fingers.

When Echo smeared it across the open cut on his head Vaughan jerked away. Echo's scowl made Vaughan stay still. "It smells disgusting."

"Mom used to say that's how you know it works." Echo smiled.

"My mom says the same thing." It must be a mom thing. Or maybe fae and witches had similar qualities.

"You have a family?" Echo asked and wiped his hand on the forest floor, trying to clean the goop away as much as possible.

When he straightened again, Vaughan wrapped his arm around Echo's shoulder, and they walked together. "The Somersets are a big family. Lots of brothers and a sister. We're all adopted or mated into the family. "

A pretty blush spread from Echo's neck to his cheeks, and he kept darting glances at Vaughan. It took Vaughan a second to realize where Echo's gaze had landed.

Vaughan would have gotten hard if not for their situation. "Sorry if I'm making you uncomfortable."

"I'm not used to so many naked men. Not to mention ones who look like you and Blue."

Vaughan raised his eyebrows and tried not to grin. His worry over Bandos stole some of the teasing, though. "We're not men, but shifters. And I hope that's a compliment."

"It's...you have a nice body." Echo went into the plane first and right to Bandos. He put some weeds into his mouth and chewed again.

Vaughan kneeled beside Bandos and rubbed his back as he watched Echo move Bandos's hair. He hadn't noticed the blood there when Vaughan had first found him. All his attention had been on checking if Bandos was alive, and then the relief of knowing he was. And then he'd had to find Echo.

Bandos had blood matting his hair and a gash on his scalp. Echo doctored his injury.

"You'll wake up soon, won't you, Blue," Echo whispered. He seemed worried about them not recovering.

"He's a shifter and a dragon at that. He'll be fine once he shifts a couple of times." Vaughan wouldn't lose Bandos. If the crash taught him anything, it was that life could take everything from him in the blink of an eye. He would do anything to keep Bandos safe.

Echo straightened and laid his hand over Vaughan's on Bandos's back. Their gazes met. "What do we do now?"

Vaughan sighed and turned his hand over, holding Echo's smaller one in his. "I wish I had the answers."

"Where did we land?"

"In the northern U.S. somewhere. I think we landed in the northeast. Maybe the Midwest area. My flight path matches up but my navigation was taken out by the blast so I can't be exactly sure."

"Do you live in this part of the country?"

Once they got back home, they would all learn about each other, including geographical information.

"Yeah."

"We were traveling to your home?"

Oh, shit. Where was the conversation going? "Yes. Bandos and I can protect you there because we'll have a lot of help. My family and clan won't let anything happen to you or Lucas."

"Lucas is the male witch? I've heard you talk of him before." Echo let go of his hand and stood, walking around Bandos and sat next to Vaughan, leaning against him. "He's your family."

"Yeah. He's mated to one of my brothers. He's kind of a big deal, just like you."

Echo shook his head. "I'm not. Only people who want something from me think so."

Vaughan couldn't argue with that. "That's true for everyone else besides me and Bandos. I think you're a big deal and don't want anything from you."

Echo met his gaze. "Don't you?"

"I want something *with* you. I think that's different. I hope you do too." By the gods, Echo was beautiful. His smile lit up his entire face.

"It is. And I do." Echo drew his eyebrows together. "And Blue?"

"That's a discussion that needs to include him."

"Agreed. So for now, let's talk about what we're going to do next." Echo wasn't as fragile as he looked. "Can you radio someone? Or call?"

"The plane's communications cut off when the engine did." At a guess, he would say they'd been taken out when the engine was, although there had to have been two separate blasts and both were small. They weren't designed to kill them, only bring them down. He had only heard one but maybe one drown the other out. Until he assessed the damage and discovered the truth it was all speculation.

Vaughan went to the cabinet. His puke bucket was still on the floor and that turned his stomach again. But he focused on finding his phone.

He needed as much information as he could get, so when Bandos woke, he had something substantial to tell him. If Vaughan's theory was correct, it meant someone might have put a tracking device on the plane when they planted the explosives.

"I can't find mine or Bandos's phone." Bandos had brought more than one computer. He'd left one behind in the forest near the castle but the other one should've been somewhere nearby if someone hadn't stolen it along with their phones. "Do you see a computer anywhere?"

Even if the computer was in pieces because of the crash, it would mean Vaughan's theory was wrong. He could chalk up the missing phones to getting thrashed around.

By the gods, he really wanted to be wrong because being right meant it was Senator Fowler, who was a human with a lot of resources. He had an entire government full of them, including the elite soldiery types who probably had at least one expert good enough to plant the explosives in the perfect way to not kill them. The scent of humans before takeoff was more evidence pointing in that direction.

Gods, Vaughan would've rather taken on a coven full of vampires. Even one as large as Delano Archer's. But Delano's involvement had ended at the castle. Vaughan was almost sure of it.

Vaughan had bought them a little bit of time by changing their course at the last minute but a day at best. That was probably how long it would take the senator's henchmen to find the plane and start tracking them.

Shit.

Echo searched while Vaughan grabbed his clothing and freaked the fuck out. He put them on and headed to the back where he kept a toolbox. He discovered the crash had scattered the tools around. It took him a good ten minutes to collect them, and even then, he was almost positive he had a few missing.

When he came back into the main area, Echo sat next to Bandos. He had placed a blanket under Bandos's head and then spread one over him. "I couldn't find it."

"Can you gather whatever food and water you can find?" Having a task helped. It kept the mind busy, or at least it did for Vaughan. "Just don't go out of sight, please."

"Should I stay here or help you after gathering the food?" Echo pleaded with his eyes. Vaughan couldn't resist.

Vaughan smiled. "I might curse and throw things. Mechanical work frustrates me, but I'd like having a pretty assistant."

"Blue will be fine once he wakes up." Echo leaned down and kissed Bandos's cheek. "Do you think he'll be scared? Should I be with him?"

Vaughan should've felt jealous. Echo was his mate and there should have been some type of negative reaction within him, but Vaughan's wolf didn't seem to mind. Vaughan enjoyed seeing the affection.

He felt the mating pull. It would have been a lot stronger if it weren't for his stress level. The protective instinct was still a thing. In fact, it was strengthening because of his suspicions.

He would think more about it later, because he needed to focus on finding proof. They needed to know what they were up against. Was it just finding civilization so they could call for help? Or were they running for their lives?

"It shouldn't take me too long to find the information I need, and I'll be right outside. But we can leave the door open and come check on him a lot. When we're finished, we'll sit with him." Vaughan grabbed the bucket on the way out, taking care of it before he did anything else.

As soon as he got to the engine, though, he knew there was no hope of fixing things, not that it was a real thought in his head. He focused his attention on finding pieces of a bomb. It didn't take him long at all.

They were fucking screwed.

Chapter Fifteen

The first thing Bandos realized was that Vaughan was cursing. The sound of metal clinking against metal came next. He was lying on something solid and cool. There was a blanket underneath his head, and it smelled like a combination of Echo and Vaughan. No humans. Thank the gods.

His eyes shifted, and his fangs dropped. His dragon came to the surface, and he acted on instinct, ready to fight when he stood.

The plane looked as if someone had ransacked it, and that put him even more on edge. The cabinets were the only things that had stayed closed, probably because the lock mechanisms were solid. Everything else had scattered all over. A pile of food and bottled water sat on the bench seat along with three duffle bags.

The plane door stood open, so Bandos headed toward it. As soon as he stepped out of the plane, he saw Echo holding a wrench and Vaughan with his head inside the plane's engine. His tension eased.

Echo turned to him, dropped the tool, and launched himself at Bandos.

Bandos hugged him close.

Vaughan had tears in his eyes when he stepped to Bandos's side. Bandos put his arm around Vaughan's waist and pulled him into their three-way hug. Vaughan buried his face in Bandos's neck. It wasn't long before he felt wetness on his skin.

"We'll figure it out, baby. It'll be okay." He didn't know if what he said was true, but they were together. That alone gave them an advantage.

"I thought you were dead." Oh. Oh, wow. Poor baby.

"Hey. Look at me."

Vaughan pulled far enough away to meet his gaze.

Echo did the same, watching them, but he seemed more curious than anything else, so Bandos focused on Vaughan again. He wiped Vaughan's cheeks with the pad of his thumb. "We made it through. All three of us."

Vaughan nodded. "Are you okay?"

"Just a headache. Nothing shifting won't fix." Bandos kissed him and then pressed their foreheads together. "I won't leave you, baby. I promise."

Vaughan cupped his nape and shut his eyes. "I fucking need you, so never do that to me again."

"I made a mistake."

Vaughan pulled back. His eyes shot flames of anger. "You stood while we were crashing, Bandos. It was dangerous and stupid."

"I'm sorry."

"Why did you do that?" Echo asked.

Bandos met his gaze. "I panicked. I couldn't handle you being scared." Just thinking about it brought his dragon to the surface again.

Echo's eyes widened, and he sucked in a breath. "You look..."

"Feral," Vaughan finished for him.

How long had he been out? Must have been a long time if they were finishing each other's sentences.

"I'm not feral. Just worried."

"You're imprinting on him," Vaughan raised his eyebrows as if he dared Bandos to disagree.

Bandos shrugged. "Dragon shifters don't call it that, but yeah, I think so."

"Good."

It was Bandos's turn to raise his eyebrows. He had a hard time believing Vaughan wouldn't get possessive over Echo. If he did, it would crush Bandos less if he expected it.

Vaughan sighed and shook his head. "Whatever, Bandos. If you're gonna make me work for the trust than I will. I don't have to be happy about it, though."

Bandos winced. "I'm trying."

"I know. And we have bigger problems anyway. Much, *much* bigger." Vaughan smiled and kissed him. And then he turned to Echo and did the same to him. Both kisses were just a peck on the lips, but it unified them in a small way. It made Bandos feel as if he had some connection with Echo other than attraction.

Bandos pulled them both closer, holding on because the crash could have been a lot worse and they all could have died. That they survived was thanks to Vaughan's cool head and piloting skills, and Echo softening their descent. "Did you scout the area for danger or any signs of civilization?"

Vaughan laid his head on Bandos's shoulder again. "Yes. And no one is around. Not anyone but us. Yet. But I think we should go back into the plane. We can all sit."

Bandos had been in there long enough already. He liked the way solid ground felt beneath his feet. Hell, if he never got into another plane again, it would be too soon. But he did what Vaughan said because whatever he had to say was big.

Bandos kept each one of them under an arm and then they walked to the plane together. He let Echo go first. And then Vaughan before following them inside. He scanned the area, taking in their surroundings for the first time. He didn't expect to see anything disturbed. Other than a plane and a bucket turned upside down next to a tree, nothing stuck out. Still, it was good to double check. That he didn't when he first left the plane said something about his panic level.

Vaughan sat on the bench seat with Echo on his lap. They made an attractive couple. With Echo's light green eyes and blond hair, and Vaughan's tall, dark, and handsome good looks, they complemented each other. All Bandos wanted to do was to protect them. That they sat together made that easier.

And they were Bandos's. Or at least his dragon thought so. His dragon didn't care that his human side was fighting getting his heart broken.

Bandos's eyes hadn't shifted from his dragon. He picked up the blankets and folded one of them, giving himself something to do while he thought about all that had happened.

Vaughan and Echo watched his every move as if they needed him to be the strong one, but his behavior told another story. Bandos sat, putting the blanket on the seat next to him.

"Tell me, baby."

"So the radio cut off the same time as the engine as you know. It was everything I could do to keep from nosediving, so I didn't really think about it at the time."

Bandos stiffened. "But."

"But once I had a chance to think, I realized how odd it was. So that's what Echo, and I were doing."

"And?"

"Someone put an explosive device in the engine and a smaller one near the communications center. I'm also pretty sure there's a tracking device as well. And by someone I mean Senator Fowler."

Bandos stood when his hands shifted into claws. He paced the length of the plane. "Did you find it?"

"If you mean the explosive, I found pieces of it, yeah. The tracking device—I haven't had the time to look yet."

Bandos stopped and met Vaughan's gaze. "Fowler. The guy Ladon and Magnus had a run it with?"

Vaughan nodded and then took a deep breath. "Do you want the good news or the bad news first?"

"Vaughan." It wasn't the time for games. Bandos was way too stressed out.

"More good news than. I changed our course. We were going to come in from the south originally, but I had to change it before we took off, so we ended up coming in from the north."

"Why did you change it? And why does this matter?" Other than knowing where they were geographically. They would need to know that to get out of there.

"Not crashing with other planes is the quick answer to the first question. And the answer to the second question is the bad news." Vaughan met his gaze. "I might have inadvertently bought us time but just long enough to reroute Fowler's soldiers here instead of southern Ohio where we would have ended up had I stayed my course."

Bandos nodded. If he did the math, Bandos figured Vaughan had bought them a day. Maybe a little more but not by much. And that was if they got started on their journey right away.

He already had a list in his mind of all the shit they needed to do to before they got the hell out of there. One of them had already gathered what food and water they had. "Explain how you came up with Fowler being the culprit."

He wasn't judging or doubting Vaughan's assessment. The exact opposite was true. Vaughan was intelligent and Bandos needed to know what he thought so they could act accordingly. One wrong move and Fowler's men would close in faster. They needed any advantage they could get because they didn't have many things helping them.

"The smell of humans back at the other airstrip first of all. I mean humans. Not vampires. That's a massive clue. And then I couldn't find our cellphones or your computer, so I figured they were probably smart enough to get our flight plan as well. The explosives were small enough not to cause massive damage or kill us. I bet you that takes a lot of skill. That kind of thing is bought and paid for by the government." Vaughan rubbed his chin on the top of Echo's head.

"They took my computer." Bandos wanted to throw something and would have if it weren't for the way Echo's eyes widened.

Vaughan rolled his eyes. "Did you hear anything else I said?"

"Unfortunately, I heard all of it." Bandos began pacing again. He needed to think.

Vaughan patted the side of Echo's ass and said, "Okay, let's leave him alone for a few minutes."

Echo stood.

"No! Stay close. Both of you." Bandos stopped and looked from one to the other. "That's the first rule. Neither of you leaves my sight. Ever. Got it?"

Echo nodded with his mouth open and his eyes wide. He let out a little squeal when Bandos pulled him close.

"Say it, Vaughan. I need to know you'll do what I say."

"I got it."

Bandos expected a little resistance, but Vaughan seemed relieved.

"Do you have canteens in here?"

Vaughan shook his head. "Just the water bottles."

Bandos nodded. "Okay, we're going to have to walk out of here, so gather whatever makes sense to take. Leave what we don't need."

Vaughan was the first to move, and he went to the left cabinet. Echo pulled away and did the same thing to the right.

Vaughan pulled an empty backpack out and handed it to Bandos. Why he had an extra pack but not a canteen was beyond Bandos's scope of reasoning. When it came to Vaughan, picking a battle wisely was key and arguing about his logic wasn't something Bandos wanted to do at the moment.

"If I'm wrong and it's a vampire coven, it'll be difficult to keep our lead. They're fast mother fuckers," Vaughan said as he pulled out rope and laid it on the floor beside him.

"You're not wrong, baby." Bandos put as much food and water in the bag as he could and rearranged the clothing to fit into one so they weren't taking so much space.

Bandos raised his eyebrows when he found lube in Vaughan's bag, but he didn't take the time to comment on it.

He left the bags there and gathered the stuff Vaughan and Echo had found.

When Bandos picked up a metal canteen, Vaughan shrugged. "I didn't know I had it."

Vaughan handed him a lighter.

Bandos packed it and grabbed the two blankets, putting them in one duffle bag.

"Echo. Come here." When Echo came to him, Bandos made a gesture for him to sit. Bandos kneeled at his feet and pulled off his shoes and socks. He put a pair of socks on first and then met Echo's gaze. "What's your shoe size?"

"Forty-one." Echo winced. "Seven. Sorry. I forget about the numbers being different in the US."

"I think these are going to be big but try them anyway." He picked up what he thought might have been Jules's shoes and put them on Echo's feet. "How do those feel, little fae?"

Echo stood and walked around. "A little big."

"Try Fane's," Vaughan said without turning from his task.

Echo sat back down, but he bent and took off the shoes, pulling some smaller ones from the pile of clothing. Echo put them on. "Better than the other ones."

Bandos nodded. "Why don't you change into something else. And take a jacket."

They could walk around in T-shirts, but nights might get chilly, and Bandos wanted Echo to stay as warm as possible. They couldn't afford for him to get sick.

He nodded and pulled his shirt over his head. His underwear and pants came next. And before Bandos knew it, a very naked Echo stood before him. As a shifter, he should have been used to a naked body, but there was something about Echo that made him think of sex even when it was inappropriate.

Vaughan's reaction wasn't any better. In fact, his eyes shifted, and his fangs dropped as if he were ready to mate right there. His gaze met Bandos, and he smiled.

Bandos would have had a similar physical reaction if his eyes and teeth hadn't already been that of his dragon counterpart. Bandos shook his head and smiled back. "Behave, baby. We don't have time for that."

Some of Bandos's stress lifted. He needed the distraction.

Vaughan chuckled and turned back to the cabinets, going to the one Echo had abandoned.

Echo pulled on some underwear that was brand new and then met his gaze. "What?"

"Nothing." Bandos couldn't help but chuckle.

"Are you making fun of me?"

That sobered Bandos up some. "No."

Echo picked up a pair of Fane's pants. "I'm not as fit as either of you."

Shit. Bandos decided to lay it on the line. "We were admiring your body."

Echo narrowed his eyes. "Truth?"

Bandos held up a hand. "Swear it on the gods."

He would've dropped his pants and shown Echo he was half-hard if necessary. He couldn't believe Echo didn't know his own appeal, but his reaction was genuine.

Echo picked up a T-shirt that probably belonged to Jules because it was pink, which was more Jules's style than Fane's. He grabbed a sweater, wrapping it around his waist and tying the arms together. And then stuffed the jacket into a bag.

When he finished, he met Bandos's gaze and nodded. "I'm ready."

Vaughan handed Bandos a small bag. "Not sure if that's essential, but it's toothpaste, soap, and stuff like that."

Bandos took it and put it into the bag with the food. It wasn't the most necessary thing, and if it got too heavy, they could always leave it behind later on. Bandos grabbed a bandanna and wrapped it around his head before grabbing his leather jacket. He counted it as essential. They already had his computer, so he'd lost enough.

He emptied some of the water into the canteen before handing the pack to Echo. While it was heavy, it would lighten up and Echo could wear it on his back.

He handed Vaughan a sweater and then a bag while he took the heaviest one. "We're ready."

Vaughan nodded but his forehead creased and his bottom lip poked out a little. "My plane."

"I'm sorry, baby."

Vaughan sighed and then focused his gaze on Echo. "Are you going to kiss it and make it better?"

Echo chuckled. "I will. Later."

"Bandos lost his computer." Vaughan turned to the door, opening it a crack and scanning the area before going out.

"That's a lot of kisses."

"Yep, so you better get your lips ready."

"Why don't you kiss each other? I enjoyed watching before."

Bandos raised his eyebrows. Most of the time, when Vaughan got going, the best approach was not to engage, so he kept quiet. Echo didn't know that yet and even if he did, Bandos seriously doubted he was capable of not pushing back.

Vaughan had his hands full with Echo too, so maybe they were evenly matched.

Chapter Sixteen

Echo's feet had never hurt more. Walking through the forest wasn't like making the trip from his small flat to the café where he had worked. He had to watch where he stepped, and straddle fallen logs that were sometimes as wide as him. It smelled better. Pine took over everything. The vegetation cleaned the air and the smell of damp earth made Echo feel at home.

After spending so long locked in a room with a single window so high on the wall he couldn't look out of it, walking through the forest was a blessing he wouldn't overlook ever again.

He stayed between Wolf and Blue. His view of Wolf's denim-covered ass made his day a lot better. He would have liked to see him naked again, but he would take what he could get.

"I smell water," Wolf said, but he didn't stop walking.

"Let's head that way. We'll camp for the night." Blue was their unspoken leader. Wolf didn't seem to mind. In fact, it seemed to calm him, which Echo could relate to.

Both shifters made him feel safe in a situation that should have sent him into fearful hysterics. There wasn't a time when he wasn't in more danger, except for maybe the initial kidnapping. Still, they brought him a contentment he had never felt before. He hadn't had a lot of time to think about it up to that point, until they'd made their way out of a plane crash and into a forest.

He didn't have answers for why, other than he knew they all needed each other if they wanted to survive. Of course, Wolf being his mate said that much, but there was also his vision. Somehow that held more weight because it included Blue.

"Do you think it's warm enough to swim?" Echo wished he would have taken Blue up on that shower he had offered back at the airport, but a dip in a lake would come in a close second.

"Just barely. The better question would be the safety of the water. There are a lot of rivers around here. The current is too strong is some," Blue answered.

"But it's possible?" Echo hoped.

"Sure."

"I think it's a lake. Smells almost like home." Wolf pointed to the change in soil from dark, damp earth to sand.

It wasn't long before Echo could see the sun reflecting off water. The trees became less dense until he had an unobstructed view of a pretty lake.

He had a sudden urge to run to the water's edge, strip, and jump in, but he held back because Blue would want to assess things first. Acting on impulse wasn't the best idea.

Echo slowed until he walked next to Blue. He laced their fingers. "I'd like a swim."

They came to a section of the forest where the trees had left a clearing. It was a few dozen yards from the water. When Wolf stopped and turned, Echo knew that was where they would camp for the night.

Echo let the bag fall from his shoulders and looked around, scanning the plant life. There wasn't much what with the sandy soil, but he could go back the way they had come and gather a few greens to eat.

"Let me shift and get a look at the area." Blue dropped his bag. "You two stay here and stay together."

Wolf reached for Echo and tucked him under his arm as Blue stripped.

Neither said a word as they watched each piece of clothing come off.

"He looks..." Echo didn't need to finish the sentence. They were both thinking the same thing.

"Yeah." Wolf sounded as breathy as Echo.

Even though they whispered, Blue was close enough to hear. He rolled his eyes. "Keep your eyes peeled."

Echo didn't know who he was talking to or if he was talking to both of them, but he answered anyway. "We are."

"On danger. Not me. Pay attention to what's around you." Blue shook his head, but the corner of his mouth lifted into a crooked smile.

"You're making that difficult." Echo had never felt more focused on something in his life.

Wolf nodded, and his eyes shifted. He looked like a predator, which struck Echo as funny, and he couldn't explain why even to himself.

Blue snorted out a laugh. "Don't start a fire until I secure the area." He shifted and walked to the water's edge before taking to the sky. The trees blocked Echo's view as Blue flew around, so Echo turned in Wolf's arms.

Wolf smiled before kissing him. "Maybe we should collect some wood. Might be wishful thinking but I bet we're alone out here. No one around for miles."

Echo nodded and began searching for sticks or even something bigger. Wolf's words eased the tightness in his shoulders. He hadn't even known it was there until it wasn't anymore. One night of peace sounded like bliss, especially since it would likely be their only one. He would take what he would get and be grateful for the reprieve, however brief.

They stayed within sight of each other as they gathered kindling.

"So you know how we're both into Bandos?"

Echo picked up a sizeable stick as he wondered where Wolf was going with that question. "And each other."

"Well, he's gonna need some incentive to jump on board with the three of us becoming a thing."

Echo stopped what he was doing and raised his eyebrows. "And you think I don't."

Wolf chuckled. "You can't play that game after the way you just looked at him."

Echo sighed and nodded. "You're right."

"Hey, it's not a bad thing. I mean, you know I'm in love with him. And we're mates. That makes it a win-win in my books."

Echo scanned for other sticks. "It all sounds complicated to me."

"Yeah, I know. But it doesn't have to be. My brother has two mates, and it works for them. Maybe it can for us too, but we have to get Bandos on board first."

"I don't know if we should even be talking about this until after we get to safety."

"I hate to be a Debbie downer but we might not make it out of this forest alive. Or get another chance. This is our one opportunity, and that's if Bandos says we're clear. I don't know about you but I feel like seizing the moments while we can." And there it was. Wolf's point. Finally.

"And how do you purpose we do that when you growl at him all the time?"

"Hey, I haven't done that in a long time and I'm not jealous or anything. Not when it's between you and him. I only growled because you're like this fragile little thing. I want to wrap you in bubble wrap."

Echo turned to meet Wolf's gaze, but he was bent over picking up a stick. He still narrowed his eyes, though. "I am not fragile."

"That isn't my point. And if we get in an argument, I won't be able to make my point in time because Bandos will come back soon." Wait. Vaughan hadn't made his point yet?

"So what, then?"

"Would you seduce him?"

Echo blinked for a full minute before saying, "'Seduce him'? That's what we're having a conversation about?"

Wolf turned and met his gaze. "It would get him on the right side of our relationship faster."

Echo had never seduced anyone in his entire life. "I don't know how."

"It's not that hard." Wolf smirked.

"You don't know me. At. All. I can assure you I'm not even a little bit capable."

Wolf waved off that comment and turned to search for more firewood. "You're irresistible. You could literally do nothing but sit on his lap and kiss him, and that would work."

"How do you know?"

"Because he looks at you the same way he does me, and all I have to do is knock on his bedroom window."

Wait. What did that mean? "Knock on his window?"

"Long story. We were kinda on the down-low until just recently."

Really? "Why?"

"We started out as friends with benefits. I didn't know how he felt. And I wasn't sure how my family would react to me being in love with someone who isn't my mate. None of it is important anymore."

"Because you found me?"

"Well, that too. But it's because I came clean right before we left to rescue you. Figured Bandos deserved more." Wolf did the right thing, even when it didn't benefit him.

"That he does." Echo learned a lot about Wolf at that moment. He hadn't had a lot of time to get to know either shifter until they could take a breath. Even with the danger looming, all three of them were in their element in the forest, and that made things easier. The walk to civilization would help them get to know each other. It was one more thing he was grateful for.

Wolf turned to him again and pleaded with his eyes. "I'm going to level with you."

Echo nodded and held his bundle of sticks in his arms like a shield.

"The mating pull is getting stronger."

Echo didn't feel it the way Wolf did. He didn't have an animalistic instinct. But he felt the attraction growing. That was undeniable. "All right."

"And I can't live without him." Wolf took a deep breath. "I want you, but I want him too."

"I'm aware." If there was nothing he understood about Wolf, it was that he wanted them both. He had made that clear.

"Maybe that makes me a dick. I don't know. But I figure it kinda doesn't because you guys want each other and me too, so that just makes me the most vocal."

"So you're asking me to decide right now how the rest of my life is going to go?" Twenty minutes of sex would work the stress out of his body, so he wouldn't deny the appeal of what Wolf suggested. But Echo wouldn't feel rushed just because Wolf wanted to move things along. Maybe Blue needed a little nudge. Maybe he didn't but Echo needed to decide what approach to take either way. Did he want to live in the moment or take his time thinking things through?

"No. I guess not." Wolf returned to the task at hand. "Sorry."

Echo sighed and dropped his sticks in the middle of the clearing. It seemed like a good enough spot for a fire. He closed the distance between them, putting a hand on Wolf's shoulder to get his attention. When Wolf met his gaze, he said, "Fae mate like humans, so rushing seems pointless. That said, I like you both. There's an attraction we all share. Maybe that's worth exploring."

Wolf smiled. "Bandos and I will make it worth it."

"So how do you think I should begin this grand seduction?"

Before Wolf could answer, Blue landed near the water. He shifted and gave them a thumbs up as he walked into the clearing. "Oh good, you guys started getting firewood."

Blue grabbed his underwear and pants, putting them on.

"Is anyone around?" Echo asked. He wanted to swim. He wanted something that would provide him some semblance of normal and yeah, maybe that meant he wasn't living in the land of reality. He knew he would have to deal with the fact all three of them were in danger but the moment felt like a reprieve, and Echo didn't want to squander it. He could feel the hope for it building in his chest.

"Nope. Not a single cabin. It's a small lake, though. Probably few people know it's here because I'm pretty sure we're on private land. And no sign of anyone. Human or otherwise."

Echo sighed as the stress left him. "Is it safe to swim, do you think?"

Blue nodded. "I'd say so."

Echo couldn't contain his excitement. He squealed and jumped on Blue.

He couldn't get his clothes off fast enough.

Blue chuckled. "Hold on. Someone needs to keep watch."

Wolf grinned. "You go. I'll start a fire and join you after I'm done."

Blue nodded and followed Echo to the beach. Echo finished getting undressed. He hesitated with his underwear, but after the conversation with Wolf, he figured naked was a good thing. After all, Blue had said he liked the look of Echo's body. Based on Blue's expression, Echo knew it was true.

Echo finished and held out his hand, wiggling his fingers as his impatience grew.

Blue shook his head but smiled. "Hold on."

Echo licked his lips when Blue took off his pants and underwear again. And then Blue held his hand. Echo's focus changed when they both dipped their toes into the water.

"By the gods, hypothermia." Echo tried to back away, but Blue snaked an arm around his waist and held him in place.

And Blue grinned, which made Echo wonder if he had ever seen him smile. The half-smile he had gotten a time or two didn't count. "You'll get used to it. Come on."

"There is no one on this earth who's capable of swimming in this water."

"Vaughan is building a fire for us, for after we get out."

"Skinny-dipping should happen when the water's warmer."

Blue scooped him into his arms before taking a couple of steps into the lake.

Echo squealed at the suddenness of being lifted off his feet. "Put me down."

To Echo's surprise, Blue obeyed. And Echo found out the reason he was so agreeable as soon as his feet touched the water. He yelled and jumped onto Blue, crawling up his body.

Blue chuckled, but he lifted him again, letting Echo wrap his arms and legs around him. He rubbed Echo's back and got very close to Echo's ass a few times, but never touched him there.

Blue waded in, sucking in a breath from the cold. It took Echo a second to realize why it had affected him more in that moment than all the others. The water touched his balls, but he never stopped going.

It wasn't until Echo could feel the water touch his legs and then his ass that he protested. "I'll do whatever you want if you stop moving."

Blue chuckled again. "Whatever I want, huh? That sounds like a deal. But I have a counteroffer."

Echo met his gaze. "Which is?"

"If you do one thing for me, I'll stop walking for five minutes. And the offer can't be repeated." Blue had an intelligence that Echo hadn't seen until their little negotiation. Had Echo known, he wouldn't have tried to make the deal.

"Five minutes is all I get?" Echo sighed. "Fine, but it can't be anything difficult. Like carrying your bag for two days. Not something like that."

"I would never make you carry my bag. It's too heavy for you." Blue was still in his prime, after all. He could hold a lot more weight than Echo.

"Well then, what's the thing you want me to do?" Echo ran his hand down Blue's soft hair before lacing his fingers through it.

"Get in the water."

Echo opened his mouth to speak but all that came out was a squeak which made Blue laugh his ass off.

"Not fair."

"I'm kidding." Blue let the last of his chuckles out, but a smile remained. "Are you ready?"

"Just tell me."

"Say my name."

Echo blinked. "Your name?" That was it?

Blue nodded. "My actual name, not the nickname you gave me."

Well, that wasn't difficult at all. "Bandos."

"My name is Conor Montgomery. Bando is slang for an abandoned house. Like a trap house, I guess. I don't know why the *s* was added."

"Why are you called that?"

"My fated mate abandoned me. Afterward, I drowned myself in shifter drugs. My friend, Sully, started calling me Bandos, and it stuck even after I got clean."

Echo wanted to cry. Instead, he whispered, "Conor Montgomery."

Bandos smiled.

"Do you mind being called Bandos now?"

"No. It reminds me to never go back." Oh, wasn't that a suitable answer.

"Conor."

Echo cupped Bandos's cheek and kissed him. He hadn't intended to take the kiss any further, but with both of them naked and pressed together, the kiss turned heated. He made demands, licking at Bandos's lips.

Bandos took over the kiss and Echo let him. He asked for everything, and Echo was happy to give it. Somehow, he worked Echo's mouth open, getting a taste.

Someone growled and for a moment Echo thought it was Wolf getting possessive again. Or protective. Whatever. It amounted to the same thing. Desperation stole his breath because he had an image in his mind of Bandos pulling away. He held the back of Bandos's head, keeping him involved.

And then the growl happened again. Echo felt the vibrations against his lips, and he realized it was Bandos. Echo would have asked questions, but Bandos gripped Echo's nape with one hand, holding him in place. He cupped Echo's ass with his other. One of his fingers touched Echo's balls.

Echo's hard length pressed against Bandos's abdomen.

It all made for an experience so heated Echo knew he couldn't ever go back. That was the moment he decided to go for it. He wanted to live in the present, especially when Bandos was in it, doing all the things that made Echo's body hum with pleasure.

A hand landed on his back right before he felt Wolf against his side. His presence made Echo's cock ache and his balls pull tight. There was a desperation that Echo hadn't felt in a long time, if ever.

Bandos responded to Wolf's presence by ending the kiss. He stiffened.

Echo whimpered and buried his face in Bandos's neck, kissing him there with little pecks and licks.

Bandos ended the intimacy. It felt like a lost experience. Echo longed for a future in which Bandos worked Echo's body like a musical instrument.

"Keep going, baby. He wants you too."

Echo whimpered. The sound slipped out as if his vocal cords belonged to someone else.

And then Bandos's hand was back on Echo's ass, along with Wolf's. "We both want you, baby. I'm hard from watching the two of you together. See?"

Echo wanted to get a look at Wolf too, so he lifted just enough to take in the hard length. As soon as he saw it, he wanted to feel the weight of it. The only problem was he couldn't touch it without letting go of Bandos, and he wasn't willing to do that. Bandos needed reassurance from them both. So instead, he did the next best thing. He hooked an arm around Wolf's neck before kissing him.

Echo was the one who deepened the kiss. He worked Wolf's mouth open. Wolf tasted good enough to eat and Echo let him know by nipping at him. He sucked on Wolf's bottom lip, taking his time.

If Bandos made him crazy with lust, Wolf made him bold. His submission was as much a turn-on as Bandos's dominance. Being at the center of that spectrum made him feel as if he fitted into an already established relationship. It wasn't something he had thought he'd worried about until he knew where he fit. Since his rescue, he hadn't thought a lot about anything but survival. The moment felt right, though.

Wolf tasted like belonging. So much so, Echo nearly bonded, but he needed permission. It was the way of the fae. And he probably would need to bond with Bandos before Wolf, if they all wanted to mate.

Why are you thinking about bonding, Echo? By the gods, slow down.

But he didn't know when they would get another reprieve or if they would live past tomorrow. Wolf was right about that. It wasn't just his safety, but the uncertainty of the rest of his life.

If people wanted him for the things he could do, then the future held danger. He would not live in fear. His life would not belong to someone else, so maybe bonding wasn't smart, but nothing was certain, and his imagination didn't extend to the future. At least not beyond dying at the hands of strangers who wanted more than he could give.

So he was going with his impulse.

Bandos growled again, so Echo ended the kiss. A reptilian gaze met his own. Perhaps they all wanted to bond.

Echo tilted his head to the side, giving Bandos permission to take what he wanted. He didn't know if the biting would hurt.

Bandos kissed him on his neck and then where his shoulder met his neck. "Are you sure, little fae?" His breath fanned over the spot he had just kissed.

"Yes." The anticipation stole his breath.

Bandos met Wolf's gaze. "And you? You're okay with this?"

"I don't know how many times I have to say how much I fucking love you, but I'll keep saying it if it makes you understand that all three of us are in this together, not just Echo and me."

Echo smiled and reached for Wolf again, kissing him. He didn't linger over the kiss like he wanted to because it was about Bandos more than the two of them. "Well said, Wolfy."

"'Wolfy'." He shook his head with a smile.

"Vaughan."

"You're so fucking cute when you say my name."

Echo grinned. "Vaughan." He met Bandos's gaze. "Conor."

"Wait. Your first name is Conor?" Vaughan raised his eyebrows.

Bandos narrowed his eyes. "Are you going to make fun of my name, because if you are, then be prepared for the consequences."

Vaughan grinned. "Don't you have a fae to bond with?"

Someone's finger pressed between Echo's ass cheeks, rubbing his hole. He wasn't sure who touched him, but he liked it. He sucked in a breath and tried to move his hips so he could get the finger inside him.

Bandos kissed him where his neck and shoulder met. "No lube, little fae. Getting inside will have to wait."

"Please." That one touch brought back the desperation, getting him worked up quicker than anything. "I'm so hard." It almost hurt.

When the bite came, it wasn't what he expected. It was so much more. It was...everything. It made him come without a single touch.

His brain short-circuited, and everything he did after that was instinctive, including putting his own bonding mark onto Bandos.

"Holy shit," Vaughan said when Echo pressed his hand to Bandos's chest. He knew he probably had an aura around him, which made him glow, but he didn't know what color it was. It didn't matter. All that did was complete the bond.

He felt Bandos in his mind, all the pain from his past and his hope, his affection for them, his protectiveness. It was all there, along with his beautiful dragon. "Blue."

Bandos didn't pull his fangs out even though he'd stopped drinking. One of their hands moved from Echo's ass and then Bandos grunted.

"That's it, baby," Vaughan whispered. He must have been jacking Bandos off.

Echo felt warm wetness splash against his ass. "Oh. That's sexy."

He wanted to see it. He wanted to see Bandos and Vaughan together. Just the thought threatened to make him hard again. He would have if he wasn't so satisfied. He needed a few minutes to recover.

A few seconds later, he felt more warm wetness on his back. That must have been Vaughan.

Bandos released Echo and then buried his face in Echo's neck. "Little fae."

Oh. Oh no. "We won't abandon you, Conor." The concept was hard to even think about. It would never happen. Not while Echo had free will.

"That will never fucking happen as long as I live," Vaughan growled.

"I know. I just...it feels good to be connected." He met Echo's gaze and smiled, kissing him before he turned to Vaughan. "I need the connection with you. It feels incomplete and my dragon knows it."

"I want that more than anything." Vaughan pressed his lips to Echo's. "With both of you."

"Echo wanted to swim."

"I changed my mind. Let's make love. You two can go first." Echo wondered if his bond mark on Bandos would set the mating pull in motion between him and Vaughan. His bond came from the natural elements, and it had felt right with Bandos. But only time would tell.

"We have time." Vaughan kissed Bandos again. "Let him swim."

Bandos grinned. They had enough of a connection for Echo to know what he was thinking.

Echo squealed right before Bandos flipped onto his back and floated, plunging Echo down with him.

Vaughan chuckled and followed them, holding his hands out for Echo. "Come here. I'll save you."

Bandos stood again and passed Echo to Vaughan before swimming deeper. He waved at them, beckoning them forward when he stopped. "Come on. The water's warmer out here."

"How is that possible?" Echo should've really demanded to walk on his own. They would carry him around like a child if he didn't, but he liked it too much to protest. He would think about raising a fuss later.

Vaughan was thinner, so it was easier to wrap around him. He wouldn't shake Echo loose if he wanted to. "Currents. I don't know."

"I think he's teasing us."

Vaughan chuckled. "If he is, he's in rare form."

Vaughan was bolder than Bandos, holding Echo up by his ass. One of his fingers rested against Echo's hole. Whether or not he did it on purpose didn't matter. Echo liked it.

"You made him happy." Vaughan met his gaze. "Thank you."

Maybe focusing on that, and not the constant danger, would help him to take back his life. "You don't have to thank me for that. And I think you do too."

"I'm with you on that. Safe and happy. That's the goal."

"You're very good at fighting. Where did you learn?"

Vaughan raised his eyebrows. "No one has ever said that to me before."

"I'm not sure why others wouldn't tell you that. It's very obvious."

Vaughan shrugged. "It's instinctive. Can I ask you a question?"

Echo nodded.

"Why do you have an American accent?"

"My mother was from Ireland and my father from the states. My father met my mother on a trip across the Atlantic. His ship ported in Ireland before heading northeast. But my mother worked in a pub down by the port and the rest was history. Dad never made it any further. He brought my mother to the states. So far west they had to go by wagon. Boy, did she have stories about that trip, and she glared at dad the entire time she told them. So I'm originally from Oregon. A small town near Portland. By the time they had me, airplanes existed, so we went back and forth, visiting Ireland all the time. When my parents died, I moved to Mom's hometown."

"I didn't know fae lived in the states."

Echo hadn't noticed how deep they had gotten or the temperature of the water. It wasn't until Bandos kissed his cheek that he knew how far out they were.

"Not many do. Not anymore." Echo smiled and then let his hands go, floating on the surface of the water, but he still kept his legs wrapped around Vaughan's waist. "You were right. I got used to it."

"Told you."

Echo shut his eyes and let himself float.

Chapter Seventeen

Sexual tension charged the air. It sang through all three of them. The need to finish the bond hung like humidity. The only thing that mattered more was Echo's safety, so getting to Saint Lakes as soon as possible was important but so was completing their connection. If they strengthened the bond, they would have an internal dialogue, which would help them in the long run. And it wasn't just Vaughan who thought so. Bandos had the same thought process. They needed each other.

They ate before bedding down for the night. Echo, with his little naked ass, foraged for food nearby. He called whatever he gathered *greens*, but they were weeds. He divided jerky and dried peas into three piles. As dinner went, it wasn't much, but it was enough to satisfy them. Vaughan would hunt the next night if they were able to make a fire. If the danger caught up with them than they would continue with their jerky and greens. They needed all the calories they could get so they would likely eat many times.

Bandos hovered around Echo, keeping him safe, but he diverted his gaze to Vaughan every few minutes. His eyes were reptilian, and his teeth had elongated. Echo's foraging led him farther from their campsite.

"Vaughan." Bandos had never yelled a day in his life until that moment. It should have been sexy, but the undertone of anger killed the desire.

"What?" Vaughan couldn't see them anymore because they had gone over a rise, but they weren't that far away.

"Come here."

Vaughan sighed. He supposed if he argued it would put Bandos into an even fouler mood. Vaughan left the food on the blanket and put his shoes on, making his way in their direction.

As soon as he went up and over the rise and his gaze met Bandos's, he knew something wasn't right. Bandos was half-shifted, and he stalked toward Vaughan as if he were about ready to kill someone.

Vaughan growled and scanned the area, searching for a threat.

If there was one, it didn't scare Echo. He never stopped searching the ground and picking what appeared to be dandelion leaves. Bandos could have been reacting to the weather for all Echo minded.

"What's wrong?" Vaughan didn't have clothing on besides his shoes, so he could shift if and when it became necessary.

"I couldn't see you." Bandos closed the distance between them and wrapped his arms around Vaughan as if he were shielding him with his body.

What was he protecting Vaughan from? They were still in their bubble of peace. Had the bubble popped?

"What is happening right now?" Vaughan hadn't meant it as a joke. He needed to know the answer to that question.

But Echo answered. "I believe Bandos is feeling the mating pull."

"What? How?"

"I'm among the natural elements. Well, everyone is, but fae learn to embrace it." That didn't explain a thing.

"You scared me to death, Bandos. By the gods." And he could barely breathe with Bandos squeezing him so tight.

Bandos growled and kissed Vaughan's temple. "You're safe now, mate."

Mate? "I was safe before too."

"His dragon is leading him. I can feel it through our bond. You're like gold. He wants to put you in a cave and keep you for himself. Well, and me too." Echo smiled.

Bandos flipped Echo off, which allowed Vaughan to take a deep breath.

Echo snorted. "It's true."

"Seriously, can one of you explain what's happening?" Vaughan had never felt smothered by Bandos in the months they had been together until that moment, and he wasn't sure he liked it.

"It's a natural progression of our relationship." Echo closed the distance between them. He didn't have shoes, and seemed to avoid getting injured by the pine needles and sticks with little effort. "My mother would say the gods have decided, but I think it's just the elements or maybe science. You feel it toward him too. Not just me anymore."

If he analyzed his reaction toward Bandos since they ended their swim, he would have to say he felt a pull, but he wasn't three quarters of the way toward feral, though.

Bandos wrapped his arm around Echo and pulled him into their hug. "Stay close."

"I have enough greens for all three of us. We can go back to camp." Echo didn't seem to mind Bandos's behavior. He leaned into them.

Vaughan, on the other hand, was a little shell-shocked. He didn't know what to think or feel at the recent development. It was what he wanted but never thought he would ever get. It felt like a dream.

The fight went out of him. Not that he was upset, but he had been a little annoyed. Getting bossed around wasn't his favorite thing. And then maybe he had wanted to stay irritable, to protect himself if Bandos decided not to mate with him.

But as they walked back to camp, Bandos's protective instinct never stopped. He kept them both tucked against him as if he thought they would disappear. A dragon hoarding gold indeed.

Hope rose from Vaughan's throat into his chest, bringing tears to his eyes.

Vaughan met Bandos's gaze, cupping his cheeks. "Is this for real?"

Bandos growled instead of answering and wiped the tears from Vaughan's eyes. "I don't like it when you cry."

Vaughan chuckled through his tears and kissed Bandos.

Echo left their little circle, which got their attention. They had the same reaction to not feeling his body pressed against theirs. As much as they wanted to focus on each other, the need to keep Echo safe was stronger.

But he had gone to the blanket and put his little bundle of weeds in the middle of the three piles. He took a leaf and munched on it as he waited for them.

They sat with him. Vaughan gave the weeds a chance and took one. It tasted bitter, but not horrible. He could stomach it if he wrapped it around jerky.

"The plants provide balance." Echo sounded put out.

Vaughan held up his hands. "I didn't say anything."

"You didn't have to."

"Okay, fine, but how about for every weed I eat, you give me something? I need a reward."

Bandos chuckled and shook his head. He seemed better, less feral, and that probably had a lot to do with their proximity to each other.

"They aren't weeds. They are plants that will provide you with certain vitamins and minerals."

"But they taste bad. And I ate plants last time."

"Irrelevant."

"How about I promise not to bitch about them the next time you make me eat them?"

He could see the wheels turning in Echo's brain, trying to figure out what Vaughan would deem a worthy reward and how it could benefit him. "How about you just eat what's provided?"

"I'm gonna need a reward afterward. I'm just saying."

Echo chuckled. "Why do you choose to pick on me over him?"

"Because you send it back as good as I can throw it at you. Bandos either rolls his eyes or he doesn't engage."

"So all I have to do is shut my mouth and you'll stop."

Vaughan shrugged. "I seriously doubt you're capable of that, but yeah, I guess."

And there was the defiance. For about five seconds Echo wanted to take him up on the challenge but then he nodded, "that's fair."

Refueling meant the sexual tension was even stronger. The only difference was they were all comfortable letting it wrap them up a bit longer. Vaughan wasn't the boldest in making love, but he leaned into Bandos, placing a kiss on his neck.

He wanted to bite down. No, he *needed* to. But all three of them wanted to make it a memorable experience. It might be their only time together. Still, he licked Bandos where he would place his mating mark, above the one Echo had left.

It looked like a tattoo. It was green and appeared almost Celtic. The image could have been anything, but Vaughan saw it as three interlocking leaves. It was high enough on Bandos's chest that it touched his shoulder.

Bandos pulled Vaughan closer. "Straddle my lap, baby."

Vaughan obeyed but reached for Echo, inviting him into their lovemaking.

Echo took his hand and knee walked over to them. His cock was hard and pressed against Vaughan's side. Vaughan wanted to take it into his mouth, but they weren't to that stage yet.

Bandos had one arm around Vaughan, his hand spanning an ass cheek while the other held Echo. He leaned into Vaughan, kissing him.

The kiss wasn't about playing but told Vaughan what he wanted. They were too far gone to keep things light, and Vaughan didn't tease. He gave Bandos what he demanded, wanting him to know that he went into the mating with his whole heart. He didn't want doubts to cloud Bandos's mind.

Their hard lengths rubbed together. And then a tongue licked across their heads. Bandos ended the kiss, and they both watched Echo taste their pre-cum.

Vaughan fought the urge to move his hips but failed when Echo sucked Vaughan into his mouth, his lips covering the head. He swirled his tongue around Vaughan before leaving him and going to Bandos, doing the same.

Bandos cursed and laced his fingers through Echo's hair. There wasn't anything more beautiful than Bandos receiving pleasure.

Echo moved to Vaughan's cock again. Only he stayed latched on like a leech, sucking Vaughan's brain cells through his cock. And then a finger pressed into his opening. It was slick and went in without a problem.

Where Echo got the lube, Vaughan didn't know, but he knew it was his finger. He knew Bandos's touch almost as well as his own. Bandos dominated. He gave Vaughan exactly what he thought they both needed. But Echo was tentative, as if he wasn't sure of his welcome. He took his time, either wanting to memorize how Vaughan felt or wanting to ensure pleasure. Vaughan wasn't sure.

Echo rubbed Vaughan's prostate.

Vaughan moved into the touch, wanting more, and Echo didn't disappoint. He stopped sucking Vaughan off and focused on making Vaughan lose his mind.

Bandos laid on the blanket. He made sure Vaughan went with him. It opened Vaughan up more and Echo worked his way behind him, putting another finger in.

Bandos cupped Vaughan's cheek. "You like his touch."

It wasn't a question. But Vaughan nodded anyway. He couldn't speak because his heart picked up its pace, making him pant as if he'd run a marathon.

"Are you ready for him?"

Vaughan nodded again.

Bandos peered over Vaughan's shoulder. "Get inside him, honey."

And then Echo's fingers left and he touched Vaughan's ass cheek before the head of his cock pressed against Vaughan's opening. He sank in slowly and then kissed the center of Vaughan's back. He left his lips there as if he thought he needed to soothe Vaughan.

"You can move, love."

"I'll come if I do." His gentle voice sounded breathless with need. It was sexy.

"Have you topped anyone before?" Vaughan held his breath as he waited for Echo's answer.

"No."

Something about that sent Vaughan into a tailspin of desire. His hips moved almost on their own, as if his brain had nothing to do with it.

Bandos grinned, exposing his long canine teeth, which made him appear menacing and sexy. "You like that."

"Yeah."

Echo whimpered and pulled out before pushing back in again. He straightened and held on to Vaughan's hips, pumping into him. "Oh. Oh my...feels so good."

Vaughan met him thrust for thrust, wanting more, and when Echo came, he pressed his hand to Vaughan's shoulder. The spot heated his blood, almost sending him over the edge, but he also wanted to prolong it as much as possible.

The urge to bite Echo was nearly overwhelming. He growled and had to remind himself making love wasn't about instant gratification. They had all night to complete the bond. Vaughan would get his chance.

Echo's mating mark heated Vaughan's skin. The rhythm became erratic and then he pressed into Vaughan as far as he could go. He collapsed onto Vaughan's back, panting. His body went slack, and his cock fell partway out of Vaughan.

Echo trailed his hand from Vaughan's hip, along his side and then around him as much as he could with Vaughan pressing himself against Bandos. He touched Bandos next, including him.

Bandos must have moved Echo's cock from Vaughan because it didn't feel as if it had fallen out on its own. Bandos replaced it with his. He pressed in so slowly Vaughan thought he would go crazy.

His need to come hadn't lessened, so when Bandos entered him, he fought the urge. "I'm not gonna last long."

Bandos didn't respond. Instead, he bottomed out and didn't waste time pumping into him. He flashed his fangs before he bit Vaughan's shoulder without a warning. The surprise made Vaughan cry out, and then he moaned as the pleasure hit him. He acted on instinct, biting Bandos.

As soon as the blood touched his tongue, he came. It hit him like a train, sending him into an orgasm quicker than he would have liked, but it was still one of the best experiences of his life.

Vaughan let Bandos go, licking at the wound. His wolf felt almost satisfied. Mating with Echo would do the trick, but he needed a few minutes to recover.

Bandos released Vaughan, licking his wound. "I knew you'd taste good."

Vaughan smiled. "You do too."

Vaughan pressed his cheek against Bandos. "Mate."

"Yes." Bandos's cock was still hard inside him.

Vaughan could tell Bandos held back and that would get to him, so he reached around, holding Echo in place before he straightened and lifted off Bandos.

Echo lifted from Vaughan.

"Come here, little fae."

Echo straddled his hips, but Bandos shook his head. He tapped his lips. "I want your ass right here."

Oh, yeah. Vaughan wanted to see how Echo reacted, so he put himself in the perfect position to get a good view.

Echo sucked in a breath and then did what Bandos wanted, seeming more than eager. He gripped Vaughan's shoulder to stabilize himself.

Vaughan could tell the exact moment Bandos licked around Echo's opening. Echo's eyes widened, and he met Vaughan's gaze. He moved his hips, rubbing against the touch before Bandos wrapped an arm around his waist, holding him in place. Whatever Bandos did with his mouth seemed to increase the pleasure because Echo's grip tightened.

Vaughan grinned when Bandos gripped Echo's length. It didn't take long for him to get hard again, which meant he had great stamina.

Echo whimpered and wanted more stimulation, but Bandos held him still, not even jacking him off, but just holding him in his hand.

Echo seemed about ready to curse when Bandos released him. He rolled onto his back, pulling his legs back, getting ready for a cock. It didn't appear that he cared if it was Bandos or Vaughan.

Vaughan wasn't ready yet and when Bandos saw that, he settled over Echo, grabbing his legs before pressing his cock inside. He watched Echo's expression and when he sucked in a breath, Bandos stilled.

"Do you need me to stop or pull out?"

"No! Gods don't go anywhere."

Vaughan chuckled and then laid beside Echo, kissing him before whispering, "He's big."

Echo nodded.

"He feels good, though." Vaughan kissed Echo's cheek. "You feel just as good."

Echo moaned and gripped Vaughan's nape. He seemed to like resting his hand there. "I need."

"He'll give you what you need."

Bandos kissed Vaughan on the cheek and then kissed Echo.

Echo panted as if he'd run a marathon. "Move, please."

Bandos pressed in a little more. Echo moaned.

"Oh gods, right there." Echo's eyes closed again, and his mouth hung open.

Bandos must have hit the right spot and kept on hitting it because Echo grew louder with each thrust. Bando scowled with concentration as if he tried to hold off, but the stimulation appeared to be too much. Echo seemed tight. It only took about four more thrusts before he came. He grunted and sagged. He almost collapsed onto Echo, but he caught himself at the last minute.

He met Vaughan's gaze. "Get in him."

Vaughan didn't normally top, but he wouldn't leave Echo wanting. He laid on his back. "Come on, love."

Echo scrambled up and didn't waste time straddling Vaughan's waist. He grabbed Vaughan's hard cock and then sank onto it. Vaughan lost his mind from the pleasure. "Gods, you're tight."

Echo took control, just as Vaughan thought he would. He moved as if the gods had made him to ride a cock.

"Gods." Bandos whispered. When Vaughan turned to meet his gaze, Bandos only had eyes for Echo. "Look at you, little fae."

Tight heat surrounded him. There wasn't anything like it, and he wondered why he had waited so long to experience it.

Vaughan needed to bond, and that would push things toward the end quicker than he wanted, but he couldn't stop it.

"Mate." The word sounded harsh even to his own ears, but Echo seemed to know what he needed because he nodded and laid on Vaughan, tilting his head to the side, exposing his neck.

Vaughan struck, holding him in place, and let the blood slide down his throat. The bite made Echo cry out, and then his ass clamped on Vaughan's cock.

Vaughan came with an intensity that matched the first time with Bandos, which wasn't something he'd expected. After coming once, he thought the second time would be less grand, but he was just as good.

Mates. It took Vaughan a minute to realize that was Bandos and he hadn't actually spoken.

He came down from his orgasm and all he wanted to do was sleep. He released Echo and licked the mating mark. After he finished, Echo laid his cheek against Vaughan's chest.

Two is better than one. It was Echo who used the mating link the second time.

Bandos wrapped his arm around them and snuggled closer to them. He kissed Vaughan before moving on to Echo. "Yeah, it is. The internal link will help us keep you safe now."

"If Vaughan's loud moaning didn't alert the bad guys." Echo smiled.

Vaughan chuckled. They had all been loud, which was a concern and something they needed to be mindful of in the future, but it wasn't an immediate issue. Still, he wouldn't have been himself if he didn't tease Echo back. *Me. You woke the dead.*

Echo pinched Vaughan's nipple, which made him chuckle even more.

Chapter Eighteen

V aughan woke up stiff from sleeping on the hard ground with just a blanket separating him from it. Morning dew made everything damp, including the blanket covering him. As much as he wanted to stretch the kinks out of his body, he couldn't move because Bandos was behind him and Echo at his front.

Bandos wrapped his big arm around him and Echo, holding them close. He growled in his sleep and each time he did, he tightened his hold. He sounded more like a wolf than a dragon.

The rising sun created a pretty glow through the trees, and the smell of morning in the forest was everything comforting in the world. Maybe the three of them lived in a bubble. Or the moment was all in Vaughan's mind, implanted by scientists trying to manipulate his existence like one of those philosophical questions some asshole used to trap another person into a debate. If that were the case, he didn't care. He counted the morning after bonding with his mates as special.

The way they all fit together like puzzle pieces was a mark of perfection. And the way Echo smiled, even in his sleep. Hell, even Bandos's protective growl made the moment perfect.

Vaughan buried his nose in Echo's neck, kissing the mating mark. It was the one Bandos had left, and something about that made him feel like he was kissing them both.

And then Bandos moved behind him. The growling stopped before he placed a kiss on Vaughan's cheek. "Morning, baby."

"Morning. Guess what?"

"What?" There was humor laced through the word.

"My ass is sore." His entire body ached for a few reasons, but it was the one in his ass that made him smile.

"Are you complaining?"

"Hell, no. It makes me want you and Echo again."

Echo turned, pressing his cheek to Vaughan's chest. He wiggled, tangling their legs together. "I'm sore too," he mumbled without opening his eyes.

"Do you want me to rub it for you?" Bandos asked.

Echo smiled. "Maybe."

Vaughan chuckled. "I need mine rubbed too."

"I'll rub yours, Wolf."

"You can make love to me any time you want." Vaughan meant every word.

"We don't have time this morning. We should get moving. The more distance we cover, the better." Bandos, always the voice of reason, had a point.

"Yeah. I know." As disappointing as it was that they couldn't linger, they would have plenty of time when they got home.

He had a new respect for his brother, Bennett. His mate, Lucas, was the only male witch in existence. Everyone wanted a piece of him.

Most wanted to exploit his unique abilities. Vaughan identified with Bennett in ways he hadn't before. Keeping Echo safe was a full-time job that Vaughan wanted, but he wasn't sure how he would make it all work yet. Not with the way Bandos had his nose in a computer all day and Vaughan flying so much.

Bandos kissed Vaughan on the mark Echo had left on his back before giving one to Echo. When Bandos moved away from them and stood, Echo groaned.

"I'm going to shift and get an aerial view."

"We'll get up and around," Vaughan promised.

Echo grumbled something Vaughan didn't understand, but the protest came through clear enough.

Bandos shifted and walked to the beach before he took off.

"We better get moving. If we're still lying here when he comes back, he'll have a few things to say."

"Will he spank you? Because I'd like to watch that."

Vaughan chuckled. "Yeah, I can see how that might benefit both of us."

"So we agree. We'll stay here."

Vaughan gave Echo a playful slap on his ass and then pulled away, standing. Vaughan's body popped as he stretched, and he groaned. "Remind me not to sleep on the ground ever again."

Echo wiggled around until the blanket wrapped around his body as if he was a caterpillar in a cocoon. He didn't open his eyes. "It's not that bad."

"I know." Still, he shifted and headed to the lake. When he shifted in his human form, his body felt a lot better. He squatted and cupped his hands, splashing his face.

It didn't take Echo long to squat beside him. He brought a bar of soap, which Vaughan had forgotten about. The soap lathered well, even though the water was cold. Echo handed it to Vaughan before rubbing his hands over his face.

Vaughan did the same. "There's a lot to be said for a warm shower."

Echo chuckled. "You're really not a camper, are you?"

"It's easier in my wolf form." He appreciated modern plumbing and electricity a lot. Like a lot, a lot.

"Why don't you shift then?"

"Because I have to carry a bag."

"Oh."

Echo wet his body with his hand. He sucked in a breath and shivered. When he took the soap from Vaughan, he made quick work of washing.

Vaughan did the same, except the water wasn't as cold for him, so he didn't have the same response. Still, he hurried as much as possible. When he finished, he helped Echo rinse the soap off, trying to get the job done quicker so he could get dressed and warm up.

When they were both done, Echo reached for him, wanted his body heat. Vaughan lifted him off his feet when he stood, holding him close, rubbing his back as he made his way to their camp. He grabbed a blanket and wrapped it around them.

That was how Bandos found them. Echo bundled in a blanket, clinging to Vaughan like a shivering monkey. The second Bandos shifted, he growled. "Hurry and get dressed. There's a campfire at the crash site. Must have just arrived. We're a day's walk ahead but our lead won't last long, depending on their trackers."

Echo stiffened. "They found us."

Bandos closed the distance between them, rubbing Echo's back. "That's what it looks like. They won't get to you, little fae."

Vaughan met Bandos's gaze and nodded, letting him know he understood it was up to them to make sure Echo stayed safe. His eyes shifted on instinct. "Did they spot you from the air?"

"I don't think so." They had covered enough ground yesterday and they may have an advantage with their pursuers being human. They might not have known to look for flying creatures.

Echo put his feet on the ground. He grabbed a bag and searched for something to wear among the different sized clothing. He pulled out one of Bandos's shirts and then put it back down again. His frustration came through and then he met Vaughan's gaze, pleading for help without saying a single word.

Vaughan took over, finding his pants and underwear first, so he set that aside. Socks for Echo came next.

He managed to find each of them clothing, one article at a time.

By the time he'd dressed, Echo had food and water for them. They killed the coals still burning in their fire and ate as they walked.

"I have a question." They had been hiking for less than an hour when Echo spoke. He kept his volume at almost a whisper.

"What's that, little fae?" Bandos led, but they kept Echo in between them.

"Why don't you fly out of here?" Echo munched on some weeds he had found a few steps back. He had picked one every few minutes. "It occurred to me while Wolf and I were cleaning up that you could have just shifted."

"I won't leave you guys."

Echo made a noise in the back of his throat and nodded. "I thought that's what you would say."

"No way will we ever leave you all alone." Vaughan hoped by reiterating what Bandos had said, it would reassure Echo.

Instead, Echo waved his hand. "I know."

"We're in this together." Bandos had a way of simplifying every-thing until there wasn't a way to argue. The only time he was like that was when he thought an argument would start, but Vaughan didn't think that Echo's goal was to get them to think of themselves first. He asked for a different reason, although Vaughan hadn't figured out why yet.

"You're putting yourself at risk by staying human."

Bandos grunted. The noise meant he'd finished with the conver-sation, but he wasn't the censoring type. Echo could continue talk-ing about the subject for the next seven hours straight and Bandos wouldn't say another word.

Vaughan found that trait annoying most of the time, but he would've liked it way less if Bandos was the type to shut things down. Vaughan would take that sort of attitude as too controlling, so for that reason their personalities complemented each other. Vaughan was eager to see how Echo handled it.

"You love Wolf a lot then."

Vaughan walked behind them so he couldn't see Bandos's expres-sion, but he would have liked to in that moment. He knew Bandos hadn't expected Echo to say that, though. Vaughan certainly hadn't, and he didn't know where Echo was going with the conversation. But one good thing about the comment was that it forced Bandos into speaking.

"I have no shortage of love." Bandos answered that like a pro.

"Is Wolf another reason you don't shift and fly back to your home?" Was Echo fishing for confirmation of their mating?

Bandos sighed. The people miles behind them probably heard it, which meant Echo annoyed him by forcing him to talk about his feel-ings, and that wasn't something Bandos enjoyed doing. "Of course. I'll protect you and Vaughan with my life."

Vaughan bit his lips to keep from chuckling. He could tell by Bandos's tone that he was about ready to tell Echo to get to the point, and something about the way Echo could force Bandos into expressing his emotions with very little effort made Vaughan's morning.

"Because you want to protect me, and you love Vaughan?" Echo's statement took the wind out of Vaughan's sails. Echo's happiness, or lack of, sat like lead in Vaughan's gut.

"Because I'm protective and I care about both of you." As reassuring as Bandos's statement sounded, Vaughan wasn't sure what Echo thought.

"Does that reassure you?" Vaughan asked. There had never been something so important than Echo's answer.

"I was just making conversation."

"No, you weren't."

Echo sighed. "Yes, it helped a great deal."

Vaughan felt responsible for someone else's wellbeing. And not just one mate, but two. And while he wouldn't ever think about going back, he had to balance everything. He needed to figure it out before they made it home because once they were there, Bandos would go back to his nose in a computer and Vaughan would start taking clients again.

Wait.

His plane was toast and a few miles north of their location. How would he work again?

Vaughan stopped walking as the full weight of his current situation hit him. He didn't know why it had taken so long.

Bandos and Echo must have felt his emotions through their bond because they stopped and turned. It was Bandos who asked, "What's wrong?"

"I lost my plane. That was my livelihood." His lack of a job solved one of his problems. He could balance having mates because he didn't have to include his work in that. Then against, if they had to rely on his income, they would all be living in the woods off the land so their current experience would prepare them for that.

"Can we talk about it after we get home?" Bandos asked.

Vaughan nodded, but he would think about it for a while. His emotional turmoil must have shown on his face.

Echo wrapped his arms around Vaughan's waist, hugging him. "I'm sorry about your plane."

Bandos sighed. "I'll buy you a new plane, baby. But we need to keep moving."

If Bandos had enough money to buy a plane, it was news to Vaughan. Whether he could afford a plane was beside the point. It was the gesture that counted.

Vaughan smiled. *Thank you for offering, but I can't let you do that.*

"We'll argue about it later." Bandos turned and continued walking.

Vaughan held Echo to his side and got them moving. "I might not have my plane anymore, but I have an offer of a new one and Baby Spice to make me feel better."

Bandos chuckled.

"'Baby Spice'. Are you referring to me?" Echo raised his eyebrows when he met Vaughan's gaze.

"You have a nickname for Bandos and me. I figured you needed one too."

Echo smirked. "It doesn't fit."

"I think it does," Bandos said. That Bandos joined in on the teasing meant he wasn't as tense as before. Maybe he figured they were putting distance between them and the bad guys.

"We like carrying you around and we like that you're spicy when making love." Vaughan wiggled his eyebrows. "The spicy part is especially true."

Echo blushed. "Just don't call me that in public, please."

"I won't make any promises."

Echo sighed but didn't respond. Maybe he was getting as wise as Bandos to Vaughan's teasing.

Chapter Nineteen

B andos didn't want to stop moving. The feeling of being followed put him on edge. Fowler's men breathed down his neck. At best, they had one more night of peace before they'd have to fight, and for that reason Bandos planned on pushing Vaughan and Echo into walking through it, which was why he decided taking a short break was necessary. Well, that and Echo looked as though he would fall over soon.

They didn't have the proper shoes to hike long distances. They hadn't thought a plane crash would happen and hadn't planned for it, but Bandos would insist on buying hiking shoes and putting them in the next plane Vaughan owned.

Bandos sat against the tree trunk with Vaughan leaning on one side of him and Echo lying on his other side. Echo had a green glow around him. It didn't take Bandos long to learn that meant Echo had used his abilities. He didn't have to wonder how for very long because the vegetation under Echo grew, creating a cushion.

"Not fair, little fae." Bandos ran his hand down Echo's arm until he got to his hand, lacing their fingers together.

Echo shut his eyes and smiled. "Do you want a cushion?"

"No, honey. I'm just teasing you."

"I want a cushion." Vaughan crawled across Bandos's lap and laid on top of Echo.

Echo grunted under his weight and whined, "Wolf."

"Baby Spice." Vaughan matched Echo's whine.

"If you stay as you are, you'll owe me something. And I'm going to make it good." Echo had an American accent but occasionally, he sounded a little more Irish. Something about the way he said that brought it out.

Vaughan kissed Echo and grinned. "What do you want?"

"I want you to teach me how to fight." Echo raised his eyebrows. His lips firmed into a straight line. It spoke of how set his mind was on that.

Vaughan blinked. "Why?"

"I should learn how to defend myself. I don't want to be locked up in a room that feels like a tomb ever again. If I fought like you, I might have gotten out of that situation."

"You're the deadliest one out of all three of us, little fae." Bandos agreed with Echo, but he had skills that didn't require learning hand-to-hand combat.

Echo met his gaze. "In the forest. If a plant is near. Away from them, I'm useless. What if you guys aren't around to save me?"

Bandos growled. "That is not a possibility."

"I don't really know how to fight." Vaughan made it sound like a confession. He pressed his forehead to Echo's.

"You're fierce, Wolf. Truly." Echo cupped Vaughan's cheek.

"You don't give yourself enough credit, baby." Bandos would talk to Ladon about Vaughan's abilities at the earliest opportunity because they underutilized him in the clan.

Vaughan stood and pulled Echo with him. "No time like the present."

Echo squeaked at the sudden movement and clung to Vaughan to stabilize himself.

Vaughan put a few feet of distance between them. "First thing you need to do is shift into a wolf."

Echo sighed. "Be serious."

"I am serious. It's all instinctive." Vaughan met his gaze. "I don't know where to start."

Bandos crossed his legs. "What's the likeliest scenario?"

"That he'll be captured."

Echo nodded. "I don't want to get stuck again."

"So how did they take you?"

"At the end of my workday. I walked home. They came up behind me. I couldn't even yell because they put a hand over my mouth." Echo shuddered as if the fear had lain dormant until he recalled the memory.

"So maybe we need to work on how to get out of a hold from behind." Vaughan's eyebrows drew together, and he bit his lip. "What I wouldn't give for Fane right now."

Bandos stood and moved behind Vaughan. "If I'm going to grab you and run, it would look like this."

Bandos put a hand over Vaughan's mouth and then wrapped his other arm around his waist. He tightened his hold as if he were genuinely holding Vaughan against his will.

Vaughan bit the palm of his hand. Not hard enough to do damage, but made his actions known. Bandos pretended to pull away. Vaughan faked stomping his foot and Bandos played along again.

Once they'd finished, Vaughan turned and smiled. "Thanks, baby."

Bandos kissed him and then sat back down.

Vaughan came closer to Echo. "So we're going to pretend you can't use your abilities this time, but you absolutely should if possible."

Echo nodded, and then his aura glowed. Vegetation wrapped around Vaughan's feet, holding him in place.

Vaughan's eyes widened, and he looked down before meeting Echo's gaze, grinning. "Exactly like that."

Echo chuckled and let Vaughan go. "I'm on my way home from work."

"When I grabbed you from behind, you're going to bite me and then stomp on my foot."

"That's it?"

"It's what I would do."

"Really?"

"You saw me with Bandos a second ago."

"It just seems so simple."

"It is. You're not a big guy." Echo opened his mouth to protest, but Vaughan cut him off. "It's relevant because it's not likely you'll overpower anyone. Use what you have. It's the same with me. If a shifter as big as Bandos attacked me, I won't be able to overpower them either. I would have a better chance shifting and going for their throat."

Bandos nodded. "Accept your limitations."

Echo sighed and nodded. "That makes sense."

"So what you have is agility and probably speed. You're smart, which means if you're able to run, you'll be able to get somewhere with plants or maybe even trees. You'll be able to save yourself by knowing your abilities." Vaughan stood behind Echo.

Echo tensed with anticipation. Vaughan must have known it because he didn't do anything right away. Instead, he leaned in and smelled Echo's mating mark.

Echo relaxed and smiled. "I doubt the bad guys are going to do that."

"They might. You smell good enough to eat." Vaughan kissed Echo's neck.

Bandos could tell the exact moment Vaughan grabbed Echo because he stiffened, and his eyes shifted as if he wasn't happy about pretending to attack.

Vaughan put a hand over his mouth.

Even Bandos expected Echo to panic, but he leaned against Vaughan and mumbled. Vaughan took his hand away. "What?"

"What am I supposed to do again?"

"You were supposed to be scared enough to act on instinct." Vaughan shook his head.

"I can't be scared of you."

Bandos chuckled. "We'll have to wait until we get home. We'll get one of the family to help with the training. Fane can take over."

"That's what I've been saying." Vaughan sounded exasperated.

"So if a stranger comes up behind me I bite them and then..."

"Stomp on their foot. Give yourself enough time to run." Vaughan picked Echo up and carried him back to his plant bed. "You should get some rest."

Maybe Vaughan knew they needed to get their feet on the ground because he met Bandos's gaze. Bandos nodded and laced his fingers with Echo's again. Echo rolled to his side and laid his head on Bandos's thigh. Vaughan settled on the other side of him, resting his head on his shoulder, and wrapped an arm around Bandos's waist.

Bandos sighed. Their pursuers would catch up to them. Still, they all needed a rest, even if it was a small one. They didn't have one single clue where civilization was so they couldn't make a getaway plan. Bandos could fly to find the right direction but he wouldn't leave Echo and Vaughan for the length of time it would take. Their option was to walk and Bandos didn't know when they would be able to stop again, so he would let his mates rest for a bit before they continued. The need for escape was important but so was making sure they stayed healthy enough to get them out of danger.

They had one last moment of peace, and they all knew it.

Chapter Twenty

Vaughan laid on the bed of vegetation as he liked to think of it, watching as Echo and Bandos kissed. It had started with Vaughan teasing Echo enough to steal his bed. Echo had ended up in Bandos's lap. Vaughan wasn't sure who'd started it, but they had kept it going for long enough they'd probably be fucking soon, although they all knew their time for leisurely make out sessions was coming to an end. Bandos and Echo's philosophy was to seize the opportunity while they could.

As much as Vaughan wanted to join that mindset, someone had to think about the pursuers closing in on them. Their bubble would pop soon. Like, very soon.

Vaughan sighed and rolled to his feet. *I'm checking things out.*

Vaughan pulled his shirt over his head and laid it on top of a bag. As he took off his pants, he leaned into them, kissing Bandos's cheek first before doing the same to Echo. They didn't stop, which meant they were into each other so much nothing could pull them away.

Echo's insecurities were unfounded, and if anything should've relieved him, it was the way Bandos forgot about the danger in favor of kissing Echo until he came. Given how tense Bandos had been and the fact that he was letting the bad guys gain ground so they could walk through the night told Vaughan how desperate Bandos truly was.

Vaughan had his doubts about out-hiking them. They would have to plan for a fight, but Vaughan would let Bandos and Echo have their reprieve first.

When he had stripped, he shifted and took off through the forest toward his plane because that was the direction the bad guys would come from.

A squirrel skittered down a tree, unaffected by Vaughan's presence. The squirrel might've recognized Vaughan as a predator, but it knew his agenda didn't include having it for dinner. He ran too fast and away from it. He would have liked to hunt, but they would have to start a fire to cook whatever he caught, and that wouldn't have been smart.

Birds squawked in the nearby trees. Maybe they'd followed the three of them on their journey. It was difficult for Vaughan to tell, but he had noticed them since the plane crash. They were in a big enough flock that the sound they made was loud, sometimes drowning out their voices as if covering their trail the only way they could so the pursuers couldn't hear them. They didn't seem to have a problem with Vaughan being in their forest. Maybe Echo was right, and they were natural beings, belonging to the forest as much as the animals around him.

He knew the birds were on his side when they stopped making noise. Vaughan laid on his belly next to a tree, listening. He kept his senses as open as possible, even as he scanned his surroundings.

The forest stilled, falling silent as if a threat stalked it. Vaughan fought the urge to run back the way he had come. But he waited, gathering evidence of the bad guys' closeness.

How far had he run? Ten miles. Not less than that.

And then Vaughan heard a human voice say something about a track being made by a shoe.

More than a few trudged through the forest. He could smell each one. Twenty to twenty-five. Some smelled similar to each other, which told Vaughan they were fucking but the combination of scents made it difficult for him to know an exact number. He had enough information to bring back to Bandos, though.

He fought the urge to attack. He was more of a predator than the humans hunting Echo, and his instinct was to hunt. He felt almost feral at the thought.

He backed away and turned, following his own trail to Bandos and Echo. He waited until he was far enough away that he didn't hear them anymore to run again.

The birds followed. He saw them in the trees ahead of him. They knew where he was going.

The fight for rationality was real the closer he came to Bandos and Echo. All of his mental energy went toward protecting them until he couldn't get to them fast enough. He tried to slow down, knowing the humans were good enough to track them, but they were also disciplined if they moved more than twenty humans through the forest faster than the three of them had gone. They were soldiers of some sort, and that made them more dangerous.

The upsides were few, but one was they wanted Echo alive. And even though they knew they were chasing paranormals, they might not understand what kind, so their knowledge had its limits. They didn't know how deadly Echo was, especially amongst vegetation and trees.

It didn't take Vaughan long to get back. When he did, he didn't shift. He couldn't. His instinct rode him hard, so he stayed in his wolf form.

Bandos and Echo weren't kissing any longer. They must have felt his stress and reacted to it because Echo had his backpack on and Bandos had packed Vaughan's clothing in a bag, and had one in each hand, ready to go.

Bandos couldn't carry the bags all night. He would need his energy when it came time to fight, so Vaughan would have to lighten his load at some point.

They're close. Ten or so miles I think.

Bandos nodded. "You lead."

Vaughan did as Bandos directed. *There's around twenty. They're all soldiers and good at tracking. Definitely human.*

"Tracking? Like our footprints on the ground?" Echo sounded breathless, and he wore his fear like a mask, but Vaughan didn't know for a fact because he was in front of him, leading their hike. Still, the thought of their sweet fae scared made him want to rip throats out.

Yeah. I heard them talking about it.

I can take care of our tracks. Echo must've meant to use the plants to obscure their footprints.

"That will help a lot," Bandos responded.

Can you make it look like we went in another direction? They might make it out of there without having to fight.

I can use the plants to make it look like shoe prints, and I might be able to break a few branches.

Do you need to see the area before you manipulate it? Vaughan didn't want to lose their lead.

Yes, because I'm not familiar enough with this forest.

Vaughan stopped and turned, shifting to human. He met Bandos's gaze. "What do you want to do?"

Bandos came up behind Echo, wrapping his arm around his chest. He pointed toward the east. "Go in that direction, little fae."

Echo nodded, and then his aura glowed green. "How far do you want me to go?"

"As far as you can, love." The endearment was deliberate.

When Bandos met his gaze, Vaughan smiled, letting him know he felt the same way. Bandos winked, making Vaughan feel a part of something bigger than all of them. They were in a hot-air balloon, floating in their feelings. No one could touch them, no matter what. They would make it through together.

Vaughan took a deep breath, letting go of his panic. His mind cleared, and he relaxed enough to shift back into his wolf.

If Echo had picked up on the change of endearments, it didn't distract him from his task. "Should I turn us?"

"Toward the right, if you can."

They stood like that for a few more minutes, letting Echo do his thing. The green glow disappeared, and Echo relaxed. "I covered our tracks all the way back to the tree where we sat."

"That will buy us a lot more time." Bandos kissed Echo on his temple and released him. "Let's get going. We'll walk until we can't anymore."

Vaughan turned and moved again. They had a long way to go. The sooner they created distance, the more time they had to plan. They needed a strategy because running like prey wouldn't get them out of danger.

Chapter
Twenty-One

D arkness took over everything. Each step was uncertain. All Echo had to do was step on a stick wrong or fall into a hole. Most of the moon had hid itself. A sliver remained. So there wasn't any lunar help either. He could barely make out Vaughan's wolf in front of him.

Vaughan and Bandos were on high alert, and tense because of it. They had no way of knowing if their diversion had worked. No one had said a word in a couple of hours, not even through their bond link. They didn't have to speak for Echo to know they expected a fight at some point.

Bandos's quietness came naturally, but only to a point. He spoke through his touches more than he did with words. Even though he kept close, he didn't touch Echo. He kept his hands free and scanned the forest.

Echo didn't complain about the dark or about the exhaustion threatening to make him fall over. And he said nothing about his feet hurting so badly each step made them ache.

Vaughan stopped and crawled on his belly through the tall vegetation. *Get down.*

Echo fell to the ground, lying behind him. He was close enough to touch Vaughan's tail, so he did, holding it. The soft fur provided comfort.

Bandos laid next to him. "What is it?"

There's a building up ahead. I can smell old wood and oil. Vaughan's senses were amazing.

"You can tell it's a building from smell?" Echo whispered and rubbed his thumb across Vaughan's fur.

Yeah, pretty much. The wood is rotten and there's a mustiness in the air. The oil has soaked into the dirt. It's been there a long time.

Do you smell people around? Bandos asked.

No. Nothing lives nearby except for a couple of snakes and a few mice. Nothing bigger for a long time.

"So it's abandoned." Echo really wanted a shower, but he doubted an abandoned building had running water. And if the wood was rotting, safety was a factor.

Pretty sure, yeah.

Scope out the area. Be careful, baby.

When Vaughan took off, Bandos scooted closer until his chest covered Echo's back like a warm shield. He couldn't divide his attention because Vaughan wasn't with them. Echo knew he didn't like it when they weren't together because he couldn't keep them safe. If covering Echo made him feel better, he wouldn't put up a fuss, not that he minded Bandos's body on top of him. Their biggest problem was Echo's backpack. The thing was in the way.

"Do you think we tricked the humans?" Echo whispered.

Bandos pressed his cheek to Echo's. "Not sure."

Bandos's scent enveloped him. He would always associate cinnamon with Bandos. The scent comforted him.

It's clear. Vaughan said through their bond link. *It's an old barn. Not glamorous and we can't build a fire. Should shield us for a couple hours, though. The biggest problem is if the humans are close, we'll be sitting ducks.*

We'll have to take the chance. Rest is needed. Thank the gods Bandos had made that decision. *We'll scout the area. Make sure our diversion worked. It's the best we can do.*

Bandos scanned the area before he wrapped an arm around Echo's waist and lifted him off the ground. When he let Echo go, he patted him on the ass and said, "There's a downed tree about two yards ahead, love."

There went that word again. Twice Bandos had called him that. Given that they were mates, Echo knew what it meant, but a part of him still didn't want to get his hopes up only for them to get crushed, so he didn't comment. The endearment made his chest ache. His heart wanted to think Bandos meant what he said.

He also wished for different circumstances. He might have asked questions and seen where they took him and his mates. But he didn't have the luxury of assurance. Not in love or with his and his mates' safety.

He made it far enough that he saw a solid black structure just past a few trees. He figured that was the barn Vaughan had found. It was too unnatural and large for it to be anything else.

Echo trudged toward it. With each step, fatigue set in.

He stumbled over a tree root and would have fallen on his face if Bandos hadn't caught him. When Bandos lifted him, backpack and all, Echo wrapped his arms around his neck and rested his head on Bandos's shoulder.

"We're getting good at this." Gods, Echo even sounded exhausted.

"At what, love?"

Echo smiled. "Carrying me."

Bandos chuckled. "I like it."

Echo did, too. "What about the duffle bags?"

"I'll come back for them." Bandos didn't sound as if the lack of sleep and the constant walking affected him.

"Aren't you tired?"

"Exhausted. We'll take a rest."

"You don't show it."

"I feel it."

"Me too." There had been a couple of times when he had pulled all-nighters, doing stupid but fun things with his friends. And then when vampires had kidnapped him and put in a crate he had been so scared he couldn't sleep for fear he would never wake up, and when he'd thought someone had saved him only to find out they intended for him to have a larger cell in a castle.

He counted his blessings because he might have stayed awake for longer than was healthy, but he wasn't nearly as scared. He had Bandos and Vaughan. He wasn't alone, and that meant a lot.

"Thank you. I don't believe I've said that yet."

"I will always come for you. You don't need to thank me for it. Just know I'll raise myself from the dead for you if I have to."

"You said more words at one time then you have the entire time we're known each other." Echo chuckled. "You could have just said you'd Echo for Echo."

Bandos chuckled. "That is by far the worst joke I've ever heard."

"I'll have to ask Vaughan to teach me."

"With your jokes and his teasing, it would be a comedic nightmare." The deadpan way Bandos said that made Echo laugh. It was loud enough that Echo put a hand over his mouth to quiet the sound. "I'd use the word reverberate. Reverberate for Echo. It sounds smarter but means the same something."

They were only feet away from the building. Vaughan's voice met his ears before he saw him. Or rather, Echo saw his shadowy form. "Shh. You're gonna draw them right to us."

That made them both chuckle because it went against what they'd said about Vaughan. Maybe they were getting punchy.

Bandos handed Echo over as if he were a duffle bag. "I'll be right back." Bandos took off into the dark, back the way they had come.

Echo wrapped his arms and legs around Vaughan and rested his head on his shoulder.

Vaughan turned and went inside. It smelled moldy, but other than that, nothing seemed off. Vaughan stood just inside the door and held him with his hands on Echo's ass. "What were you guys laughing about?"

"Nothing important." But Echo needed to express his appreciation. He met Vaughan's gaze in the dark. "Thank you for coming to save me."

"Thank you for saving *me*." Vaughan kissed him.

"But I wouldn't have had to save you if you hadn't come for me." By the gods, Echo was too tired to keep up with Vaughan.

"That's true, and I'd do it all again."

"Reverberate for Echo." Echo grinned.

Vaughan chuckled. "Funny. And gorgeous."

Echo snorted out a laugh. "Blue told me it was bad."

"He has no taste in jokes. But he has great taste when picking mates."

"Agree. He also said you and I together are a comedic nightmare." Echo wanted to see what Vaughan would say to that.

"We're in his sexy dreams and he knows it. Don't let him tell you any different."

Bandos nearly sent Echo through the roof because Echo didn't hear him come inside until he plopped what had to be the duffle bags on the floor beside them. "That's also true."

Echo sucked in a breath and jumped into Vaughan's arms.

"Sorry, love." Bandos kissed Echo on his cheek before he bent, opening one of the bags and rummaging through it. The sounds of Bandos spreading the blanket out on the ground met his ears, and then Vaughan set him on his feet.

Vaughan guided Echo to it. It was dark in color so Echo couldn't see a shadow in front of him. He took his backpack off and set it down before sitting beside it. He tried to find the jerky by feeling for the shape of the packaging and managed that rather well.

Bandos sat beside him and Vaughan on Bandos's other side.

Echo handed each of them some food before taking some for himself. He was too tired to eat but he needed to refuel so he went through the motions anyway.

Vaughan ate as he dressed, stopping between bites but holding the jerky in his teeth as he put on articles of clothing. Not that Echo could see him very well, but he could hear it and guessed at what he was doing.

When Echo finished eating, he laid on his back, shutting his eyes. His body relaxed.

Bandos curled next to him. His deep rumbling voice soothed Echo, lulling him into a half-sleep in which he was aware of his mates but not much else.

"You did good today."

"Thanks." Vaughan must have kissed Bandos because the sounds met his ears. "How long should we stay here?"

"I don't know. Long enough for Echo to get some rest. His body is like a human's. We need to pay attention to him. Make sure we don't exhaust him. If we fight, he needs to be strong enough to do his thing. It's the only way we'll make it out of these woods alive. No way can you and I take on so many humans at once."

"Yeah, he's a little badass."

"I think we may have to stop running at some point and face them. Take the humans by surprise."

"When?"

"I don't know. I need time to think of a strategy. For now, we rest and then keep going."

Echo rolled toward Bandos, throwing his arm around his waist, only to find Vaughan curled against him on his other side, so his hand ended up resting on Vaughan's side. "Sleep now. Talk later."

Chapter Twenty-Two

They wouldn't make it very much longer. Their supplies were running out, and with the humans so close, making a fire was next to impossible, so hunting was pointless. Survival aside, the situation with the humans couldn't stay as it was. Something would happen, and soon. They had to gain the advantage.

All of it weighed on Vaughan's mind. He cuddled against Bandos, listening to Echo's soft purr of a snore and watching the moonlight shift through the crack in the door. He couldn't sleep. His mind raced with what-ifs.

He sighed and then kissed Bandos on the cheek. "I'm going to scout the area."

He knew Bandos was awake. He hadn't slept the whole time, which was another problem. Bandos was the brains of their operation. If exhaustion set in and he couldn't function when the time came, they would all pay the price. It wasn't just Echo Vaughan had to worry about where exhaustion was concerned.

"Be careful."

Vaughan stood. "I suppose it's too much to ask you to get some sleep."

"Yes, because I think we should head out when you come back."

Vaughan nodded. "I won't be gone long."

"See if you can find some form of communication. Maybe this barn means we're headed toward an occupied area."

Vaughan winced. "I've flown over this part of the country lots of times. Houses are spread apart by miles sometimes."

"Yeah, I know. Lots of off-the-grid people and no cell towers." Sometimes Vaughan forgot Bandos had had a life before coming to Saint Lakes. He had traveled most of the country. Maybe even the world, before they'd met. He'd had adventures.

Did he ever want to go back to that life? If he did, mating with Vaughan and Echo made that near impossible. Well, maybe not. They were traipsing around the northern United States together, getting chased by humans. Finding adventure wasn't a problem.

Whether Bandos liked the adventure wasn't in question. Vaughan could tell he didn't, through their link. So maybe he wanted to get back to boring Saint Lakes as much as Vaughan did. The most adventurous thing they would do is swim in the lake and fuck on Vaughan's back porch.

And when had he stopped mourning the loss of his plane long enough to think about domesticity?

Oh yeah, about the time the humans had started following them. When it had become less about the things he'd lost and more about saving the people he loved.

Vaughan shifted and headed out. He made a large circle around the barn, going wider each time. By doing so, he could find out what was nearby more thoroughly. Otherwise, he would have to pick a direction and hope luck was on his side.

The run helped slow his mind. He concentrated on where he put his feet, scanning ahead. He used his nose for most of it. Fallen, rotting trees had a different scent than one still standing. His eyes had adjusted hours ago so he could also see well enough. Still, using his sense of smell was second nature. He relied on it more than his other senses.

Where are you? Echo sounded sleepy even through their link.

Circling the barn and looking around.

Are the humans nearby? Echo sounded as if he intended to get moving if necessary.

The birds stuck with him as he ran. He could smell them when the wind shifted. They were as constant a companion as the bond-link made his mates. *I don't sense anyone.*

He wasn't sure how far he'd went. Maybe a mile all the way around. He wanted to go farther out, just to be sure.

That's a relief. Whatever Echo was doing, it wasn't relief he felt. His horniness came through well.

What are you doing, Baby Spice?

He's rubbing his cock against my thigh and licking my nipple. Bandos liked it. Vaughan could tell.

You guys are teases. You don't have time for anything more than a quickie. Vaughan's cock was half-hard and growing. Not that they had time for sex. It would relieve some of the tension and maybe take their minds off of their situation, but Vaughan wasn't so sure that was a good idea. They had to keep their eyes on the prize, and that happened to be staying alive.

Even through their bond-link, Bandos's chuckle came through. He knew what he was doing. *I am not. I intend to follow through. And I'll make it quick.*

But you made me hard and I'm not there, so you're a tease.

Echo chuckled. *Come back so I can suck you.*

Shit. Vaughan wanted to take him up on it, but he would be another half an hour at least, maybe a little longer. *It's more important to make sure the humans aren't close.*

I know. You're right. But what if they're not?

Lots of foreplay. Lots and lots of foreplay. And try to keep the sex noises down. We don't want to alert them.

The birds are too loud. Humans can't hear us through all their racket. Bandos must have noticed too.

How about I describe what he's doing? Most of the time, Bandos was a serious person who indulged Vaughan in all things. When he let loose a little, he became the sexiest shifter on the planet but his timing was for shit. One of them had to make sure they stayed out of harm's way.

Great idea. Vaughan would make it as quick as possible. *I won't be that long. Less than an hour.*

Better hurry. He's moved on to my other nipple already.

This time Echo chuckled.

Did you wake up horny, Baby Spice?

No. I want both of you all the time. I can't think about anything else. Maybe sex was how Echo coped with his stress. If so, than Vaughan wasn't complaining other than he wished they kept vigilant.

Damn, that's hot.

Very hot. Bandos sounded as if he was about to take over the foreplay. When that happened, it wouldn't take long for him to enter Echo. They would finish before Vaughan got back. *I'll scout from the air if you just get back here.*

You can't, baby. Fowler's men might spot you from the air. They might be closer now. We don't know for sure.

You're right. Make sure we're clear. We'll wait.

You're ready to bury yourself inside him already. I can tell. Vaughan chuckled. *Good job, Baby Spice.*

Vaughan went four miles out and didn't sense anyone, human or otherwise. They could make love if they didn't take too long, not that Bandos and Echo waited for him. He could feel it through their bond.

Being newly mated made them want each other as often as possible, but their circumstance made that difficult. Vaughan couldn't wait until they made it to Saint Lakes. As soon as they did, they could fuck like rabbits.

By the time Vaughan made it back, he was hard as a rock.

One of the sexiest things in the world was seeing Echo and Bandos sitting chest to chest in the middle of the blanket. Bandos's cock was inside Echo. The muscles in Bandos's arms rippled every time he lifted him, creating a rhythm.

Vaughan met Bandos's gaze. His eyes were reptilian, and he looked almost feral. Bandos had always had a bad boy appeal, even though he was anything but. He drove a motorcycle and wore leather more times than not. The hard edge in his gaze spoke of a life not always easily lived. In reality, Bandos was the nerdy type who would rather play with his computer than with guns. Still, the image held true most when he was making love.

Dangerous. Possessive. Dominant.

"Shift and come here." Bandos's tone sounded rough and made demands Vaughan wouldn't refuse.

As soon as Vaughan shifted and was within reach, Bandos pulled him close enough his dick was in Bandos's face. He took Vaughan all the way into the back of his throat in one suck.

Vaughan cried out when the sensations became overwhelming. He placed his hand on the back of Bandos's head, needing to touch, and tried not to come so soon.

And then he felt wet kisses on his thigh, which was as close as Echo could get to his cock, especially with Bandos in the way.

Bandos pulled off, using his tongue to caress Vaughan's cock on the way out. Echo licked around the tip. Where Bandos was forceful and took what he wanted, Echo was sensual, making demands one lick at a time. By the time Echo took Vaughan into his mouth, he whimpered. Begging crossed his mind.

Bandos chuckled, but it sounded breathless and strained. "Now he knows the struggle."

Yeah, yeah, waiting for him hadn't been easy. He got it loud and clear.

Echo had skills for sure. He took his time, going at his pace, which was a little faster than if Bandos wasn't fucking into him. It worked out for Vaughan because it was a perfect rhythm.

Echo moaned around Vaughan's cock and gripped his thigh tighter. He pulled off and buried his face in Bandos's neck, moaning past the pleasure.

"So pretty when you come." Vaughan ran his finger down the side of Echo's neck to his shoulder.

And then Bandos took over sucking Vaughan again. His no-nonsense approach was to get both of them to come at the same time and clearly, he was close.

"Shit. Bandos." Gods, he couldn't think when Bandos did that thing with his tongue where he cradled Vaughan's cock, all while sucking him.

It didn't take long for Vaughan to fall over the edge, and when he did, Bandos never pulled off. Vaughan shuddered.

It wasn't until he came down that Bandos let his own happen. He released Vaughan in favor of biting Echo. Echo cried out at the suddenness and the pleasure. It looked as though he might have come again, although Vaughan didn't know how that was possible. Baby Spice was a little machine.

Bandos fucked into Echo and then stilled as if he were trying to hold his come inside, getting it as deep as it would go. He came down a little at a time. When he pulled his fangs out of Echo, Bandos laid on the blanket again.

Echo went with him, clinging as if he couldn't fathom being anywhere else.

When Vaughan snuggled next to them, they both wrapped an arm around him, pulling him closer.

For the first time in Vaughan's life, he found silence comfortable for a few reasons. The most important one was how their sex noise may or may not bring all their enemies closer. Hopefully Bandos was right about the birds drowning out the sound.

And then Bandos said, "Male fae can't get pregnant, right?"

Echo sat up just enough to meet Bandos's gaze, scowling. "What kind of question is that?"

"I'm just checking." In other words, he hadn't researched it because he hadn't thought it was relevant before they left.

Vaughan knew some male paranormals, depending on the kind, could. There was a bat shifter in Wingspan who'd given birth recently. He'd mated to a dragon shifter. They were family friends.

Echo lost his scowl right before his eyes sparkled with mischief. "And what if I can? What then?"

Vaughan wanted to laugh, but he held it in, focusing on Bandos's reaction.

"Then that puts another layer onto our current situation."

While Vaughan agreed with Bandos, he didn't think it was an issue. Echo reacted as if he didn't know male pregnancy was a possibility for some, which meant it wasn't for his kind.

"There are so few fae left in the Upperworld, how would I know for sure." Echo grinned, which gave away the fact that he was teasing.

"Would your giant dragon shifter spawn fit inside him, anyway?" Vaughan asked.

Bandos sighed. "Get up and get dressed. We have to head out."

Vaughan chuckled.

Echo braced himself with his hands on Bandos's chest, and he leaned forward until they were inches away. "Do you want children?"

"I haven't thought about it." Oh, that wasn't true. Vaughan could tell by the way Bandos didn't want to have the conversation anymore.

"You have."

"My true mate rejected me. I haven't thought about it since."

Echo's face hardened, which Vaughan had never seen before. And when he spoke, he had an edge to his tone. "We are your true mates."

Bandos didn't back down, and that was probably a mistake. His intelligence made him right about a lot of things. It also closed him off sometimes. "You and Vaughan are my mates, but we're not fated."

Echo stood. He went to the duffle bag and rummaged through it, pulling out a shirt that wasn't his. He huffed in frustration and threw it in their direction.

It landed on Bandos's thigh, so he sat up and grabbed it. He held it, assessing it before handing it to Vaughan. "It's yours."

Vaughan took it before standing, pulling it on. He went over to Echo, squatting beside him. "Can I help?"

Echo moved out of the way, pushing the bag toward Vaughan before sitting and pulling his legs up to his chest.

Vaughan found clothing for each of them. The tension increased along with the uncomfortable silence. It would spill over at some point.

If he could've disappeared, he would've.

They all dressed in silence and packed everything before getting underway.

"You lead," Bandos told Vaughan. It was the first thing anyone said.

"I'll lead." Echo adjusted his backpack before gripping the strap. "Which way?"

"Vaughan can lead, little fae." Oh man, Bandos was an idiot. He needed to grovel. Telling them both how much he loved them would also help a lot, but that probably wouldn't happen. He would have to feel it first.

And there Vaughan went, letting Bandos's words hurt him even though he tried to push it down.

"Which way?" If there was anyone Vaughan never wanted to piss off, it was Echo.

Bandos sighed. "I'd really like it if you would stay between us."

"And I'd really like it if you loved us, but we don't always get what we want." Echo's comment broke some of the tension. "So which way?"

Echo might as well have slapped Bandos. His reaction would have been the same.

Bandos opened his mouth, but nothing came out.

Echo turned to Vaughan, raising his eyebrows.

Vaughan pointed in the direction they needed to go and watched as Echo turned, stomping off.

Bandos followed, shaking his head. He hadn't realized how his statement had made them feel until Echo had pointed it out. The remorse poured off him like water, drenching them all. And then he pushed love through their bond-link, which somehow pissed Echo off more, although he didn't stop walking.

Vaughan brought up the rear. By the gods, he didn't want to talk about it. He would have to deal with his feelings if he did, and they were feelings he'd had since before Echo had come into the picture. The time for the discussion might not have been perfect because of their situation, but it had to happen at some point.

Vaughan knew how things would play out with Bandos. He wasn't so sure about Echo. They were still getting to know each other. Vaughan could handle Echo's anger, but what happened if he let the hurt take over? A crying, sad Echo would make Vaughan's heart ache. And yeah, maybe Bandos was the one in the hot seat, but Vaughan was in the relationship too.

So I have a question. Speaking through their bond-link would help Vaughan make his point.

"For which one of us, baby?" The weariness in Bandos's voice was unmistakable. But knowing he'd fucked up and fixing the problem weren't the same thing.

Why did you bond with us? You know, knowing we were second best. There had always been something holding Bandos back. Even when he said he loved Vaughan it was as if not all of him did.

He expected a growl and Bandos turning the truth behind Vaughan's words into an accusation. What he got was silence, and it stretched for so long they nearly walked a mile.

Echo's anger embed and he stopped walking. The reaction Vaughan feared the most was unmistakable. Echo's hurt matched his own.

Bandos stopped a couple of feet from Echo. When Vaughan passed him, Bandos grabbed his arm, holding on as if he expected Vaughan to disappear.

Vaughan knew if he took one look at Bandos's crestfallen expression he would give in.

Echo turned and closed the distance. He had tears in his eyes when he pressed himself against Vaughan. With his free arm, he wrapped him up as best as he could.

Bandos pushed at them again, sending love through their bond-link. *Look at me.*

Vaughan shook his head, but Echo ended the embrace so he could face Bandos.

"Vaughan."

"No." And then Vaughan did the thing he'd said he wouldn't. He turned and pulled his arm out of Bandos's grip. "I've been competing with a fucking ghost the entire time we've been together. All I want to know is how long I'll have to do it. I think that's a fair question. But you just stand there and pretend it's not true, that way you don't have to answer it. And I'll wait. Like I have been since the day I met you. Because I don't have any choice anymore."

Vaughan took off Echo's backpack before pulling him closer. So yeah, he used Echo like a shield. Not that it would work. Nothing would guard his heart. Not where his mates were concerned. But what he said felt like a confession.

Bandos pounded a fist on the tree next to him and then leaned against it. "I love you both so fucking much it hurts. I never felt about him how I feel for you guys. Not once. But I ended up almost hating him. Do you have any idea what it's like to feel compelled toward someone, at the same time you dislike them so strongly you wouldn't want to be in their presence?"

Vaughan tightened his hold on Echo a bit. "No. I don't. But I know what it's like to want to be important in someone's life."

"By the gods, Vaughan. You're missing the damn point."

Vaughan didn't mean to raise his voice. He didn't want to alert the bad guys to their location. But he couldn't seem to keep his volume down. "Then what, Bandos? Because I'm just going on my experience here."

Echo stiffened as if he thought they were going to come to blows.

"Your experience." Bandos shook his head. "Your experience includes me never letting you get beaten near to death. Your experience includes kindness and love, Vaughan, despite what you think."

He couldn't deny any of that. He knew it did.

"You're so young, Vaughan. So idealistic. You haven't lived long enough for someone to break you, and it won't ever happen. You know I won't let it. And do you know why?"

Vaughan shook his head.

"Because I would die first."

"Your true mate would have let you die," Echo whispered.

Bandos nodded. "That won't happen to either of you. And you're right. You two are my true mates. In every way that counts."

"It won't happen to you either, baby." Walking with Echo in front of him wasn't graceful, but they made it over to Bandos.

Echo wrapped his arms around Bandos. "We won't hurt you." And that was the heart of the issue. It was the reason Bandos held back.

"We're not him," Vaughan said. By the gods, Vaughan had gotten it all wrong.

Bandos nodded and hesitated before he put his arms around Echo. "You could hurt me so much worse than he did."

"There's a difference between him and us."

"Double the fun," Echo whispered.

All three of them chuckled.

"Well yeah, that, and the fact we're proud to call you our mate. I don't care who knows. Not even the clan. It's the three of us together from now on."

"Yes." Echo's simple agreement said more than any speech.

"I'll try to be more open with you guys." That was about all they could hope Bandos would say.

"I'll try to not get so mad." Echo closed his eyes.

Vaughan smiled. "That's your big takeaway here."

Echo didn't move from Bandos's chest or open his eyes when he asked, "What should it be?"

"If I tell you, are you gonna get pissed?" He had a large chance of starting another argument, so maybe he should just keep his mouth shut.

"Just say it straight."

Vaughan widened his eyes, and he met Bandos's gaze.

Bandos chuckled but otherwise didn't comment.

"You are absolutely right, Baby Spice. Your big take away should be about your temper." Vaughan might have agreed, but even he knew it was too late.

"Your takeaway should be to stop while you're ahead."

Bandos laughed even harder.

Yeah, Vaughan probably should. Before he could agree, Echo's aura glowed and then a tree branch bent. A leaf from the tree covered his mouth, cutting off his words.

"I haven't had enough sleep to put up with your teasing, Vaughan."

Bandos grinned. "Wow. He called you by your actual name. He must be serious."

"Yours either, Conor." Echo pulled away and picked up his backpack, putting it on before walking again.

The leaf left Vaughan's mouth.

Vaughan and Bandos followed.

"For the record, I'd like to have kids," Bandos said.

"Yeah, me too." Vaughan could talk to his mom about it. She could steer them in the right direction in terms of adoption.

"To answer your earlier question. No, male fae can't get pregnant. I'd like to raise a family, though," Echo said, without turning around.

"Let's revisit the conversation when we get home then." Bandos sounded a little lighter, as if a weight had been lifted from his shoulders.

If Vaughan had had anything to do with that, then he was glad they'd had the discussion, even if he didn't feel as if he had a lot to prove. Maybe Bandos should know Vaughan wouldn't ever hurt him, but emotions didn't always make life easy.

Chapter
Twenty-Three

Humans smelled distinctive, like sandalwood and soap. Not unnatural except in the northern woods where everything smelled like pine. When the wind shifted, Bandos could smell them, and he knew Vaughan could too because he put his nose in the air, sniffing it, much like his animal counterpart. Vaughan's eyes shifted, and he bared his teeth as if the humans were within sight.

Their reprieve was over. It was too late to plan some grand escape or strategize a fight.

Bandos growled.

Echo stopped and turned. He wore a smile, but it died when he saw their faces. "What's wrong?"

Come here. Bandos moved to Vaughan, standing with his back to the scent and the direction of the humans. When Echo closed the distance, Bandos grabbed him around the waist and pulled him between them. *I'm going to check it out. I want you both to stay here and stay hidden.*

As soon as he said to stay hidden, Echo's aura glowed and the plant life around him shifted, growing as if seconds had turned into months while they stood and watched. There was a nice natural-looking wall that came up to Bandos's waist. It was tall enough for them to crouch and wait.

That'll do, little fae. Bandos cupped his cheek and kissed his forehead.

"I should go. I'm able to hide better," Vaughan kept his volume so low Bandos wouldn't have heard him if he weren't so close. "My wolf blends into this environment."

You're not getting close to them. Neither of you are. No one will see me. I'll go on foot. In human form.

Vaughan sighed, and to Bandos's surprise, he nodded. "Your dragon's close to the surface."

Bandos had nothing to say to that. He was protective of his mates and wouldn't apologize for it. "Stay here. Stay hidden," he repeated for good measure.

He gripped Vaughan's nape and kissed him, keeping it quick. He bent enough to give Echo a kiss next. And then he turned, following the scent through the forest.

Be careful. Echo's distress followed him, taking each step with him. It built his anxiety until his gut told him it wouldn't be easy to get out of the forest. The humans would make their lives hell.

The intuitive thought made him want to puke.

Crows. They'd been with them since the plane crashed. Vaughan had noticed them too. They stayed camouflaged in the trees, but he saw a hint of them as he made his way through.

Bandos had a stealthy team at his back. They would alert him to any trouble.

He tried to stay low as he made his way through the forest. As the human scent strengthened, Bandos's body reacted. His dragon came out the closer he got, hands turning into claws, and scales grew on his chest. He had to repress the urge to shift all the way when he heard them walking.

They sounded like a herd of buffalo, even though they were trying not to make a sound. Or Bandos assumed that because they didn't speak to each other.

While Bandos didn't see them yet, he didn't want to. If he spotted them, they would see him too. He didn't want to give his position away.

He turned, heading toward Vaughan and Echo again. He only made it about halfway to them when he heard Vaughan snarl. The sound was faint, but it traveled on the breeze straight to him. And then crows squawked.

He shed everything from his waist down and started running, pulling his shirt over his head as he picked up speed. As soon as he did, he shifted, taking to the air when the trees thinned enough.

A gun went off, the sound blasting through his eardrums right before pain knifed through his side. The pain threw him off-kilter and he struggled to stay in the air. When he flapped his wings, trying to gain height, the movement took his pain from an eight to eleven and he nearly passed out, so he stopped trying.

He thought he would crash when he went in for a landing, but he managed it, even if it lacked finesse. He shifted and cried out when the change tore at his wound. He fell to his knees and must have blacked out because the next thing he knew humans were passing him, leaving him as if they thought he was dead.

He laid as still as possible until the last one passed him and then shifted. Ignoring the pain, he took to the air. He hadn't been that far away from Vaughan and Echo, so he saw what was happening.

Vaughan fought two guys at the same time, while more came at him from behind. Bandos swooped down, heading off those closing in on Vaughan. They were the same ones who'd passed him earlier.

Nine more, including the two who fought Vaughan, plus the ones who came from the opposite direction. He hadn't expected them to split up but Bandos was almost sure that was what had happened.

Shit.

Bandos bit at the closest one to him, taking his arm off even as he raised his gun. He wasn't able to get a shot off, but the one behind him did. It missed Bandos, but only by centimeters, because Bandos felt the bullet whiz past him. He lifted off the ground enough to knock two guys to the ground before biting another in half.

The two who he had knocked over, scrambled to their feet. One made it past him but the other, Bandos caught between his teeth and shook until he stopped struggling.

The pain made him lightheaded as he maneuvered around bullets and took out as many as he could. When he heard Vaughan yelp, he forgot everything except getting to him. Instinct kicked in and his dragon took over.

There wasn't any pain, even when a bullet entered his body. He took to the air and came down on top of one human, taking his head almost all the way off. The last man standing limped away. Bandos landed and stomped after him, biting his injured leg until he fell. Once Bandos had his prey on the ground, he bit him around the middle.

Bandos turned, searching for his mates. He found Vaughan lying on the ground, as still as death. A soldier stood over him with the butt end of a gun raised above Vaughan.

Bandos didn't hear his own roar, although he knew he made a sound. The guy turned with wide eyes. He raised the gun, but Bandos grabbed it with his mouth, flinging it away before closing his teeth around his enemy's torso. The man fell like a stone, lying partly on Vaughan.

Of the nine, one had gotten away. There were a few more coming from the opposite direction.

Bandos's chest ached as he scanned the area for Echo, but he was pretty sure Fowler's men had captured him.

He closed his eyes and wished for the possibility of time travel. He would have done things differently if he had known their pursuers had split up. He should have guessed they would.

Bandos grabbed the human's leg with his mouth and dragged him away from Vaughan.

Mate.

Bandos shifted and went to his knees next to Vaughan, pressing his face into his fur. He could feel Vaughan through their link, so he knew he was alive.

Where are you, little fae? Bandos hadn't cried in a long time, but the lack of response from both of his mates sent him over the edge.

He wrapped Vaughan in his arms and let his tears flow. It was what he had to give because he didn't know what to do. He couldn't leave Vaughan. What if another group of humans came back to finish him off while he was unconscious? But he needed to find Echo. Those bastards had his precious fae, and something about that made his stomach knot.

He wasn't sure how long he laid there, but as each minute passed, his adrenaline faded, and the pain came back with a vengeance. He had almost forgotten his injuries.

He rolled onto his back, ignoring the stick poking into his skin, and probed where most of the agony was centralized. When he touched wetness and a small hole, he sucked in a breath and grunted when it felt as if a thousand knifes entered him.

It was a bullet wound, which meant it would take time, and shifting, to heal.

It was as he moved to feel around on his back that his shoulder burned. He hadn't realized he had gotten shot a second time.

"Shit." He curled into Vaughan again, grunting when the action made his wounds burn. He waiting for the radio silence to end or the forest to swallow him whole.

Fur turned to skin under Bandos's arm. Vaughan whimpered and put a hand to his head. He tried to speak, but the pain must have eaten through the words because he ended up curling in on himself and shifting again.

"I'm here, baby. You'll be okay. You have to."

Echo. Vaughan shifted back, and that seemed to lessen his discomfort enough to uncurl his body. *Echo, Bandos.*

"I think they took him. We'll get him back." Or Bandos would die trying. He wouldn't let Echo become a science experiment, or worse. Armageddon.

Vaughan cleared his throat. "They did something to him. Knocked him out before he could get to more than one of them."

"Did they come from behind?" Bandos needed confirmation.

"There were around ten of them, I think. Maybe twelve. No more than that." That seemed about right. It matched with what Bandos suspected.

"One got away from me." And Bandos felt that one the most because he was pretty sure that person had shot him.

"Echo is still alive. I can feel him." But he wasn't vocal, which scared Vaughan. He could feel it through their bond link. Words mattered to Vaughan in ways Bandos was just understanding.

"Is shifting fixing your injury?" The sooner they could stand, the faster they could save him.

"Yeah." Vaughan shifted to his wolf and then back again before he spoke. "Are you hurt?"

For a second, Bandos thought about lying. He knew how Vaughan would react to his injuries, and it wouldn't get them moving faster. Vaughan deserved the truth, though. "I'll need Lucas's help."

"What!" Vaughan sat and immediately put his hand to his head as if holding it on his shoulders, but he seemed to recover enough to turn.

He found Bandos's shoulder wound first and growled. "You're fucking shot."

Bandos grunted in answer.

Vaughan leaned over him, searching for the exit wound, and that was when he saw the wound on Bandos's side. "They shot you twice!"

"Oh, I'm very aware." He felt every hole in his body that he hadn't been born with because they burned like a bitch.

Vaughan took a deep breath, and that seemed to calm him enough get past the pain and think of ways to fix Bandos. "So, I'm not a medical person, but I've seen enough television to know there's not an exit wound on your shoulder. The one on your side has two holes, so you're good there. Unless the bullet tore your insides."

"That one's healing when I shift." He could move and that was all that mattered. "I'll make it through rescuing Echo."

Vaughan scowled and his eyes shifted. "Fuck you, Bandos. You make it for the next two hundred years. After that we can renegotiate our mating."

Bandos smiled, cupping Vaughan's cheek. "I'll need Lucas's help. Eventually."

Sometimes honesty sucked. The bullet being stuck in him was a problem that would kill him if he didn't get it out. That was a fact Vaughan needed to know so they could work together to get themselves out of the mess.

Vaughan laid his forehead on Bandos's chest. "We gotta hurry."

"Yeah, baby."

Vaughan nodded. "So, I'll shift a few times and then let's go get our Baby Spice."

Bandos smiled. "That sounds like a good plan." It was the one Bandos had too.

Chapter Twenty-Four

- -

E cho couldn't move his arms. His neck hurt and he couldn't figure out why until he tried a different position. He must have fallen asleep sitting up, and the position he was in caused his muscles to ache.

He panicked, jerking and struggling against whatever held him captive. When he couldn't free himself, his chest hurt.

The tree bark rubbed the skin on his wrist raw. And that made him stop. He tried to regulate his breathing so he could think, but his lungs seized until he fought for each breath.

Where were Bandos and Vaughan? Had they died?

Oh gods.

Just the thought left Echo nearly hysterical, which cut off what little oxygen he brought into his body.

Please. He wasn't sure who he intended that for. Bandos. Vaughan. The gods. It didn't matter. He just knew he wanted his mates safe.

Nothing else mattered, not even being tied to a tree by people who would ultimately use him to preform mass murders. After they finished using him for that, they would either study or kill him.

The sun had fallen, although Echo couldn't tell the time. The humans had a fire going, but they didn't speak to each other. They didn't pay attention to him, even though he had made enough noise with his struggles for them to know he had woken.

The longer he couldn't breathe, the more his survival mechanisms kicked in and he struggled again. He wanted to cry out for help, but he couldn't get sound past his closed throat.

We're coming for you, Baby Spice. Just hang on.

And just like that, Echo's throat opened, and he sucked in a deep breath.

Calm, little fae. Keep calm.

By the gods, the relief brought tears to his eyes. Bandos and Vaughan were alive. He couldn't think about anything else because nothing mattered as much as that.

Echo rested the back of his head on the tree trunk. *Thank the gods.*

I feel you calming down. Good job, little fae. Bandos. Gods, Echo wanted to kiss him just for staying safe. *I'm going to need you to focus on your surroundings.*

Echo could do that. *Where are you?*

A couple of miles away. We plan on striking when they're sleeping. It was dusk. The sky was still a deep blue, but it was darkening a little at a time.

It occurred to Echo that he could kill the humans within seconds. It hadn't entered his mind until that moment because the uncertainty of Bandos and Vaughan's safety clouded his thoughts. Since he knew they were alive, he couldn't see a downside. *I can kill them. They tied my hands around a tree. I can't get loose. But I can kill them, and then you can untie me.*

Are you sure you can get them all before one of them gets a shot off?

No. But his arms hurt and all he wanted was to get to his mates, so he would take the chance. Bandos wouldn't allow even a slight risk. He would see it as unnecessary. And as impatient as Echo was, he would follow Bandos's lead. He knew Vaughan would do the same.

He could still argue his point, though. *How do you know they have guns?*

Vaughan and Bandos both had a reaction to that question that Echo didn't understand until Vaughan explained. *Don't freak out, but they shot Bandos. Twice.*

Echo's chest ached again, and his lungs tightened, squeezing the air out of his body.

He hadn't seen or heard guns. Obviously, he had been unconscious when all hell had broken loose. But he was awake and near enough to the humans to see if they had any weapons. *They have guns. Handguns. I'm not sure how many.*

Between the encroaching darkness and the fire casting shadows, it was difficult to see every single one. They had strapped him to a tree a few yards away, as if they thought of him as unworthy of their presence.

How many humans?

We injured one. Including him, sixteen, I think. They have a fire going. They're mostly all just sitting around it. One is leaning against a tree between me and everyone else.

How far away are they from you?

Ten meters, maybe. Echo's information made Bandos happy. He could feel it through their bond.

Idiot humans. They don't know how easy they just made it.

Does that mean you'll let me kill them?

Bullets travel fast and further than ten yards, love. We'll do it together, but we won't wait for them to sleep. We're moving toward you right now. Bandos wanted Echo with them sooner rather than later. Echo could feel that through their link. *Tell me how they got to you.*

Echo knew what Bandos was really asking. How did the humans get him before he killed even one? *We were behind our hiding spot. Vaughan shifted.*

I smelled humans close by. I didn't know how close, though. Vaughan contributed.

I turned around when Wolf did, but something came over my mouth. I remember a chemical taste and some type of fabric, but that's all until I woke up here a few minutes ago.

Do you feel okay? Can you function normally?

I'm scared.

I am too, Baby Spice. But we'll be together in a few minutes.

Can you take out the guard? Oh, Bandos wanted to know if the chemicals they used on Echo affected his abilities.

Echo didn't have the emotional capacity to think past his panic. Thank the gods for Bandos and Vaughan, who could plan an attack.

Echo manipulated a tree branch, making it sway as if it were moved by the wind. *I'm able to kill all of them.*

Not until I say, love. Just kill the guard but do it when I say.

Echo sighed so loudly the guard looked his way. *Fine.*

I can see the fire through the trees. Vaughan let him know they were close.

Echo's heart rate increased with anticipation.

There was a flutter in the trees. The crows were drawn to Echo. They'd always been close by his entire life, like best friends. They reminded Echo of something else as well. *You don't die, Blue.*

I don't plan on it, love.

No. What I mean is, I would have had a vision. And I didn't. Echo could tell Bandos was in pain, though. Enough that the feeling grew through their link.

We'll worry about me once we get you to safety. That meant his injuries were bad.

Once they were together, Echo never wanted to be away from them again.

Chapter
Twenty-Five

The fire crackled nearby, casting a glow. The guard had grown lax in the last ten minutes. He leaned against a tree, standing under the huge pine branches. A snake slithered past him. Echo could barely see its big dark body. The snake didn't care, and the human remained oblivious to its presence. If he discovered it, he would create enough of a ruckus to wake the others.

Most had bedded down. One human poked at the fire with a stick, stirring the hot coals beneath the logs. Another sat staring at it as if he could see the future inside it. "Do you think Hall's right and the other two are done?"

Echo knew what he meant. Hall must have been the leader, and he'd declared Bandos and Vaughan dead.

"If Hall says they're dead then they're dead."

The other human sighed. "I know. But I just keep thinking—"

The man pointed his stick at the other one. "That's your biggest problem. You think too much."

The other guy's back was to Echo so he couldn't see his facial expression, but Echo imagined there was a spark of rebellion in his eyes. "We don't know enough about their kind to know if we killed them. If they're not and they come for him, we're as good as dead. You saw the way they fought."

The poker man's brow creased, and he scanned the area as if looking for the soldiers who'd died, counting them in his mind. "Yeah."

The next time he spoke, it was at a whisper. Echo could hardly hear him. "I don't get this mission. It's all fucked up." He ran a hand down his face. "We have a human being tied to a tree, man. That's fucking wrong."

"Keep your voice down," he whispered and then leaned forward. "And he's not a human being."

"You know what I mean. He's got a soul and all that." The poker guy shook his head and turned his gaze to the fire again.

The conversation waned.

Echo focused on the guard, wanting his reaction to their conversation. The guard stayed as watchful an observer as Echo.

Echo sighed and shut his eyes, trying to forget the pain in his arms. His muscles protested the odd movement.

Tears threatened when he heard crows flutter in the trees. The ones with Bandos and Vaughan coming to join those who'd stayed with Echo. He vibrated with anticipation and he couldn't help imagining a hug from each of them.

The image must have been strong enough for Vaughan and Bandos to see, because they each responded. Bandos pushed love at him.

Vaughan licked his hand. At first, the feeling startled him, but then the relief took over so thoroughly, tears rolled down his face.

Something big flapped its wings overhead, but with the moon at a little more than a sliver and the tree branches blocking most of his view of the sky, he couldn't see it. Not even a shadow. Still, he wanted to believe it was Bandos.

Kill the guard, love. Wherever Bandos was, the order came through loud and clear. So did his pain.

Echo took a deep breath and then another. He knew his aura became visible to everyone when he grew closer to nature, so he had to make it quick. And he wanted to do it in a way that wouldn't cause a lot of sound.

He focused on the tree, asking it to aid him. One of the lower branches acted as an extension of Echo, seeming almost human in the way it moved. It covered the guard's mouth so fast he didn't have enough time to react. The limb was big enough to conceal most of his face.

The guards tried to pry it off, but before he could make a lot of noise, Echo made two more wrap around him. Pine trees made up most of the forest. Their branches weren't perfect for penetrating flesh without a lot of sound, so Echo made what little vegetation there was climb up the guard's body and into his ears.

Vaughan must have been waiting for the guard's attention to be diverted because halfway through incapacitating him, Echo felt warm skin as Vaughan cut him free. They used zip-ties, and the plastic was thick enough that whatever sharp object Vaughan used took time.

Vaughan cursed under his breath. "Bandos will need you to do your thing, Baby Spice. I'm supposed to be done by now and helping him."

Echo didn't wait for Bandos's order. Instead, he let Vaughan's touch and the knowledge he would be free soon soothe him.

Echo focused on the vegetation and trees around the campfire. *Do you want any left alive?*

The flapping noise came again. *No.*

Most of the humans were already sleeping. Blankets covered all but one. The vegetation worked its way under the covers, trapping them as they slept. The process was slow and deliberate. If one of the two humans still sitting around the fire turned, they would've seen something snakelike move. Neither did, which made the attack silent.

Each sat stuck in their own silent struggles. Echo wasn't sure what made Poker struggle with his conscience, especially after chasing them through the forest. Maybe that was a good thing. Killing him while he considered the part he played might help him find favor with the gods in the afterlife. Or maybe Echo should defy Bandos and keep him alive. It wasn't until the sound of Bandos's wings alerted the two men to the danger that Echo decided what to do.

The other human stood, pulling his gun from its holster. The gun pissed Echo off, and he acted on instinct. The branch sent him sailing and as he landed so did Bandos. Bandos bit him in half before shifting.

Vaughan got Echo's hands free and when he did, he shifted, coming around Echo to stand in front of him.

Echo stood and let the trees do their thing to Poker. The human scrambled to his feet and backed away with his hands in the air. Two branches circled the man's waist and suspended him off the ground.

Bandos took Poker's gun out of his holster. He walked over to the nearest sleeping human and pulled the blanket back. When he saw the human struggling against the vegetation, Bandos raised his eyebrows as he met Echo's gaze. "I'm not leaving them alive."

Echo nodded and wrapped his arms around Vaughan, clinging to his wolf's body from behind.

"Turn your head away, love." A fine sheen of sweat covered Bandos's face. His skin had a grayness to it.

Echo rolled his eyes but did what Bandos wanted. He helped the process by killing a few with the vegetation making their brains mush. Four shots went off, deafening Echo.

Echo latched onto Vaughan like a monkey, fearing someone would tear him away. There wasn't anyone left except Poker.

Bandos had the gun trained on Poker. He kept his finger around the trigger.

"I was a medic in the service. I can help you." The man shook.

Bandos dropped the gun, and he swayed before his eyes rolled into the back of his head.

Vaughan pulled Echo off him and would have run to catch Bandos, but Echo's actions were quicker. Tree branches braced Bandos from behind, giving the vegetation time to create a soft bed so when he fell, the landing wasn't as hard.

Vaughan got to Bandos first, but Echo wasn't far behind. When their gazes met, Vaughan said, "There's a bullet in him. He can't heal until it comes out."

The human breathed as if he were hyperventilating. He appeared in his late twenties, but his fear made him seem younger. Coming so close to death had aged him within minutes.

Echo didn't know what to do, and if he contemplated it too much, he became more uncertain. The humans' conversation while sitting around the fire came to mind, and he met his gaze. "If I let you go and you hurt either of my mates, I'll make sure your death is slow and painful."

The human nodded.

Vaughan blinked as if Echo had grown two heads. And then his expression hardened. "Let him go and then come here."

Echo nodded and moved to sit on Vaughan's lap.

Vaughan wrapped an arm around Echo and then reached for the gun Bandos had dropped.

Bandos groaned and tried to roll onto his side, but Echo pushed on his chest, stopping him. He let Poker go without paying attention to him. His entire focus was on Bandos, although he heard Poker hit the ground with a curse.

Echo laid his cheek above Bandos's heart so he could hear it beat.

Bandos put a hand on Echo's back. "I'm okay, love. Just hurts a lot is all." He sounded as though he gargled with glass.

"I think I can help with the pain." Echo let Vaughan anchor him.

His gaze met Bandos at about the same time the human came into his line of sight. Bandos's gaze turned reptilian, and he growled.

The human shook, but he focused on Bandos's wounds.

"Echo. Damn it." Oh, Bandos made sure he felt how pissed he was.

Echo ignored him. He had bigger problems. When Bandos's anger became his biggest issue, he would deal with it. Until then, he would help Poker fix Bandos.

Echo patted Vaughan's arm around him. "I need you to let me up."

Vaughan had the gun trained on Poker and didn't waver when he spoke. "No fucking way."

"I need to find plants that will help with the pain. I'm positive they grow here. It seems like a cold enough climate." He thought for sure that would get Vaughan to release him.

"No." Vaughan had never been so stubborn.

Poker ignored them, probing around Bandos's body, finding his wounds. "Through and through. Might have hit an organ. How are you alive still?"

"You don't get to ask questions, kidnapper."

"It would help to know, so I know where to concentrate. He has two separate wounds." Poker's voice shook, but he seemed to put his fear aside. If he thought of Bandos as less, it didn't show. He worked on him as if his life mattered, and it did. Bandos mattered very much to Echo.

"Just get the bullet out." Vaughan gestured to Bandos's shoulder with the gun.

"If he has organ damage, he needs a hospital." Poker moved to Bandos's other wound.

"He doesn't need a hospital." Vaughan didn't want to give information to the enemy, but Echo had to wonder if Poker was ready to jump ship and side with the paranormals.

"His liver is in that area." Poker seemed to think he could argue for the welfare of his patient. Echo liked him a bit more.

"Just get the bullet out," Vaughan said again.

"Fine. I'll do that first, but his other issues will have to be addressed at some point." Poker met Vaughan's gaze. "I'm going over to my bag. I have a knife and a few basic medical supplies. I'll need both if I'm going to help him."

Vaughan nodded. "You try anything, and I'll shoot you through the head. Got it?"

Poker held up his hands. Bandos's blood covered them. "Yeah. I got it."

"You travel with medical supplies?" Echo asked.

"Like I said, I was a medic in the service. I was the designated doc for my division here too." Poker grabbed a bag that sat over by the fire. Echo could tell he tried not to look at his dead teammates. And he hurried back to them, kneeling next to Bandos. "I guess you could say I have a calling. Wanted to go to medical school after the service, but I got pegged for this. The pay was good."

"Not everything is worth the money," Echo leaned against Vaughan, but touched Bandos with his leg.

"A-fucking-men to that, man. A-fucking-men." When he spoke, he focused on Bandos and his shoulder wound, pulling stuff out of his bag as he went. "So I need to clean the area. It'll hurt."

"Just do it." Bandos gritted his teeth. He was already sweating.

"Let me get him something for the pain."

Vaughan and Bandos both said, "No" at the same time. But it was Bandos who followed it up with, "I need you to not leave my sight, love. Not for a while. Fucking hell." Bandos panted when Poker started cleaning around the shoulder wound.

"Sorry. I'll try to make it as quick as possible."

Echo leaned forward and took Bandos's hand. He watched everything Poker did. "My name is Echo."

Bandos cursed. Echo didn't know if he did it because of the pain or because of Echo trying to make friends.

"Taylor." Taylor smiled but didn't let himself get distracted from his task. "Nice to meet you. Wish it would have been under different circumstances."

"Me too." Echo brought Bandos's hand to his lips and kissed the back of it. "It'll all be over soon, Conor."

Bandos narrowed his eyes and actually growled at Echo. "Stop making friends with the enemy."

"He's not the enemy. If he was, he wouldn't be fixing you."

"I literally have him at gunpoint, Echo." So Vaughan chose Bandos's side. That just figured.

Echo deflected because he knew they had a point. Not that his gut feeling about the human wasn't valid, but still. "Okay, first, he's right there. Stop talking about him like he's not. And second, he knows nothing about us. And you know how humans fear what they don't know. Scared humans are more dangerous, not less."

Vaughan held the gun out farther, threatening Taylor. "Exactly."

"I'm going to have to poke around inside the wound to look for the bullet," Taylor cleaned a knife with some of the same stuff he'd used to clean Bandos's wound. The knife was long and seemed more for hunting than doctoring.

Seeing Bandos in pain was bad enough but listening to him scream wasn't possible. Echo leaned forward, getting inches from Bandos. "Please."

Bandos sighed.

Echo's chest tightened when the tears built in his throat, threatening to spill over. "I can make it better. Let me help."

Vaughan was the one who gave in. He moved his arm from around Echo. "Go. Stay within sight."

Echo scrambled up, searching the ground for what he needed.

Vaughan mumbled, trying to keep it under his breath, but Echo heard. "We're gonna give him everything he fucking wants. Every damn time."

"I shouldn't have to ask for permission. I'm not a child." Echo didn't stop his search.

It was a combination of two different plants. They had magical qualities that, when combined, worked on paranormals. Paranormals abused them, selling the product they made to those who wanted to get high. The plants didn't work very well on humans and witches. And Echo didn't feel the potency as strongly as other beings. But they would work on shifters.

Echo found one right away.

"Just so you know, you're in a lot of trouble. So I wouldn't be so quick to start an argument," Vaughan said.

"Like I say. I can do what I want. I'm not a child." Echo found the second plant he needed and started over to them again.

"You don't get to say that to me." Vaughan had never been so upset. "When I came to, you weren't anywhere in sight and Bandos was shot twice. Some sick fuckers had you." Vaughan pointed at Taylor with his gun. "Namely him. For all I know, they were doing all kinds of shit to you. The thought of you or Bandos getting tortured doesn't exactly make me feel good. And I'd say the way they tied you to that tree sent me pretty close to the edge of insanity. So you can sit there and declare your independence all you fucking want, but that doesn't change the facts. You're a part of him and I. Fact. We fucking love you more than everything. Fact. And we'd die for you." He gestured to Bandos's wound. "Fact."

Damn.

Echo sat in Vaughan's lap again. Vaughan's arm came around his waist, holding him steady. He turned to Bandos and put the plant to his lips. "Chew them together. They'll make you high, but it'll work out of your body in a couple of hours."

Bandos nodded and let Echo feed him the plants. When he had enough in his mouth and started chewing, Echo met Taylor's gaze. "Should only take about five to ten minutes."

Taylor nodded. "I'm sorry, y'all."

Echo smiled, but he took Bandos's hand and kissed it before turning on Vaughan's lap. He laid his cheek against his chest, listening to his heartbeat. "I love you both just as much. And I'm as protective of you. It's why I let him live. But Vaughan, I killed everyone else. I'm not being reckless here." Well, technically Bandos killed some, but that was semantics and didn't make a difference to his point.

"Yeah, you're a little badass. I know." Vaughan rubbed his back. "You're not the one who has to prove himself. That would be our new human prisoner here."

Taylor sighed but didn't speak. He was smart, which may or may not make him more dangerous.

"Well, you and Bandos don't either."

Bandos chuckled. "My little fae needs a spanking."

Echo met his gaze. Vaughan did that blinking thing, which meant Bandos had stunned him. When Echo turned to Bandos, he had a smile on his face.

Taylor took Bandos's little declaration to mean he was ready for the probing. When he got started, the sight turned Echo's stomach.

And then Bandos let go of his hand and crooked a finger. "Come here, love."

Echo bent, getting closer. "Are you in pain?"

Bandos snorted out a chuckled. "No." The next thing he said, he whispered exaggeratedly. "Never give this stuff to Vaughan."

Echo chuckled. "Why?"

"Picture that in your mind for a second." Bandos's eyes widened.

Echo rested his forehead on Bandos's chest. "Frightening."

Vaughan chuckled. "Bandos is right. You need a spanking."

"I think I got it," Taylor whispered.

Echo could hear the knife digging around in Bandos's flesh. "Oh gods. That's turning my stomach."

"You killed my team by plant but think this is gross. Paranormals are weird."

"He has a point." Bandos agreeing with Taylor was a minor miracle.

"I wish I had a camera. I'd video tape him and use it against him at my leisure." At some point, Vaughan had put down the gun, resting it on his thigh.

"Now Vaughan needs a spanking." Bandos yawned. "Hurry up, human."

Taylor rolled his eyes. "I have a knife inside your body. I think going slow is the right approach here."

"I think killing you is the right approach. And that could still happen."

"Yeah, I got that from your conversation with your husbands."

"Mates."

"What?"

"They're my mates. Not my husbands. We're not humans, human."

"Okay. Sorry." Taylor focused on his task. His brow creased. And then he held up a small, mangled piece of metal, grinning. "Got it."

Vaughan lifted Echo around the waist as he stood. "Might want to move, Taylor. He's gonna shift."

Taylor scrambled up and Echo thought for sure he was going to run, but he just grabbed his bag and moved around Bandos, standing next to them.

Bandos shifted.

"That's fucking wild, man."

"Don't run. He might chase you," Vaughan whispered.

Echo rolled his eyes.

But Taylor stiffened. "Seriously?"

"No." Vaughan said the word with a straight face.

Echo smacked him in the arm. *Stop teasing him.*

Taylor looked at Vaughan with wide eyes. "What?"

"He's completely cognizant. All shifters are."

"Oh." Taylor watched Bandos shifted into his human form again. "So he's as aware as when he's human."

"He's not human. Like at all."

"Right, but he looks human now."

"Yes, but he's not. He's a dragon shifter."

Bandos shifted again.

"I can see he's a dragon, man. I'm staring right at him. What I'm trying to do is understand."

"Not a dragon. A dragon shifter." Vaughan held Echo with a hand on his ass. "Do you want some advice?"

"Yes. I'll take what I can get in this situation."

"Stop thinking like a human. You'll live longer." That was actually good advice.

Echo wrapped his arms around Vaughan's neck and laid his head on his shoulder, closing his eyes. He yawned.

Chapter Twenty-Six

V aughan led the way through the forest with Taylor behind him and Echo and Bandos bringing up the rear. He wasn't even sure he knew where he was going, but Taylor knew. Apparently, his division had intended to take Echo to a small airstrip. "How far?"

"A few steps less than the last time you asked me. My god, you're like a little kid." Taylor was a fun target for Vaughan's teasing.

Bandos and Echo were in the back, making out through the bond link. The images they sent made Vaughan's dick hard. They tried to one-up each other. It had started with Echo sending an image of him riding Bandos. It made Vaughan remember when Echo had ridden him. So sexy. Bandos's image was of him eating Echo's ass. It escalated from there.

Vaughan was so horny he wanted to stop and let one or both of them fuck him against a tree. Who fucking cared about tree rash? Not him.

"It's a sad, sad day when I'm the responsible one in this relationship." Someone had to act like an adult and while it was usually Bandos, he was still as high as a kite, so Vaughan was it. The gods knew Echo wasn't about to adult.

Echo sent an image of Vaughan bent over Bandos's legs with his ass in the air. They were both naked, and Bandos smacked Vaughan's ass so hard he felt it for real.

Vaughan stopped and turned, meeting Echo's gaze.

Echo grinned and said, "I love you."

Taylor lifted his eyebrows but didn't speak. He didn't butt into their business, despite all his questions.

"You better, Baby Spice." Vaughan turned back around and started walking again.

"You're the one who needs a spanking, love. Naughty boy," Bandos growled, but he chuckled right after. And then Echo laughed hysterically, running past them with Bandos hot on his heels.

Vaughan shook his head. "So did your division rent a plane or what?"

"Nah, it's something one of the guys owned. Why?"

"I know someone who can strip it and sell it when we're done." Vaughan thought of Amos. But he knew a couple of people who were capable. "Where are we?"

"Upper Peninsula of Michigan. A team took out your technology, I take it."

Vaughan had thought there were slightly east of their location. For not having the instruments to tell, his guess had been close.

"Phones. Computers. Everything gone. And they blew up our communications and navigation at the tail end of our flight." Vaughan was surprised Taylor didn't know that but maybe his leaders told him what he needed to know and nothing more.

Taylor shrugged. He didn't seem to care about what had happened to the plane, but Vaughan did because he didn't want to go to jail for stealing it. He also didn't want to take anything that belonged to someone just trying to make a little extra cash by renting their plane out. It wasn't that poor person's fault he'd rented to kidnappers. But if the plane belonged to one of Taylor's dead division members or some very shady politician then it was fair game as far as he was concerned.

"So how does the mating thing work exactly?"

Vaughan sighed. He might as well answer. He had nothing else to do besides walk and watch Bandos throw Echo over his shoulder and carry him through the woods. "A paranormal, and a human too if they pay attention, knows their mate upon meeting them."

"How?"

"I guess that depends on who you are. I'm a wolf shifter, so I knew Echo by scent. Shifters usually use their nose. I think for vampires it's different. Not sure about Echo." Vaughan looked at Echo, who was upside down over Bandos's shoulder. "Hey, Echo. How did you know I was your mate?"

"I saw you and Blue in a vision." Echo chuckled when Bandos smacked him playfully on his ass. "Hey!"

"But if you hadn't seen me in a vision."

"It's a feeling. Like a human would get."

"What about Bandos?" Taylor asked.

"Echo and I chose him."

"So you didn't get a feeling or smell him or whatever?"

"Oh, he gives us feelings. Lots of sexy feelings." Echo chuckled and then let out a squeal when Bandos pulled him off his shoulder. Echo strapped himself to Bandos's front. He put his arms around Bandos's neck and then kissed him. "Sexy dragon."

Bandos covered Echo's ass with a hand, holding him in place.

"I smell water close by, baby." They all needed to take a break. Vaughan wanted to give Bandos enough time to work the effects of the plants out of his system.

"Human." Bandos didn't take his eyes off Echo when he spoke.

"What?"

"Will your people send another division after us?"

"No one is left alive who will radio into them. It will take them a couple of days to send someone to investigate, and if they do, it will be one or two guys at first. Once they figure out Echo escaped, they'll send another division to track him." Taylor's candid response surprised Vaughan.

"We'll camp by the water then," Bandos said. He carried Echo, leading the way toward the water. Maybe he smelled it too.

"What will happen when they find out you're still alive?" Vaughan asked.

"I'm as good as dead. I can't go back to my life. I knew that when Echo let me live."

That was what Vaughan thought he would say. "Guess we fucked you, huh?"

"Yeah. I'd rather go out doing the right thing than live forever terrorizing innocent people. And I fucking mean that, man. Y'all didn't deserve none of what happened."

Vaughan smiled. "You made it right. Saved Bandos's life. I can't tell you how grateful Echo and I are."

"Glad I could be of use."

"My people will help you."

"I appreciate it, but I'm not looking for favors. I did wrong by you and I'll pay the price for it."

"How the hell did you end up with your job?"

"Got recruited because of my experience as a medic. Serve your country in secret. That was their pitch. I figured I would save lives and fight the bad guys. And that's what it was at first. Or so it seemed. I don't know when it became a fucking witch hunt, but I won't be a party to hurting the very people I signed on to protect." Taylor didn't trust his superiors.

The revelation hit Vaughan like a train. As a shifter, he lived inside a certain culture that he didn't share with humans. At least, he didn't share it with very many. But he was still as American as anyone else, which meant he shared an overall culture, even with humans. So on some level he understood how Taylor had lived the past few years. His military experience would've changed him in a lot of ways. Not questioning those in command and following orders were automatic. So if Taylor lacked trust, it had been slowly seeping away over months, or maybe even longer. He had to have a reason for the lack. Based on what he said, it sounded as if kidnapping Echo had challenged his values.

"Who do you work for?" Vaughan didn't want to know the answer to that.

"The government. I suppose I don't work for them anymore, though."

Shit. A part of him wanted to be wrong about it being Fowler after them. It meant Echo was safer if it wasn't him. But an entire government after Echo meant he would never really be safe. Lucas wouldn't either. And while he knew that, the truth hadn't sunk in.

"You're all top secret and shit, right?"

"Only a few know about us."

"So not the whole government."

"Technically, yes. Your tax dollars pay my salary. But really, we only take orders from a few people."

"Senator Fowler," Vaughan whispered the name under his breath, but Taylor must have heard.

"I'm just the soldier on the ground. My division leader took orders from his superior, who was someone in Washington."

"My people will want to ask you questions." The paranormal council would need to know what Taylor knew. As soon as Vaughan found a phone, he would call Forrest and Angel. Since they worked for the council, they could facilitate all of that.

"I'll tell y'all what I know."

Vaughan could see the water through the trees. He stopped when he saw Bandos and Echo lying in the grass next to what looked like a small lake. They laid on their side, facing each other. Echo cupped Bandos's cheek. His expression was one of complete and total tenderness.

And then he spoke through their link. *You and Vaughan are everything.*

You and Vaughan are my *everything too.* Bandos repeated Echo's words with a conviction Vaughan had never heard from him before.

The moment, as small as it seemed, was pivotal in their relationship. It made the whole thing more real. Or maybe it was the lack of danger around every tree that allowed them to slow down and understand what they meant to each other.

"So go that way." Vaughan pointed to his right. "Things are about to get very...sexy. Damn." Just as Vaughan spoke, Bandos rolled onto his back and took Echo with him. Echo laid over him and they kissed. "Yeah, so go that way. Give us an hour."

Taylor chuckled. "No problem. Y'all enjoy yourselves."

Taylor headed through the forest. He stopped once, breaking a small branch off a tree, but kept walking. Vaughan watched him until he settled on the lakeshore with his back slightly turned. He stood and opened his bag. He fished around for something, but Vaughan didn't wait to see what. He just wanted to make sure Taylor wasn't a witness to his and his mates' bonding.

Vaughan sat beside them, putting the duffle bag on the sand. He braced himself on his hands with his legs crossed in front of him. Interrupting Bandos and Echo wasn't his goal. He was content to enjoy the kissing sounds and Echo's whimpers and look out at the water.

The lake, if they could classify it as something so big, wasn't one Vaughan would swim in. The water appeared almost black. Aquatic plants were visible from the top. He could see enough to tell they went all the way down to the bottom. There was an old wolf shifter who gathered some of it and ate it. Echo would probably love her.

One minute he was watching the long, green stands of vegetation sway with the water current, and the next he had a fae sitting on his lap and a dragon shifter snuggled in behind him. Vaughan leaned against Bandos and smiled at Echo.

Echo cupped Vaughan's cheeks and kissed him as if his intent was to show next-level tenderness.

Bandos kissed Vaughan on his mating mark, licking across it as if he wanted to bite. He continued to love on that area instead. When he did finally move on, he kissed up Vaughan's neck and then whispered in his ear. "Mate."

The assault made him feel loved and a part of something bigger than himself. It wasn't about protecting Echo anymore, or it wasn't only about that. They all took a collective deep breath. For the first time, they could focus on their connection. And maybe after the scare of almost losing Bandos, they needed to reconnect.

What would their relationship look like when they got home? Or maybe another question was what would domesticity look like? All those questions had different possibilities since the immediate danger had left. Being in Saint Lakes would mean even more protection, and they could focus on other things. Raising a family didn't feel like such a pipedream.

Echo trailed kisses along Vaughan's jaw until he met Bandos's lips. They shared a kiss, but they kept it brief. Vaughan tugged on Echo's shirt. Echo lifted his arms, letting Vaughan take it off.

Bandos did the same thing for Vaughan.

Vaughan could feel the fabric of Bandos's shirt. And then Bandos's bare skin touched him.

Echo pressed against his front.

Vaughan hadn't realized he still had tension left in his body until it all went out of him. He pulled on Bandos's hands until he included Echo in his embrace and then he wrapped his arms around Echo too, rubbing his back.

"Mates." Bandos's dragon was close to the surface. It could have been the drugs still in his system, but Vaughan liked to think he felt the importance of the moment too.

"Mates," Vaughan agreed.

Echo rested his forehead against Vaughan's. He reached past Vaughan, and must have touched Bandos, although Vaughan couldn't tell how or where. "Mates."

Bandos undid Vaughan's pants and then Echo's, exposing their cocks. When Bandos jacked them off, he did so with a slow and lazy rhythm. He made sure they knew they weren't in a hurry. It wasn't about bonding or trying to find some way to destress. It was about feeling close to each other.

Echo moaned. His mouth opened, and his forehead crinkled a little, as if he were concentrating on not coming.

The sight of him, coupled with what Bandos was doing to his body, sent a jolt of heat through Vaughan. "Bandos. Please."

He gripped Echo's nape, drawing him into a kiss. He couldn't breathe or think to breathe, so he kissed the life out of Echo. Except after a few seconds, Echo took control, devouring Vaughan's mouth as if he couldn't get enough.

Someone whimpered. He wasn't sure if it was him or Echo.

And then Bandos stopped. Vaughan wanted to cry at the loss, but Echo pushed him onto his back, never ending the kiss. He cupped Vaughan's cheek, holding him in place.

They got naked. Bandos did most of the work.

Echo slid down Vaughan's body until their pelvises aligned. Bandos's big finger probed Vaughan's opening. The finger was slick. The familiarity of Bandos opening him up had Vaughan spreading his legs almost as if they had a mind of their own.

Echo's eyes widened in surprise, and then pure pleasure crossed his face. He chased the touch.

Vaughan couldn't keep still either. While that had a lot to do with Bandos fucking him with his finger, an equal part had to do with knowing Bandos fucked them at the same time.

Echo whimper when Bandos added another finger. Vaughan knew that was what caused it because he did the same to him as well.

His breathing was shaky, giving away just how needy he had become.

Bandos pulled his fingers out.

Echo made a sound of protest.

And then Bandos let his hand slide between them. Bandos bypassed Vaughan's cock and worked Echo's, slicking it. Vaughan could feel Bandos' jacking Echo off. The back of his hand brushed Vaughan's cock.

Vaughan knew what came next. He panted as if he'd run a marathon. The anticipation made him shake.

Echo moaned and moved his hips, letting Bandos know he liked what he was doing. And then Bandos took his hand away and Echo hurried to get into place.

Echo held his cock in his hand as he placed it at Vaughan's opening. Their gazes met as Echo pushed inside. Vaughan moaned as Echo entered him. It felt as if it were one centimeter at a time.

Bandos came into view when he laid over Echo. He whispered in Echo's ear, but Vaughan heard it. "Does he feel good, love?"

Echo nodded and panted. The strain of holding back showed on his face. "Don't...can't hurt you."

Vaughan hadn't realized that was why Echo went so slow. "Feels good."

Bandos kissed Echo on his mating mark. "When you bottom out, I want you to hold still."

Echo pulled his hand away from his cock once he got in far enough. He braced himself on Vaughan's chest. "I don't...I don't know...if I can."

Bandos's eyes turned reptilian, and his fangs dropped. He nipped at Echo's mating mark. "I'll get inside you after you're all the way in."

Echo moaned, and he fell forward as if his arms couldn't hold him up anymore. He laid on Vaughan and his cock entered him in one long push.

It was Vaughan's turn to moan and when Bandos met his gaze, he nodded, letting him know Echo was all the way inside.

Bandos hissed with pleasure, focusing on his cock.

Vaughan felt the exact second Bandos entered Echo because his cock seemed to swell, and he pulled out part way when he wanted more of Bandos's cock quicker.

When Bandos bottomed out, Echo pressed into Vaughan again. They all needed friction after that, Vaughan especially. With Echo fucking him and his cock trapped between them, he wouldn't last very long.

Echo started a rhythm, taking Bandos and Vaughan along for the ride. He made demands. His ability to get his way in all things, without having to compromise, extended to their lovemaking.

He was like a sensual piston. He did most of the work because the three of them linked made it awkward. Vaughan wouldn't have wanted it any other way, though.

And then Bandos bit Echo on his mating mark. Their bodies weren't their own. They belonged to the moment, and it carried them along the path toward ecstasy.

Echo's movements grew erratic and when he stilled, he pressed into Vaughan as far as he could go. He moaned. People miles away could have heard. His expression was the thing Vaughan would jack off to in the shower when he got home. Of course, with two mates who were so insatiable, he probably wouldn't ever have to jack off again. Or that was the goal, anyway.

Echo reached between them, touching Vaughan's cock. That was all it took for him to spill. Bandos held Echo still with his bite and fucked into him. Their gazes met and held the entire time he took Echo, and when he came, Vaughan knew. Bandos in the throes of passion created more jack off material for sure.

My mates.

Vaughan smiled and cupped Bandos's cheek. "We're yours."

Chapter
Twenty-Seven

The pain relief plants gave Bandos a headache from hell. Even at his worst, he'd never had a hangover. Back in his addict days he'd stayed high all the time, so that could have been why. Still, he hadn't expected to feel like shit.

"You're a bad influence, love." Bandos held Echo's hand as they walked. Sometimes it wasn't possible for him to touch one of his mates while they hiked through the forest. Between dense foliage and obstacles in their path, it was single file most of the time. He took advantage when he could.

He needed the physical contact because he didn't feel great. Maybe that made him a big baby, but he didn't care. He hadn't been sick very often thanks to his shifter genetics, but he had injured himself a few times. Echo and Vaughan hadn't experienced that side of him yet. Getting shot didn't count because he couldn't take the time to whine and complain. But he didn't have that problem with his headache, and he planned on taking advantage of it.

"Why do you say that?" Echo smiled, but that died when their gazes met. He scowled and seemed to concentrate on something, slowing down until they both stopped walking. "Wolf!"

"What?" Vaughan had a piece of jerky in his mouth, so when he spoke, he talked around it. He also didn't stop walking.

"Blue isn't feeling good." Oh, their little fae was going to mother-hen him. That would satisfy Bandos.

Vaughan stopped, which forced Taylor to, as well. They both turned. "Let me guess. You have a booboo on your dick, right?"

Bandos smiled and shook his head at Vaughan's ridiculousness. It was funny and he would have played into it but doing so would hurt his head even more. "I'll be fine."

Vaughan's smile fell and started over to them. "No, he's right. I can feel it now. You don't feel good." When Vaughan got to him, he cupped his cheek. "What's wrong?"

"Got a little headache." He had a lot of headache but neediness aside, he didn't want to worry his mates. That hadn't been his intent.

"Shifters don't get headaches, baby." If Vaughan scowled, then that meant he was taking control of a situation and he wasn't messing around.

Bandos sighed. The last thing he needed was Vaughan ruling over him for the next day and a half. "Pretty sure it's the pain relief plants."

Echo shook his head. "No. That can't be. It has to be something else."

"It's just a headache." Okay, all the attention was nice. One of his mates fussing over him would cure a lot of things, but both of them just annoyed him. And his headache was getting worse.

When Taylor came over, Bandos growled. He tried to pull away from all of them, but Vaughan and Echo kept him in place with their scowls. Taylor was inches away, lifting his eyelids. If there was anyone's attention he didn't want, it was the human's.

Taylor sighed, and he stopped touching Bandos. "Make your eyes go back to human."

Then Vaughan got in his face. That made his eyes shift back. There wasn't a reason for Bandos to show aggression toward Vaughan. Vaughan was his mate, his baby, one of two people he loved more than life itself. "Listen, your eyes are glassy, and your skin feels warm. It's not just a headache. Let him examine you."

Echo wrapped his arms around Bandos's waist and held on as if he thought he'd float away.

"I don't feel bad other than the headache. I think it's just a hangover, maybe." He didn't feel that bad. But maybe he appeared worse than he felt.

When Taylor got in his face again, Bandos rolled his eyes, but he let him do whatever he thought necessary. "When did it start?"

Bandos opened his mouth to answer, but then closed it again. He had to think about it. "When the pain plants wore off is when it got a lot worse. Pretty sure it's been hanging around even before that."

"How long before, Bandos?" When Taylor sounded scared, Bandos took the headache seriously.

Bandos met Vaughan's gaze and tightened his hold on Echo. When he met Taylor's gaze, he said, "Around when the fighting ended."

"So after you were shot?"

"Yes. After. For sure."

Taylor cursed and then sighed. "A few nights ago, I saw two of my team mates messing with the bullets in their guns. Taking them out and then putting them back in again. I didn't think anything of it. Hell, I didn't even remember it until right now."

Vaughan shook his head. His scowl deepened as he waved his hand. "What are you saying here?"

"He's saying they coated the bullets in some type of poison. Right?" Echo let Bandos go and paced along the path they made. He stopped once and focused on Taylor. "Do you know what poison they used?"

Taylor shook his head. "No. I don't remember seeing anything. Hell, I'm not even sure that's what happened. I mean, they could have been just cleaning their guns. It's just odd that they would, considering they hadn't fired them at that point. The whole thing was weird enough that it came to mind. I could be wrong."

"No, it makes sense. Whatever they used, they didn't get it from this region. Nothing that grows here would poison a shifter." Echo started pacing again.

"You think it's a plant?" Bandos asked. He still felt nothing except for a headache.

Echo threw his hands up. "I can only hope. That's all I know. If it's anything else, I'm useless."

"You are never useless. Not to me. I need you for a lot of things, not just your plant knowledge." Bandos wiggled his eyebrows, trying to make light of the situation, but it was lost on Echo.

"It's not a joke, Conor. You could be dying. Again."

"Okay, so let's assume it's poisoned bullets. And let's assume the chemicals are biological." Bandos was nothing if not an analytical thinker. He wished he had a computer.

Taylor raised his eyebrows.

Vaughan relaxed visibly, as if Bandos getting involved provided him some comfort.

Bandos pulled him into his side and kissed his temple. "Everything will be all right."

Vaughan buried his face in Bandos's neck and wrapped his arms around him. "Just figure it out."

Echo stopped pacing and focused on him. He still wore a scowl, but he was listening.

Bandos met Taylor's gaze. "You just saw two humans take bullets out of their guns and the put them back in?"

"Yeah."

"What can you tell us about the humans?"

"Delacruz and Chambers. They had a military background, same as me. Both came to my division from another one that got assigned to a medical facility, but the building blew up or something like that. I remember them talking about it because they seemed to be the experts on paranormals. Particularly dragon shifters. Apparently, one attacked the facility. They weren't supposed to talk about it but did when our DL turned his back. The news spun the whole incident as an electrical accident. Most knew that was bullshit. If they assigned a division to the facility, that facility did something to paranormals."

Vaughan whispered, "He's talking about that place where Ladon rescued Magnus."

"What's a DL?" Echo asked as he started pacing again.

"Division leader. Sorry. I'm used to the acronyms." One thing Bandos learned about Taylor the longer he spent time with him was that he was intelligent. And he didn't bullshit people. That combination was helpful and would probably keep him alive when the paranormal council started questioning him.

Bandos nodded. "They saw themselves as experts on shifters? What was their job at the facility?"

"They were guards." Taylor rolled his eyes. "No one took them seriously. They were just exaggerating their role in the whole thing. Trying to be cool around the rest of the division because they actually saw someone shift into an animal and lived to tell about it."

"It's likely one of them found some information about poisons strong enough to keep a shifter down." While that was a logical conclusion, he didn't know if it was true.

Taylor shrugged. "It's hard to say if my assumptions are even right. If they are, they came by the information somewhere."

"So it's possible."

"I think we need to keep walking." Vaughan moved from him just enough to meet his gaze. "We can talk as we move. But we're nearly to the airstrip. The sooner we get home, the sooner my mom and Lucas can get involved. We may need them."

Bandos nodded. "How close are we?"

"Maybe half a day's walk." Taylor supplied the information.

Bandos met Vaughan's gaze. "You can cover that in a third of the time. You should go ahead of us and get the plane ready."

The second the suggestion was out of his mouth Vaughan shook his head. "No fucking way am I leaving you."

"No. You're clearing the way. Making sure no one is waiting for us." Taylor opened his mouth to speak, but Bandos held up a hand. "I know you're gonna say no one is there, but you have no idea who might know about your little trip to kidnap a fae. I can think of at least two possibilities off the top of my head where that would be the scenario and neither bode well for your division. One is a vampire coven led by Delano Archer. Archer has a lot of money and even more resources. We'll all be in trouble if he's waiting in the wings to take Echo. The other is the council enforcers. If they suspect we're in trouble, they'll come to help."

"Echo is that important to the paranormals?"

"Yes. He's that important." Bandos had never hated something more than the thought of people hunting Echo as if he were hidden gold. He wasn't a thing to covet. He was Bandos's mate, and, by the gods, Bandos swore he would never treat him as anything less than a person with feelings and thoughts of his own.

"I'm right here." Echo didn't stop walking when he said it. Apparently, he'd decided Vaughan was right. They needed to get moving.

Bandos smiled. "Sorry, love."

Echo waved the whole thing away as if it didn't matter.

Bandos met Vaughan's gaze. "Scout the area. Make sure it's safe and if it is, get the plane ready." When Vaughan protested again, Bandos put a hand over his mouth. "It'll save time, baby."

When Vaughan sighed, Bandos pulled his hand away. "Fine. But you better not die. If you do, then I swear to the gods, I'll have Echo give me that shit that made you high and make your life miserable."

None of what Vaughan said made sense, but Bandos agreed anyway. It would shut him up faster. "Crystal clear, baby."

Taylor chuckled but didn't contribute to the conversation. He was a very smart man.

Vaughan dropped his duffle bag and took off his clothing, shoving each piece inside.

Taylor turned and jogged to catch up with Echo. Nudity was difficult for non-shifting being. For Bandos and Vaughan, it wasn't a big deal. Plus, seeing Vaughan naked always did it for Bandos.

When Vaughan shifted, he licked Bandos's hand before taking off. When he caught up to Echo, he did the same thing.

Bandos bent and lifted a bag in each hand, following Echo and Taylor. He still didn't feel bad other than a headache.

As he drew closer to them, he heard Taylor ask, "How do you know so much about the medicinal properties of plants?"

"My parents worked a lot. Our next-door neighbor babysat for me. She was a retired botanist and a witch. She must have seen something in me. Plant knowledge comes easy for me. Maybe because I'm chlorokinetic." Echo shrugged. "Whatever the reason, she taught me everything I know. Even when I was old enough to not need a babysitter, she remained my teacher. She died right before my parents did. Of natural causes."

"I'm sorry for your loss."

"Thank you."

"Can I ask how your parents died?"

"Accident." The one word was the truth. But Bandos had gathered Echo's information. He knew Echo hadn't told even a fraction of the story. "It's traumatic for me, so I would rather not talk about it."

"I'm sorry to pry."

"You didn't. It's fine."

Bandos would have to talk with Echo about it at some point.

Are you still feeling okay?

"I'm fine. Just a headache. Like I said." He must've looked pretty sick, but he didn't feel it.

Echo stopped and turned, making his way around Taylor, heading straight to Bandos. He tried to take one of the duffle bags, but Bandos wouldn't let it go. "Let me help."

"It's too heavy for you, love." Bandos smiled, trying to soften his response because he didn't want an argument.

Echo held on to Bandos's arm and they started walking together again. "I've been thinking."

"Uh-oh."

Echo smiled, but that was his only response to Bandos's teasing. "So if I go over your symptoms. Your headache and red glassy eyes would indicate an allergic reaction."

"His fever might be his immune system fighting it off," Taylor contributed. He didn't turn when he spoke. "Assuming he functions like a human, that is."

"Yeah, so if that's the case than it could be anything." Echo winced. "But I've been thinking about the humans poisoning you. There are a lot of nightshade plants that are toxic to animals but don't really do that much to humans. Like tomato plants, for example. And then there's hemlock." Echo shuddered. "Let's hope it's not that. There's no antidote."

"It's not that. He doesn't have the right symptoms. But you're on the right track. It makes sense that they would think that. They weren't exactly Einstein," Taylor said.

"So what do we do?"

"I don't know. I'm hoping it's an allergic reaction. Maybe something by that pond where we made love. If it was the bullets than there're endless possibilities." Echo laid his head on Bandos's arm as they walked. "It's good that you aren't feeling worse than you are, but if you do, promise me you'll tell me."

"I promise."

"I mean it. It's important that I know." Echo gestured to Taylor. "That we know so we can get you help if needed."

"No heroics. I swear." And he meant it. He would rely on his mates.

Chapter
Twenty-Eight

W hatever was in his system made his stomach cramp. He had never puked at all in his entire life but by the gods, when the feeling came upon him it was overwhelming and it happened fast. He couldn't let Echo know as he had promised. He just bent over at the waist and let loose. He'd never tasted or smelled anything so foul either. He was a shifter, for the love of the gods. He didn't puke.

It made him angry enough that when Echo handed him a bottle of water to wash his mouth out, he snatched it out of his hand. And getting angry at his body's betrayal and taking it out on Echo and the poor plastic water bottle pissed him off even more.

Bandos swished water in his mouth and then spit it out. "Sorry."

"It's okay." Echo rubbed Bandos's back.

"It's not. I'm taking it out on you when I shouldn't be."

Echo smiled with indulgence.

Bandos kept his mouth shut. The last thing he needed was an angry Echo.

It seemed Echo could handle Bandos's moods. Of course, Bandos was putty in Echo's hand. Even when he was an overly dramatic puking mess, something about Echo calmed him.

I'm ready when you guys are. In other words, Vaughan was telling them to hurry because that was the third time he either asked how far away they were or said something similar.

We're almost there. Echo answered, but he didn't take his eyes off Bandos. Maybe he needed the reassurance. And then his expression fell, as if a sunny day turned to a thunderstorm with the snap of a finger.

Bandos had dropped his bags when his stomach let loose, so it didn't take much to catch Echo when he launched himself at Bandos. Tears soaked Bandos's neck where Echo had buried his face.

Taylor came over to them and lifted both of Bandos's bags. "We're close. I think it's just on the other side of those trees."

Bandos nodded. "We'll be along in a minute."

"I'll let Vaughan know." Taylor gave them a look of sympathy. For the enemy, he was a pretty nice guy.

"Vaughan knows. We have an internal link with him. All mates do." It was the first information Bandos volunteered. It might have taken Taylor saving his life and hiking two solid days through the northern forest, but the man had earned his trust enough to give some information about paranormals.

Taylor's eyebrows went up. "I would like to know more about that. Later."

When Bandos nodded, Taylor turned and started walking again.

Bandos rubbed Echo's back with one hand and held him by his ass with the other. "It'll be all right baby."

"You're getting worse." Echo's voice hitched as if saying it aloud made it more real.

"Or maybe the poison is working its way out of my system." One could only hope that was true.

Echo shook his head, which was awkward because he didn't pull his face back from Bandos's neck. "It's the effects of the plant poison. A lot of them cause vomiting. Like a lot, a lot. I...I don't know what to do."

"How about we have Vaughan save the day this time? He makes a pretty sexy hero, and we can reward him for it when we're home." Bandos figured he might as well make light of the situation. The dramatics weren't helping. Not from either of them. Worrying about it wouldn't slow the poison.

Echo chuckled through his tears. "He deserves a reward."

"Yes, he does." Bandos's stomach rolled, so he started walking. Maybe moving would allow him to hold off the next round of vomiting a little longer. It would upset them both all over again.

"It's taken a long time."

"What?"

"For the poison to set in." If Echo's energy was directed on working out a solution again then he wasn't letting his fear rule him.

Problem-solving was what Bandos did best. With Echo's knowledge and his investigative skills, they might come up with something that would help. Bandos needed all he could get because he was pretty sure he would puke again soon. "Probably because I'm a shifter."

Echo met his gaze, his eyes widening. "Right. Because humans wouldn't have taken that into account."

"The way Taylor made it sound, the men weren't all that smart. Like I said before, it has to be something commonly known for its poison." Not that Bandos was on board with the whole poisoning thing. Maybe it wasn't much of a stretch, but it seemed a little out there. Especially for special ops soldiers. The only reason he entertained the possibility was because they'd worked in the lab where the humans had held Magnus captive. Some people were twisted enough to think they knew a lot of shit when they didn't.

"Something that would poison a human. Something common." Echo played with Bandos's hair in such a mindless way, Bandos doubted he was aware of the action. "Oleander might give you a headache. It's rare that it would, but with your shifter DNA it's hard to say how some plants would affect you."

"Maybe they were even stupider."

"How?"

"Maybe you were on the right track before. They might have used something common for animals because I'm a shifter."

Echo's eyes widened. "Like Monkshood. But that's not even native to North America. That's a European plant."

Bandos didn't know what that was, but he nodded anyway. "They can get some version of it easily."

Echo nodded. "If it's that, then the humans weren't as dumb as we assume. Aconitum is poisonous to animals as well as humans. In fact, it's commonly known as wolfsbane. There's a reason for that."

"Well, I'm neither one of those things."

"It was thought to kill werewolves back in the day."

"I'm not a werewolf either. Hell, I'm not a wolf at all. I'm a dragon shifter."

"Yes. Yes, you are." Echo wiggled, wanting down.

When Bandos put him on his feet, Echo grabbed his hand and pulled him along. "Let's hurry. The faster we get there the faster Vaughan can fly us toward some help."

Bandos followed Echo until the need to puke took over. By then they were on the edge of an airfield with Vaughan in the pilot's seat of the plane, watching them make their way out of the forest.

When Bandos finished and swished his mouth with water, he met Vaughan's gaze. The plane window and distance separated them, but that wasn't enough to keep them from knowing what the other was thinking. They also didn't need their bond link. Vaughan was scared. Maybe as scared as Bandos.

Get on the plane, baby.

Bandos nodded and grabbed Echo around the waist, moving at a fast walk. When he went around to the other side where the door was, Taylor held the door open for them.

Bandos lifted Echo to Taylor, who helped him inside before giving Bandos room to enter. As soon as Bandos was inside and the door closed, Vaughan began taxiing down the runway.

It'll take about an hour to get to Saint Lakes.

Stick to the original plan. We can't risk leaving this plane in Saint Lakes.

I can drop it off after we get you to my mom and Lucas.

No. Bandos sat next to Echo, putting his seatbelt on. He met Taylor's gaze. "I need a bucket and a computer."

Taylor had to brace himself, but he stood, reaching into a compartment above them. The next thing Bandos knew, he had a laptop in his hand. He ran his hand over the flat surface before opening the lid.

Bandos.

We found a computer. Give me twenty minutes and I'll have the family meet us. Just tell me where we're going.

Bradwall. Vaughan's anger came through their bond link like a tidal wave. *You fucking said no heroics.*

Bradwall is a twenty-minute drive from Saint Lakes, baby. It's not heroics. The only one being a hero is you by flying us home.

Shut up and make contact. If you can't, let me know. I'll radio Amos and have him get the message to them.

By the gods, he'd missed technology so much he forgot about his request for something to puke into until Taylor set a paper sack on the floor beside him.

Bandos focused on the computer and then went about disabling the tracking system inside the thing. It took ten minutes, and it held his complete attention.

Echo rested his cheek on Bandos's shoulder. "What are you doing?"

"Rerouting our signal."

"Why?"

"Because a good hacker can use it to find out where we are. Or where this computer is."

Bandos brought up a messenger program. It was one he'd taught Shawn to use. Their signal would stay scrambled, along with any messages. *Guess who's going to be Superman.*

I like Batman better. He had more money. And where the hell have you guys been. The whole family is going crazy with worry.

Well Vaughan is Superman today. Tell Mother Estelle and Lucas to meet us at the hotel closest to the airstrip in Bradwall. Hang on. I'll get the hotel name.

"Are you talking to someone?" Echo leaned closer to the computer.

"Yeah." Bandos found information for the nearest hotel to the airstrip. Bradwall wasn't exactly a metropolis, so there were two choices. He sent the name to Shawn.

"Who?"

"Vaughan's brother's mate, Shawn."

Echo nodded. "Why does the screen look weird?"

"I'll explain the program later, okay, love."

Echo waved his hand. "Who's Mother Estelle?"

"Vaughan's mom. She's a witch."

Echo sucked in a breath. "Ask her if she knows of anything that will slow down the effects of Monkshood? Ask her if she can bring peppermint and..." Echo pursed his lips and furrowed his brow. "Let me think."

Bandos smiled and then read Shawn's message. *Who's hurt?*

I am. Poisoned. Echo thinks it's Wolfsbane. Although he called it two other things.

I'll tell Mom.

Echo nodded and pointed to the computer. "Yes. That's good. She'll know how to help, I bet."

"Yes. And if not, then Lucas can use his magic."

Echo didn't respond to that. "Aconitum is fatal in large doses. But it's a situation if a dog gets a hold of it. And with you being a shifter, I don't know if that makes you better or worse off."

Vaughan turned and yelled. "You guys can take off your seatbelts and relax."

They're on their way. And fyi, the whole damn family is coming. Except for Owen and Damian because they're in Blackwing. And Sully and Anna because they're on a rescue mission.

Bandos rolled his eyes. He really only cared about one person besides Mother Estelle and Lucas. *Rocky?*

Is on his motorcycle. He left before everyone else.

Bandos looked away from the computer and sighed with relief. Sometimes a person had to accept their limitations. Since rescuing Echo, Bandos had understood where his strengths lay and where they didn't. Taking on the role of leader wasn't necessarily in his wheelhouse. He had always deferred to Rocky. He and Sully both did because Rocky was good at it. And he would never take that for granted again.

He didn't even care that Rocky would give him a dressing down. Rocky didn't have to say a word either. It was all in his stare. Rocky was and had always represented strength.

Nausea rose in his throat, so he handed the computer to Echo and grabbed the bag. He needed Rocky's strength.

Chapter
Twenty-Nine

E very time Vaughan heard Bandos toss his cookies, he wished
he had Lucas's ability. If he could've made a ball of light cure
Bandos, the way Lucas could, he would've done it in a second. The
only thing he had was his ability to fly a plane. It didn't feel like
enough.

He didn't feel like enough.

He hated the helplessness more than anything. When he landed on
the tarmac at Bradwall, he didn't waste time parking the plane. It was
the quickest shutdown he had ever done.

He'd been at Bradwall a few times. The airstrip was about the same
size as Saint Lakes, but the human who ran it wasn't always on the up
and up. Vaughan would go through Bradwall instead of Saint Lakes
whenever he took a questionable load, which he wasn't above doing
as long as he wasn't trafficking human beings, guns, or drugs.

I'll be right back. Just gotta get the plane situation taken care of and get a loaner car. Vaughan didn't waste time. The sooner he talked to Frankie, the sooner they would get to the hotel.

They have car rental at this airport? It doesn't look big enough. One thing Vaughan loved most about Echo was his innocence. He could get kidnapped and held captive, and he still was naïve enough to ask that question.

Not exactly. Vaughan chuckled and knocked on Frank's door with the side of his fist. "Frankie!"

"Hold your horses. I'm comin'." When Frankie opened the door, she had on gray work coveralls and heavy boots. She was one of the best mechanics Vaughan had ever known. She was also in her mid-fifties, although she appeared about fifteen years younger, and she was a hellacious flirt. She also knew about paranormals, not that Vaughan had asked her how. "Well, hello handsome."

The airstrip was about as busy as the one in Saint Lakes, which wasn't a whole hell of a lot. If flirting with her made her day a little brighter then it was the least Vaughan could do.

Except not that day. He had a mate who would puke up his spleen at some point in the near future. "I need two things. For a plane to disappear. I don't care what you do with it, just don't let the feds find it. And I need a car."

Frankie's gaze moved past him, taking in the rest of Vaughan's crew. "You got one with a medical problem. He ain't contagious, is he?"

"No. He was poisoned. I have to get him help." Vaughan turned to assess Bandos.

Echo had his arm around Bandos's waist and Taylor was on his other side, although he didn't touch him. Taylor had their bags, all except the backpack Echo wore. Bandos had a gray tint to his skin and appeared as if he either wanted to sleep or die. One or the other would make him feel better, no doubt.

When Vaughan turned back and met Frankie's gaze, he said, "He's my mate. The other one too."

Frankie was a romantic. He knew that based on the fact she referenced a couple of romantic comedy movies once or twice. Hell, if he'd gone into her house, he bet he would've found a few romance novels too, and he also bet they'd be the juicy kind, because Frankie didn't do anything halfway.

When Frankie went back inside but left her door open, Vaughan knew she would help them. She came back with a set of keys and handed them over. "You can keep the car if you let me scrap the plane for parts. It's a fair deal in the long run."

Vaughan nodded and then leaned in to kiss her cheek. "Thanks, Frankie."

"Yeah, yeah. Just don't go tellin' anybody I helped ya. I got a reputation to uphold."

Vaughan smiled and nodded. "As long as you don't associate the plane with us."

"You got yourself a deal, Somerset. Car's in the hangar there." She pointed to the building closest to the house. "Don't steal my plane." And with that, Frankie shut the door in his face.

Vaughan jogged over to the other three and wrapped his arm around Bandos's other side, leading them over to the car. "We'll be at the hotel in ten minutes tops, baby. You hang in there."

If Vaughan had any question about which hotel, they were meeting the family at, Garridan, standing next to one of the room doors with his arms crossed over his chest, scowling, would have been a heavy clue. As big as he was, he stood out.

The scowl wasn't his usual one either. It was the same one he'd had when Stavros had kidnapped Jules and the one he'd had when he'd thought Ladon and Magnus had taken too long coming home after rescuing Magnus.

The hotel was one of those that a guest entered their room from the outside. It was an older place, but it seemed well-kept, with flower boxes separating the parking lot from the rooms and a sitting area outside every door. It was quaint and feminine, which added a hominess to the place.

Ladon stood next to him. His alphaness had grown around him since his first shift. It made Vaughan take a deep breath then let out the stress. His alpha was here to take control of the situation.

The past few days crashed through him, hitting him in the chest until it ached. His bravery seeped out of him.

As soon as he parked the car, both Ladon and Garridan moved toward them. Ladon pulled the back door open and, without a word, lifted Bandos in his arms, carrying him inside.

Echo trailed behind them, but he turned and met Vaughan's gaze. His eyes were wide when he darted his gaze to Garridan, who stood outside Vaughan's door, ready to haul him out of the car. *Are you okay?*

Vaughan wasn't sure if Echo asked about Garridan, who appeared as if he were about ready to rip someone's head off, or if he was asking about Vaughan crying. *Everything will be okay now.*

Echo nodded. *I love you.*

I love you too, Baby Spice.

Echo smiled and entered the room, shutting the door behind him. Vaughan could feel how overwhelmed he was when he realized the entire family was in the room.

Vaughan chuckled. Talk about immersion therapy.

Garridan wanted to talk to Vaughan so, for that reason, he stayed in the car.

"Why are you laughing?" Taylor sat beside him.

"Echo just met my entire family. It's not a small group in there." Vaughan might as well give Taylor some clue about what he was walking into. "Well, Forest and Angel might not be inside. I don't know. If they were in the area, they will be. Plus, I have a brother out west."

Fear rolled off Taylor in waves, and he couldn't blame him. He would be walking into a den of...well, paranormals. For a human, especially one who worked for an organization hell bent on killing them all, he should feel the way he did.

Garridan growled and pulled Vaughan's door open. He wasn't known for his patience.

As soon as Vaughan got out of the car, Garridan hugged him. He didn't say a word but held him tight. Vaughan had difficulty breathing.

Vaughan sank into the embrace of the only father he had ever had.

"Do you want to know how I know he'll be all right?" Garridan whispered.

He didn't even realize how worried he was until Garridan asked the question. "How?"

"Because Lucas and your mother are in there."

"He's not supposed to be sick. Ever." And that scared him the most. His strong Bandos had fallen. It shook Vaughan's world in ways he didn't want to think about, but the situation forced his hand.

"Maybe you should tell him that."

Vaughan chuckled, which wasn't the reaction Garridan had been after, but it was the only one Vaughan had. "Oh, I can just see how that will go. I'll say it and he'll give me that look he always does. It's the one that means he thinks I'm being ridiculous. Echo will probably side with me because I'm right. Together we'll annoy him until he tells us to knock it off."

Garridan actually laughed. It didn't happen very often, but when it did, it felt like a gift. "You should get in there."

Vaughan turned and waved to Taylor, telling him to get out of the car.

Garridan growled at Taylor. His eyes shifted, and smoke came out of his mouth as if he were about to set Taylor on fire. Sometimes Vaughan forgot Garridan produced fire. Until someone or something pissed him off, it wasn't something he used.

"Taylor, this is Garridan. Father to all Somersets. Garridan, Taylor. He saved Bandos's life from a bullet."

"They shot Bandos?"

"Twice, and it's been a shitshow ever since."

Taylor nodded. "Pretty much."

"He's got some intel for the council." Telling Garridan would free Vaughan to focus on his mates, which he very much needed to do. Garridan would get Forrest involved or tell Ladon, who would get it done.

Vaughan forgot about everything when Echo's stress level went through the roof. "Shit."

He ran to the room. He had to search to find Echo. His smaller size made him hard to see because he was stuck in the corner. When Vaughan saw him, he pushed Gabe and Shawn out of his way and pulled Echo into his arms.

Echo nearly climbed him like a tree. His arms and legs wrapped around Vaughan. He had tears streaming down his face and sobbed.

"What happened?" Vaughan tried to find the source of the problem but, beyond Bandos lying on the bed with Lucas and Mom working on him, he couldn't tell what had made Echo so stressed out.

Bandos watched them as if he would spring from the bed to fix whatever needed fixing. *He's overwhelmed. Bring him over here, baby.*

Vaughan nodded. "Hey, mind moving for a second, Gabe."

Gabe turned and seemed surprised they were even there. He stepped aside, taking Shawn with him. "Sorry, brother. We didn't see you there."

Echo's stress decreased, and he relaxed in Vaughan's arms. "No worries anymore. Right, Baby Spice?"

Echo shook his head without moving it from Vaughan's shoulder. "I didn't know what to do."

That was the first time he had ever showed uncertainty. With that statement came the realization that they might've been safe in the arms of the family, but Echo had a few hurdles to jump because of his time spent in captivity. Or that had been Vaughan's guess, anyway. Why it hadn't manifested itself until that moment had everything to do with living in solitary confinement for so long and then being around so many people. Alone in captivity did bad things to the mind.

"Don't like groups?"

Echo shrugged. "I don't know. Just want it to be you and Blue again."

Since they needed every single person in the room, the most Vaughan could give him was the physical closeness of both of his mates. "How about we pull a chair over to the bed? That way we can all be together but not get in Mom and Lucas's way."

Vaughan got Ramsey's attention and darted his gaze to the chair, nodding to the bed. Ramsey, thankfully, understood. "Thanks."

"How are you, brother?"

Vaughan smiled. "A little shook up, honestly."

Ramsey patted his arm. "Well, you're found now. We won't let you out of our sight for a while. Especially Mom. Just a heads up."

Vaughan could get behind receiving a little of Mom's attention. She would fuss over all three of them and ply them with food. Where was the downside?

"I'll deal with you in a minute, Vaughan Patrick Somerset." Mom never lost focus on her task. It seemed she was chanting something.

Vaughan sat in the chair and grabbed Bandos's hand, putting it on Echo's thigh, and then covered it with his own.

Echo met his gaze. He wiped away his tears with the back of his hand. "Your middle name is Patrick?"

Vaughan narrowed his eyes, but he couldn't keep up the pretense. He tried not to smile but couldn't stop. "What do you have to say about it?"

Bandos chuckled, but it sounded as if he were in pain.

"I'm just asking."

"No, you're not."

"I can't find a way around the poison." Mom's words sobered them, and Echo shook.

"If it's Wolfsbane, there isn't an antidote," Echo's chin went to his chest and his fingers tightened around both of theirs.

Mom turned and focused on Echo. She smiled at Vaughan, tears coming to her eyes. At first, Vaughan freaked out because he thought it was because they couldn't cure Bandos. But then Ramsey's words finally registered.

The family thought Vaughan had disappeared. They didn't know what happened. "I'm safe, Mom. I swear."

Mom nodded and then focused on Echo. She put a finger under his chin and lifted it. She smiled when he turned to meet her gaze. "Hello. I'm Vaughan's mom."

Echo returned her smile. "I'm Echo. His mate. And Blue's."

"Blue. That fits Bandos very well."

Echo nodded.

Mom held out her hand. "How about we get to know each other the old-fashioned way?"

Echo put his in hers without hesitation.

It didn't take Mom long to see whatever it was she wanted. She didn't let go of Echo's hand when she turned to Lucas. "You're up, honey."

Lucas nodded and concentrated on Bandos.

When Mom turned back around, her gaze went from Echo to Vaughan and back again. "I'm afraid my magic won't help, and I see yours won't either, so we'll rely on Lucas now. The poison has worked well enough that it will be painful for him. He'll probably sleep for a while afterward."

Bandos cursed, having heard every word. "Just do it."

A ball of light seemed to appear out of nowhere. Lucas held it in his hand and then pressed it into Bandos.

When Bandos's eyes widened and he screamed, Echo scrambled off Vaughan's lap and onto Bandos, lying over him as if protecting him from everyone in the room.

Mom moved when Vaughan's wolf rose to the surface. His eyes shifted and his fangs dropped. He couldn't help growling, and even though his instinct was to attack Lucas for hurting his mate, he was cognizant enough not to do that to the only person who could save Bandos's life. Instead, he sat next to Bandos and tried to calm his wolf.

Bandos stopped screaming and he went limp.

Bennett pulled Lucas away, leaving the three of them on the bed. It felt more like a stage with everyone staring at them as if they were actors in a play.

When Echo's aura turned green, Vaughan darted his gaze to the plant on the side table. It was one of those viney things full of bright green leaves. His mom had one like it in her kitchen.

Sure enough, it started growing, covering the bed and them. Leaves covered Vaughan from the waist down.

The entire family, except for Mom, had one collective expression on their face and that was astonishment.

"He has a few unique gifts." What more could he say? They were Somersets—family of the weird and strange. They should have been used to it.

Lucas chuckled. "Thank the gods I'm not the only one anymore."

Lucas was Vaughan's partner in teasing at least half of the time. Their relationship had grown into a friendship. Mostly it was all fun and games, but Vaughan couldn't help but get serious. "Thank you, Lucas."

Lucas smiled and nodded. "I'm glad I could help."

"You did more than that." Vaughan could feel that Bandos rested peacefully. And it was the first time since they had left to rescue Echo.

He reached for Echo's hand and laced their fingers together.

Everything was going to be all right. He could feel it.

"Either Bandos or I will introduce everyone to Echo individually." And there wasn't any compromising on that. He wouldn't be the center of attention. He didn't seem to like that very much.

"You mated both of them?" Ladon asked.

"Yes. Is that a problem?"

"Nope. Just making sure I understood the situation correctly. Congratulations, brother."

Vaughan smiled. "Thanks."

Mom touched Vaughan's shoulder. "How are you and Echo?"

"We're not hurt."

"Good. Because if you ever do anything like that again, you will be in *so* much trouble, Vaughan Somerset, that it will rock your world." It had been a long time since he'd gotten a dressing down from his mother. If there was anyone who could reduce him to his childlike state, it was her during a lecture.

He apologized, even though he did nothing wrong. "Sorry, Mom."

Those siblings who were in the room wore sympathetic expressions, which made the entire experience almost embarrassing. Everyone else eyed Mom as if she'd banged her head on something hard. Rocky stood in the corner by the bathroom door. He was the only one who didn't have an expression.

Echo's head popped up above the plant like a prairie dog in a grassy meadow. His eyes were wide, and he looked from Vaughan to Mom and then back again. *Are you getting in trouble?*

"I think so."

"What?" Until Mom asked that, Vaughan hadn't realized he spoken aloud.

"Echo asked me if I'm getting in trouble."

"Of course, you're not in trouble." Mom hugged him, forcing him to let go of Echo's hand so he could hug her back. "You had me worried sick is all. My baby was in danger and I didn't know where you even were."

"I thought I was your baby, Mom." Ladon grinned.

"Shut up, dear. We're focusing on Vaughan right now."

Ladon chuckled.

"Technically, I'm her baby," Jules said as he leaned against Thomas. Thomas had his arms around Jules's waist, hugging him from behind. Hacen stood next to them with a scowl that rivaled Garridan's.

Mom laughed and pulled away. "You and Ladon both will be in trouble if you don't stop."

"Plus, that's my area of expertease. Get it. Tease." Vaughan grinned.

"Pun-ny. Very Pun-ny," Jules said with a straight face.

Echo snorted out a laugh. It was the first one since Bandos fell ill that he had.

Vaughan winked at Echo.

Wolf. The word was like a caress to Vaughan's soul.

Everything is going to be all right, Baby Spice.

Chapter Thirty

E cho didn't even realize he'd fallen asleep. The last things he remembered were people talking, Vaughan holding his hand, and the steady beat of Bandos's heart as Echo settled in, expecting to ride out the effects of Bandos's healing. When he woke, he noticed the indistinct murmur of voices and the plant didn't cover them anymore. Instead, the blankets reached to the center of Echo's back.

Someone had taken off his clothing, leaving him in his underwear. Bandos was also in his underwear. Echo hoped Vaughan was the one who'd stripped them and not one of his family members. He didn't exactly like the thought of Vaughan's mother seeing him almost naked.

He didn't want to wake up yet, so he stayed still.

And then Bandos spoke. He whispered, but his deep, rumbly voice was like music to Echo's ears. He still didn't move, though. He would probably never be out of touching distance from Bandos again.

"He can fight, Rocky. At least in wolf form."

Someone chuckled. "That doesn't surprise me. The kid pays attention to everything. And he's smart. Saint Lakes is full of wolf shifters.

He's probably been watching the clan for years. Don't tell him I said that."

They were talking about Vaughan. Echo wasn't sure why Rocky—was that the guy's name—didn't want Vaughan to hear his praise, but it was a nice thing to say. And then Rocky said, "For someone who picked their mates, you could have chosen one who doesn't annoy me."

Bandos chuckled. "I did. Echo isn't annoying. And besides, the wind annoys you if it shifts wrong."

Rocky grunted. "That's because my mate is across the lake and I can smell him. He's very good at avoiding me."

Bandos rubbed Echo's back. "I'm sorry, man."

"It'll work itself out. Look at you. Your fated mate rejects you, gets you beat near to death. Yet, you found two mates who fit better."

"You think Vaughan fits?" Bandos thought the concept was humorous. Echo would hear it laced through his words.

Rocky snorted. "You two weren't fooling anyone. You've never looked at anyone the way you do him. Except for maybe that one."

Echo lifted his head, meeting Bandos's gaze. *How are you feeling?*

Never better. Bandos ran the back of his finger down Echo's cheek. *You promise?*

"I promise, love."

Echo nodded and laid back down again, only he faced Rocky, meeting his gaze.

Rocky had a red bandana covering his head and a beard that made him appear as if he hadn't bothered to shave for a few days. It didn't seem as if he was actually trying to grow one. It appeared he hadn't slept well and somehow, Echo knew that came from worry for Bandos.

"Don't tell Vaughan I said that." He pointed at Echo and raised his eyebrows. He wore leather gloves that exposed his fingers. He also wore jeans that had seen better days and a black leather jacket. He looked like a total badass.

The hotel door opened, and Vaughan came through. "Tell me what? How much you love having me around your house. I already know."

Vaughan grinned and winked at Echo.

Echo covered his mouth when he laughed because Rocky was almost as scary as the guy Vaughan called the Somerset Dad.

Bandos chuckled.

Vaughan had changed his clothes and might have showered at some point. Echo sat up and then stood on the edge of the bed when Vaughan got close enough that he could smell how clean he was. The mattress bounced with each step, but he crooked a finger at Vaughan.

Vaughan carried a food bag from a chain restaurant, but he set it on the table before doing Echo's bidding. Echo wrapped himself around Vaughan, who held him up by his ass.

Echo buried his nose in Vaughan's neck and pulled in his scent. "You smell delicious."

"There's homemade herbal soap in the shower." Vaughan wiggled his eyebrows. "Did you know you're nearly naked in front of Rocky? It's a good thing the rest of the family left."

"He's seen someone in their underwear before, Wolf." Echo turned and met Bandos's gaze. "You should smell him. So good."

"I did right after he got out of the shower. And I can smell him from here." Bandos shifted his eyes, letting Echo know he had good senses because he was a shifter.

"Show off." Echo turned and kissed Vaughan before he wiggled around, trying to get him to let him down.

"No way am I giving you up now." Vaughan grinned.

Echo chuckled, but he laced exasperation through it. "Stop. I want to shower."

"You wet and soapy. I think I need another shower too." Vaughan started toward the ajar bathroom door.

Bandos sat against the headboard, keeping the blanket around his waist. He chuckled, but he didn't make a move to help Echo.

When Echo shrugged. "Is the shower big enough for the both of us?"

"We'll make room."

"In other words, no, it's not." Echo rolled his eyes. "Will I even get clean?"

"Squeaky. I'll soap up all of your nooks and crannies. Especially this one." Vaughan kicked the door closed behind him at the same time his finger pressed along the crack of his ass. *You're missing it, baby.*

I'll be there in a minute. Bandos sounded amused through their bond.

"Where's Taylor, Wolf? Is he okay?" Echo hadn't seen him since they arrived at the hotel.

"He's fine. My brother, Forrest and his mate came. They were only a couple of hours away. They're taking Taylor to the paranormal council. But they promised to stay with him the whole time he's there." Vaughan set Echo on his feet.

"He'll be safe?" Echo knew he was only giving the council information about his division. Hopefully it would help save lives.

"Yep. Forrest and Angel have his back." Vaughan turned on the water and adjusted the temperature. The shower wouldn't hold all three of them, but who needed to get under the spray to get fucked. Not Echo.

"And if something happens, you'll save him, right?"

Vaughan turned to Echo with his eyebrows raised. "Was that a question or a demand?"

"A demand." Echo gave Vaughan a pointed look, making sure he knew he didn't have a choice. "You and Bandos do a pretty good job of rescuing people. And even Rocky said you were a good fighter."

The door opened and Bandos came inside. He closed it behind him. "You weren't supposed to tell him that, love. Good thing Rocky left for home."

"Positive reinforcement." Echo shrugged.

Bandos wrapped his arms around Echo and lifted him off his feet. "You have a big mouth, love. You unleashed a beast."

Vaughan chuckled, but he didn't comment.

Bandos looked toward Vaughan. "See. He's quiet. You know what that means, right?"

Echo chuckled. "What?"

"He's considering all the ways to annoy Rocky."

Vaughan pulled his shirt over his head as he laughed. "I actually was."

Bandos met Echo's gaze. He had a sparkle in his eyes that Echo hadn't ever seen before. "See what you started."

Chapter Thirty-One

T he car they drove was the one they'd gotten from the airport in Bradwall. The thing was a boat with a huge bench seat. The three of them sat together in the front with Echo in the middle.

"Conor, can I ask you a question?" Echo rested his hands on both of his mates' thighs.

Bandos drove. When he spoke, he didn't take his eyes off the road. "Sure."

"Why did Rocky stay when everyone else left?"

"He's sort of my alpha."

"I thought the big, young guy was the alpha."

Vaughan put his hand over Echo's. "Ladon. He's the youngest Somerset."

"Yes. Him."

"He is. When my clan kicked me out, Rocky and Sully went with me. We traveled for a lot of years. Only just settled in Saint Lakes recently."

"What did you do while you were traveling?" By the gods, Echo hoped it wasn't something illegal.

"We're investigators. Sully is on assignment right now. You won't meet him for a while yet." Bandos stopped and then turned when the way was clear.

"Oh...Ooohhh." Bandos was the computer guy. "Wait. You're a computer geek?"

Vaughan chuckled. "Don't judge a book by its cover. Bandos is the hottest, sexiest biker computer nerd on this plant."

"'Biker'? You have a motorcycle?" Echo was finding out so much about Bandos. The leather jacket made sense.

Bandos smiled. "I'll take you for a ride later this week."

Echo grinned and turned to Vaughan. "Does he look sexy riding it?"

"It's going to make you hard." Vaughan said it with such conviction Echo laughed.

Bandos shook his head. "You two better stop. We're almost to Mother Estelle's house."

"Just in time for the family meeting."

Family meeting?

The days were getting longer, so it wasn't quite dark yet. They had probably stayed longer than they should have at the hotel, but it had felt good not to have to worry about danger around the next corner, so they'd taken their time.

When a lake appeared, the sun almost met the water. Echo pointed to it. "How pretty."

Vaughan smiled. "Slow down a little."

Bandos complied, stopping in the middle of the road. No one was behind them, so they were safe and not in anyone's way.

Vaughan pointed to something. "You see that dark green house across the lake."

Echo nodded. "The one with the dock and boat?"

"That one's ours."

"Are you serious?"

"Very."

"It looks so peaceful." It was a good spot to call home. He could picture all three of them relaxing on the deck.

"I'm glad you think so. We could do with some peace." Vaughan kissed him on his forehead.

"Yes, we can," Bandos agreed. "But first we have to survive the family meeting."

Vaughan chuckled. "My mom made food."

Bandos got the car moving again.

"Are the meetings bad?" Echo took a deep breath, trying to calm his nerves.

"Nah. It's just me picking at Ladon because he's so fucking touchy about where he sits. Gabe and Shawn make out the entire time. Kristin always wants Lucas to give an hour-long concert. Lately she has a jar of peanut butter, which the whole town can practically smell. I like peanut butter, but not right after eating a big meal. Tim and Josh piss each other off at least once. Fane gets blunt and usually pissed Tim off. And I usually lose about five dollars to the curse jar. I swear to the gods, Mom earns a living wage with that thing."

Bandos chuckled. "That about sums it up."

"What's a curse jar?" As soon as Echo asked, he regretted it. He knew Vaughan well enough to know he shouldn't have opened his mouth.

"I'll give you a blowjob if you say the word fuck in front of my mom."

"You love my cock. You'll give me a blowjob, anyway. So no deal."

"Please. Just once."

Bandos turned down another road. It turned into dirt part way down.

"I'm not making an ass of myself in front of your mother." He had to make a good impression and saying the f-word certainly wouldn't help that goal.

When Bandos pulled into the driveway of a big, two-story white house, Echo's focus changed. "The landscaping is so perfect."

Echo undid his seatbelt and climbed over Vaughan to exit the car. He wanted to see the plants while he still had enough light. He turned back toward Vaughan, who followed him out. "There's lemon verbena. And peppermint."

"I think you just made a best friend in my mom."

Bandos grabbed Echo's hand and then Vaughan's and they all walked toward the house.

"She'll show me around her gardens sometime, then?"

"I'm pretty sure we'll lose you to her once she figures out how knowledgeable you are. If she didn't at the hotel already."

Echo could hear voices as they headed around the side of the house. He moved closer to Bandos. He recognized most of the faces sitting outside on a patio. A sliding glass door led inside.

A dark-haired slightly pregnant lady ran toward Vaughan, hugging him.

"Did you miss me?" Vaughan said with a smile, hugging her back.

"Nah, I'm showing support. I heard about Mom's little lecture." She grinned and then cupped his cheek. "I'm glad you're safe, brother."

"Me too." Vaughan patted her belly. "How are you and the baby?"

"We're just fine." She went over to Bandos and drew him into a hug. "Real glad you made it through. Thanks for having my brother's back."

Bandos hesitated before hugging her, as if he weren't used to affection, but Echo knew that wasn't true. Bandos always touched Echo and Vaughan. "He's my mate."

She pulled back. "I heard that too. Congratulations."

When her gaze landed on Echo, she smiled. "Hi. I'm Kristin, Vaughan's sister."

"Vaughan mentioned you. I'm Echo."

"What did he say about me?" Kristin put her arm over his shoulder and led him toward the others.

"That you love peanut butter and concerts. Particularly when Lucas gives them."

Kristin chuckled. "I heard you can do some pretty neat stuff with plants."

Echo nodded, but the closer he got to all the people, the tenser he became. She must have felt it because she let him go and stood next to a handsome younger shifter who had a cowboy hat on and jeans so tight, they left little to the imagination.

"We're right here, Baby Spice." Vaughan wrapped an arm around Echo's waist.

Bandos stood next to him, kissing his cheek. "No one here will hurt you, love."

"No. I know." He *did* know that. Besides the fact that he recognized all of them from earlier in the day when they had come to their rescue and helped save Bandos's life, they were his mates' family, which made them his family. "Not used to so many people."

"How about I make you a deal?" Vaughan said.

Echo sighed. "I am not cursing in front of your mother, Vaughan."

Everyone heard him. They were only a couple of feet away. But he hadn't thought about that before he said it.

Vaughan chuckled. "That's not what I was going to say."

Echo sighed. "Then what?"

"How about you lean on us when you need to? And we'll lean on you."

"Like we've been doing." Echo turned and drew both of his mates into a three-way hug.

"Yeah, love. Just like we have been doing," Bandos whispered.

"Deal." Echo wouldn't have had it any other way.

****

Keaton has a chance to change his life. It turns out his mate is a lot older than him and his new boss. Click Here to find out what happens next in the romantic Saint Lakes series.

****

All battles leave scars. Some differ from others. ***Redefining Normal*** is yours FREE when you sign up for my newsletter. Claim your copy. Or scan the QR code.

****

Honest reviews of my books help bring them to the attention of other readers. Leaving a review will help readers find the book. You

can leave a review here: https://www.amazon.com/review/create-rev
iew/B01N5QOER2

About the Author

April Kelley is an author of LGBTQ+ Romance. Her works include *The Journey of Jimini Renn*, a Rainbow Awards finalist, *Whispers of Home*, the *Saint Lakes* series, and over thirty more. She's a major contributor at *Once and Books*. April has been an avid reader for several years. Ever since she wrote her first story at ten, the characters in her head still won't stop telling their stories. If April isn't reading or writing, you can find her taking a long walk in the woods or going on her next adventure.

If you'd like to know more about her work, visit her website and sign up for her newsletter https://authoraprilkelley.com/

Printed in Great Britain
by Amazon

29858419R00157